# ONE BITE WITH A VAMPIRE

A Hidden Species Novel

## LOUISA MASTERS

One Bite With A Vampire

Copyright © 2021 by Louisa Masters

Cover: Booksmith Design

Editor: Hot Tree Editing

All rights reserved.

# ONE BITE WITH A VAMPIRE

*Getting kidnapped was never part of my life plan. But being rescued opened up a whole world of crazy.*

It's not easy being the only human at the Community of Species Government—and especially not when you're the rescue case. Two years ago, I was planning to go to college, have a wild time, then settle into a normal life. Instead, I was kidnapped, spent months being a test subject, was in hiding for nearly a year, and then found out that my whole existence is a science experiment conducted by the bad guys. It's definitely time to reassess.

My rescuers at CSG have been awesome… mostly. They gave me a job, a home, and a support network. But the whole demons, vampires, shifters thing is not easy to get used to. Especially when one particular vampire makes me want to take up stake sharpening for a hobby. How can someone be over eight centuries old and have the maturity of a drunk frat boy?

The thing is, teenage mentality or not, Andrew is a fierce protector. With the bad guys still on the loose, I need someone like that on my side. Plus, did I mention that he's not hard to look at? I could stare at him all day if only he never opened his mouth.

As we race to find my former captor before he can find me, life takes another twist and upends my world all over again. This time, though, I'm ready—after all, I've got an eight-hundred-year-old vampire at my back. What could possibly go wrong?

# CAST OF CHARACTERS

**Community of Species Government - CSG**

**Malia** - God, Head of State of the Spiritual Plane
**Percy Caraway** (felid shifter) - the Lucifer: Head of State of the Physical Plane

**Senior Investigation Team:**
**Sam Tiller** (human/felid shifter) - Team Admin, Gideon's boyfriend [Demons Do It Better]
**Gideon Bailey** (demon) - Sam's boyfriend [Demons Do It Better]
**Elinor Martin** (hellhound)
**David Carew** (sorcerer)
**Lily Heath** (succubus) – killed by Tish
**Andrew Turner** (vampire)
**Alistair Smythe** (hellhound)

**Noah Cage** (human) - CSG intern
**Aidan Byrne** (felid shifter) - Shifter Species Leader

**Coalition for Community Advancement - CCA**
*Terrorist organization responsible for genetic manipulation experiments*

**Dr Francis Tish** (sorcerer) - Lead scientist; Sam and Noah's childhood doctor

# CHAPTER ONE

## Noah

"I HEARD he's here to test whether a human department would work."

"Really? Isn't Sam proof enough of that? He's been here five years."

"Sam's a special case. I mean, he somehow got Gideon Bailey to settle down. He's clearly not a regular human."

I roll my eyes at my computer screen. Sam's not human at all, which Gossip #1 seems to realize as soon as the words are out of her mouth.

"Not that he's human... anymore. Does anyone know exactly what happened with that? I would swear he was human for five years, and then six months ago, he suddenly became a felid shifter? How is that possible?"

Hah. *You have no idea.* Lucky her.

"Anyone who knows is keeping it quiet. All we've heard is the official story—that Sam has been a shifter all along but a birth defect resulted in latency. That was corrected by a team of doctors."

It's a weak story. I told Sam and the others that, but it's not like they had many other options. The truth was deemed too risky.

The gossips are quiet for a moment, then Gossip #1 says, "Nobody really believes that, right? Latency in shifters isn't possible. The shifter gene always dominates."

*Shows what you know, honey.* Although… I guess in the end, it did, since Sam's not human anymore.

"Well anyway, I don't think *he* could be here to start a human department. He's too young for that, even for a human. Is he even an adult yet?"

Jesus fucking Christ. They're not even bothering to lower their voices. And do they seriously think I'm a *child*? I mean, I know I'm young, but would I be working here full-time if I wasn't an adult?

"Why else could he be here? Unless… do you think he's a spy for the lucifer?"

"What would he be spying on? He doesn't talk to any of us, just comes in, does whatever it is he's been told to do, then leaves. And anyway, if the lucifer wanted to spy on any of us, he'd just use the magic."

As if her words conjure it, I feel the magic—the fabric of existence—brushing up against me. It's the weirdest thing ever, and I say that as I sit with a demon at the next desk and a vampire talking on the phone over by the window. I never felt it before in my life until—

The sensation of the magic around me sharpens… thickens, almost. Like water brushing against my skin. Man, this is eerie shit.

Pissed off and creeped out, I spin in my swivel chair and look right at the gossipers. I recognize them—they don't even work in this part of the office. They've literally just come here to gape at me and speculate.

"I can hear you, you know. I'm human, not deaf. Take your disruptive selves somewhere else."

The one on the left looks abashed and takes a small step back, as if preparing to leave, but the other one sneers. "Perhaps you shouldn't be eavesdropping on private conversations, human."

A hush falls. Everyone who's close enough to hear is suddenly straining to listen while at the same time trying to look casual. Part of that is because Gossip #1—whose name I think is Nikita—just used the word "human" like it was a slur, and CSG has a pretty strict nondiscrimination policy.

The other part is because I've been an asshole to them all before and they know what's coming.

I get up and look her up and down. I'm pretty sure she's a succubus, but it's hard for me to tell the difference between species sometimes—most times. Still... some insults work across all species.

"Look, I get that someone with limited power like yourself might not have sensitive hearing, but those of us who have more power or are human don't have that problem, so when you shout, *we all hear you.*" I raise my voice a little, as though to make up for her hearing loss. "And I know everyone under—" Fuck, at what age do members of the community start to look old? "—a thousand must look like a child to a mature woman like yourself, but I can assure you that I *am* an adult. I'm also trying to get work done, so maybe you can fuck off back to the dementia society and leave us in peace instead of wasting time with stupid gossip." I drop back into my chair and spin to face my monitor, my skin crawling with awareness as I ignore all the eyes on me in the dead silence.

My only warning is the sudden brush of the magic against me, and then my chair is being jerked around and Nikita is looming over me, her *otherness* now sharply defined. Most members of the community can pass as human—you've probably walked past hundreds of them and never known. Maybe you even live near one, or work with them. But when they embrace their innate selves, it's so incredibly clear that they're not human, even if not much seems to change on the surface.

She's definitely a succubus—there's a magnetic attraction to her features, even with the vicious glare she's giving me, and I can tell she's dialed up the pheromones from the way my body reacts. I'm not even into women, but my dick is still standing to attention. It's purely physical, though, and I feel a sick sense of disgust that she'd do this without my consent—weaponize lust because of a petty office squabble.

At the same time, I'm pretty sure I'm not supposed to be able to think this clearly. Isn't there supposed to be some kind of mental euphoria with a succubus whammy? That's meant to be part of the attraction—or so my sketchy research has told me.

"What's going on here?" The sharp voice cuts through the tension in the room like a whip strike, and Nikita stumbles back from my chair. There's a sudden flurry of people doing their jobs.

I look over at the man striding toward me. His habitual wicked grin is missing, and there's a grim set to his face that makes him look seriously fucking scary. Or maybe that's just because I know he's a centuries-old vampire and a member of the deadly senior team that reports directly to the lucifer.

"Well?" He comes to a halt about two feet from me and looks between me and Nikita.

I keep my mouth shut for once. Andrew pisses me off anyway, so why would I voluntarily want to talk to him? Plus, I'm no snitch.

He raises a brow at me, then rolls his eyes when I set my jaw and turns on the succubus trying to edge away. She freezes and starts to stutter excuses. It's hard to tell what she's saying, what with how jerky and broken the sentences are, but I can't really blame her for being terrified. If I remember right, she works in the accounting department, and she's currently being faced down by the community equivalent of a Navy SEAL or Green Beret—or whatever those scary military types are— while knowing that she just broke a whole bunch of rules.

Andrew finally loses patience. "Go back to work," he orders. "Someone will speak with you later."

She literally runs away. If I wasn't so annoyed by the fact that Andrew's in my space, I'd have enjoyed watching that.

Meanwhile, Mr. Big Bad Vampire is looking around the open-plan area at all the people trying so hard not to meet his gaze. "If it turns out that she was attempting to use her abilities to intimidate Noah, which is what it looked like, and you all were just watching, there's going to be serious disciplinary action. So you may want to very carefully consider your next steps."

*Way to threaten a dozen people I need to work with, dumbass.* Well, work next to, anyway.

The flurry this time is vaguely uneasy. I sigh, haul

myself up from my chair, and jab my index finger in his direction.

"How about you stop trying to boss people around and let everyone do their work? What did you even come down here for?" He and the rest of the lucifer's crack team, including Sam, who likes to think he's my mentor, work on a different floor.

He looks down at my finger and grins his stupid grin. Ugh. Does he seriously think that being a centuries-old silver hottie who acts like a teenager is *attractive*? I can't even. It's like when your dad tries to be cool.

Well, not my dad. Other people's dads. My dad never bothered with shit like that.

Plus, he isn't actually my dad.

And smooth, refined Andrew in no way reminds me of him.

"We're having a meeting, and Percy wants you there," he says.

Sighing, I turn back to lock my computer. Percy is the lucifer, and since it's his beneficence that got me this internship-slash-job and the apartment I live in, I like to stay on his good side. Plus, he's been nice. I've found it a little hard to trust anyone after what's happened these last few years, but if I was going to trust, Percy would be on the short list.

"Come on, then." I stalk ahead of him, and I hear him mutter something as he follows, though I can't make out what.

Are you confused yet? Need a cheat sheet? Let me give you the CliffsNotes version of my life since I turned eighteen.

My name is Noah Cage. Except it's not, really,

because the people I thought were my parents were actually only fostering me on behalf of a terrorist organization, the Coalition for Community Advancement (CCA). About forty-five years ago, the CCA decided that it wanted to enslave humanity—oh, wait. I'm getting ahead of myself. Let me give you the dirt on me first.

So, two days after my eighteenth birthday, about three weeks before graduation, I came home from school to find three huge men who looked as though they liked to rip people apart for fun at my house. My parents were packing bags. The men told me I was going with them. I asked my mom what was going on. She said, "I'm not your mom. You're eighteen now, and we've been paid."

I freaked out. The scary dudes seemed prepared for that, because next thing I knew, I was waking up in a lab, strapped to a table.

Ever had that happen? I do *not* recommend it.

While I was trying to work out if my parents had actually sold me or what, and if so, to whom and why, my doctor walked in. Yes, seriously. My parents had always been kind of freakish about medical checkups, so once a month Dr. Tish would visit our house and give me a physical. In retrospect, it's weird, but when that's literally all you've known your whole life, it's normal. So at first I was relieved to see my lifelong doctor—and then I realized he was the root of all my problems.

The next eight months were brutal. Most of the tests they ran were minimally invasive—things like vision and hearing tests, physical stamina and endurance. And the blood tests, of course. There were so many damn blood tests. And it was the same thing, day after day, sometimes with increased stimuli to cause stress. The doctors and lab assistants talked freely in front of us. Once I realized that meant they didn't think we'd ever be able to repeat what they were saying to anyone else, it was pretty fucking terrifying. But it means I know a lot about the tests they ran, even if they never really talked about why they were running them. The base knowledge was something they didn't discuss, and it frustrated the crap out of me not to know why they were doing this to us.

Because, yeah, I wasn't the only one there. I'm not actually sure how many of us were being tested, but the cell-slash-dorm I lived in had three other guys in it, and the hallway it was in was lined with doors. I guess I could find out the number now if I really wanted to— there are records—but knowing how many others were victims like me isn't going to make me feel better.

I stab the button for the elevator, trying to block out the sound of Andrew chatting with… someone.

"…keep telling them that if they didn't bring the cookies, I wouldn't eat them. That makes sense, right, Rania? It's not my fault they bring delicious cookies that mesmerize me into eating them!"

Ugh. Seriously? It's enough to make me want to take the stairs. Except I have no doubt he's much fitter than I am and would probably talk to me all the way up.

Fortunately—unfortunately?—we're not the only people who get into the elevator, so even though I still have to hear his voice, at least he's not talking to me.

So… where was I? Right, imprisoned by my childhood doctor for tests I didn't understand the purpose of. Like that wasn't horrible enough, there was something really weird about all the people at the lab compound. Like, weirder than you'd even expect for scientists and guards who were conducting medical tests on unsuspecting teenagers. At first I thought they were doing some kind of cosplay with fake fangs and horns, or that I'd ended up in the middle of one of those creepy Dracula-worshiping cults. Or maybe Satanists—I mean, if you wanted to worship the devil, you'd probably be okay with wearing fake horns, right? But then one day I saw one of the guards change into a huge dog. If shapeshifters were real, that meant the vampires and demons probably were too. Which made the tests they were constantly doing even scarier.

And then came a day when one of the lab assistants and two guards came into our dorm and started injecting us with some shit. It wasn't the first time— usually after the injection we'd have to do something physical, and then they'd take blood. But it *was* the first time my roommates dropped unconscious to the floor after they'd been injected. Major creep out, right? So when there was a distraction and nobody was looking at me, I just dropped and pretended to be unconscious too. Whatever was in that syringe, I *did not* want it—and I can't emphasize enough how damn lucky I was that day, because I found out about twenty seconds later that my roommates weren't unconscious, they were dead. The testing was done, and we weren't needed anymore.

Ever been dragged through hallways to an incinerator? Also not on my must-repeat list.

My amazing luck kicked in again, because the guards decided to bring all the test subjects down before loading us in, and as soon as they left, I was out of there. I never considered myself a lucky person before then, but I can't argue with the fact that something was on my side that day.

And for almost a year after. Because while I managed to escape being incinerated, I couldn't find a way past the guards at the entrance to the complex. The place was huge, though, and as long as I slept in short snatches and kept moving around, nobody knew I was there. I had a few close calls, and every time I heard a guard or scientist muttering about the "human stink trapped in the HVAC system," or one of the kitchen staff complaining that supplies were short, I'd break out in a sweat, but they were so damn arrogant that it never occurred to them that one of their test subjects might have survived.

The elevator doors open, and I stride out, leaving Andrew behind. He knows where he's going, and I don't need to hang around so he can finish talking about the time he made cookies and "accidentally" used salt instead of sugar, then brought them to work and gave them to the hellhounds in one of the investigative teams. Although after having to deal with those hellhounds, I would have paid money to actually see it.

I head down the hallway, peering into each meeting room as I pass until I find the one I need. I knock on the open door.

"Hi. Uh, you wanted to see me?"

Percy smiles at me from across the table. "Yes. Thanks for coming, Noah."

I enter the room and make for an empty seat at the table—coincidentally, beside Sam, who's taken me under his wing whether I want to be there or not. And I can't tell him to back off, because his boyfriend is fucking terrifying, even for a demon. The only time Gideon smiles is at Sam—the rest of the time, his face makes my balls shrivel back into my body. So yeah, not going to hurt his boyfriend's feelings and risk his wrath.

David, one of the other members of the senior team, looks toward the door. "Where's Andrew?"

"Talking about cookies." I can't quite keep the disdain from my voice, and I bite my lip. These people all *like* Andrew.

Alistair growls. "He better not be telling the story about the time he tried to *poison us*! That low-down son of a bitch."

Well, Alistair might not like Andrew. Come to think of it, they do bicker a lot.

Suddenly I like Alistair a whole lot more.

"I'll go get him," David mutters, but he's grinning as he leaves the room.

Sam leans in. "Everything okay? You seem tense."

That makes me tense up even more. There's no real privacy amongst the community—half the time they can smell what you've been doing or your feelings. Or sense them in some weird way. I didn't even know that tension had a smell until I met these people.

I force a smile, because even if Sam is overbearing sometimes, he's the reason I'm here and not still trapped in the lab complex—plus, his heart's in the right place.

And Gideon is sitting on his other side, listening.

"I'm good," I murmur. "Just, ah, some office politics downstairs."

He frowns, but I'm saved from having to say anything else when David comes back, followed by Andrew. They close the door and take their seats, and suddenly all eyes are on me.

"Noah, we've been talking about your situation, and I want to thank you again for all the information you've provided for us. I know your time at the compound was traumatic for you, and I wish it had never happened, but the bits and pieces you picked up while you were there have been invaluable."

I don't know what to say to that, so I just nod awkwardly. These people freed me from the underground lab complex and gave me a job and a home. Telling them what I overheard while I was trapped there seems like a small price to pay.

Percy smiles his gentle smile that makes me feel like I should want to be a better person and continues. "We also appreciate having your permission to review the test results and other information that was in the file Dr. Tish and his team had compiled."

I shrug, still feeling awkward. "None of the information in it would have made sense to me, and I wanted to understand what... I wanted to understand."

Because I don't. I don't understand. Even though it's been explained to me several times, I can't quite grasp it.

The CCA wanted to enslave humanity.

To do that, they needed to improve the fertility level of the various community species so humans wouldn't outnumber them. Community fertility is substantially lower than human.

They used sorcery to modify half-human, half-other fetuses in utero.

Then, two decades later, they took egg and sperm samples from those modified people to create the next generation—my generation—and see if we were born human.

Apparently, that's what all the testing was for: to see if any of my/our community genes had survived. The way it's been told to me, if a person has any community blood at all, it will dominate. So if your six-times-great-grandfather was a demon, you will be a demon, even if his partner was human and all his descendants procreated with humans.

Which means the fact that I have a vampire grandfather but am completely, entirely, one hundred percent human violates the natural order of things. The way the world works, I should be a vampire.

I don't know how I feel about that. I hate everything that's been done to me, and I definitely don't like the idea of being the result of an experiment, but I was raised human. The thought that I should have been—should be?—a vampire is… creepy.

This whole situation is just fucked-up.

On the plus side, the CCA has been all but disbanded. Most of the players are in prison awaiting trial. Their bases have been raided, all property and data files seized, funds frozen. The only ones still on the run are Dr. Tish and some of his senior sorcerer scientists.

Not gonna lie. That fucking terrifies me.

I trusted that man for most of my life. Then I found out he's a monster—and not because he's a sorcerer. And now that I'm free and have the chance to pick up the pieces of my life… he's still out there.

There hasn't been a peep from him, so nobody knows where he is and what he's doing. Sam keeps assuring me that they'll get him, that Tish has nowhere to go. And even if he did, he doesn't know I'm alive. But I still wake up at night terrified he's going to find me.

Sam pats my knee reassuringly, which means he's somehow guessed that my mood has changed. Probably by scent. I really hate this lack of privacy.

"Now that we know more about the research Tish and the CCA were doing, we're confident that you're going to be fine, Noah. Obviously you've undergone trauma, but physically, there should be no repercussions. And if you find yourself concerned about anything, any changes, CSG will handle your medical care. You have only to reach out to us."

My gut freezes. "That sounds like you don't expect me to be around," I say carefully. I don't want to be here long-term, true, but I haven't quite figured out what normal is going to be for me. I'm not ready to leave my safety net—especially not while Tish is still on the loose.

Percy immediately shakes his head. "Not at all. You've been doing a great job here at CSG, and if you want to stay, we'd be happy to help you gain some formal qualifications and look at career progression." The look he gives me says pretty clearly that he knows that's not what I want. "We just want to make sure you understand that no matter what decisions you make, CSG will provide care for you if there are any repercussions from what the CCA has done."

Well. That's… nice of them. After all, Sam didn't do his human-to-shifter transition until he was nearly forty. Percy says there's no chance of that with me, that he could see Sam was supposed to be a shifter but that I look completely human.

Still, you never know.

"Thank you. I appreciate that. Though I hope I never need it." Does this really have to be a group meeting? I'm uncomfortable having the others sit in if we're going to talk about my future medical needs—and my future in general.

Smiling still, Percy says, "Which leads me to the

point of this meeting. We've talked about the fact that the magic has been paying very close attention to you since you came here. The fact that you can feel it is very unusual."

I barely hold in a snort. The first time I ever felt existential magic, the force that basically runs the universe, was the day Sam was brought to the labs. It was the weirdest thing, but the second I started sneaking around the lab where he was, trying to eavesdrop on the techs, I felt… something. Like water against my skin, but less resistant. It creeped me out. Since then, it's been with me almost all the time. It was Percy who told me what it was—as the lucifer, he has a connection with it. He made an offhand comment about how the magic seemed to like me, as it was wrapping me up in the metaphysical equivalent of a hug, and when I stupidly said, "Oh, so that's what it is," everyone got all excited. Apparently, humans don't feel magic that easily. It takes training and effort. So they thought maybe my community DNA would eventually dominate after all.

Turns out, I'm just defective as a human.

"Uh, yeah. It… still seems to be hanging around."

"While we're now absolutely certain that you're human, we think there's a possibility that you might have inherited some recessive traits from your vampire ancestors, and that's why you can feel magic the way you would if you'd actually been born a vampire."

Say what now? "Oh-kay…"

His smile widens. Is he amused by my hesitation? These people. Seriously.

"We'd like to test this theory—"

I open my mouth to protest—no more fucking tests —but he raises a hand.

"—no, no more medical tests. We want to see if you can pick up any vampire abilities. It would be some meditation and physical activities, the same things vampire adolescents do when they first begin to come in to their abilities."

Well… that doesn't sound too bad. Although… "Would I have to drink blood?"

Andrew snorts. "Only if you find yourself wanting it."

I'm pretty sure that's not going to happen. I haven't said anything, but the sight of blood squicks me out. I'm used to it after so many blood tests, but that doesn't mean I like it.

"Okay, I can do that."

Sam pats my knee again, this time with approval. "Hopefully, you'll find you have some latent abilities we can bring out. I'd feel more comfortable if you had an innate ability to defend yourself."

I hadn't even thought of that, but fuck yeah. I might not want to be a vampire, but even I can admit that they're badass scary motherfuckers. If I could develop vampire charisma, speed, or strength—or even just enhanced senses—I'd be in a much better position to defend myself if Tish comes back. Maybe I'd even be able to sleep for more than thirty minutes at a time.

"Sure. Sounds good." I'm totally on board with this.

"Great. You and Andrew can work out the details. I think it would be easier for you if the first attempts, at least, are made without an audience."

Oh, fuck my life. Andrew? I look over at his stupid, smug face. Damn it, I should have guessed he'd be the one assigned to this. He is the only vampire on the team, after all.

I did not think this through.

"Uh, does Andrew have a lot of experience guiding adolescent vampires?" I make a desperate attempt to retrieve the situation. "Maybe someone who actually has kids…" Crap. *Does* Andrew have kids? He's been around, according to gossip, for over eight hundred years, so maybe they're all grown up. Maybe he has dozens. I mean, I can't stand him, but that doesn't mean he's not seriously hot. People would want to have sex with him. Hell, if he was gagged and had a bag over his head, I'd even think about having sex with him. And while everything I've overheard points to him liking men, if I'd lived for centuries, I'd probably give women a try—just to see what it was like.

Everyone is staring at me.

"Do you not want me to help you?" Andrew asks. On the surface, he sounds concerned and a little hurt, but there's a twitch to his lips and a sneaky gleam in his eyes that tells me he's screwing with us.

Fucking dick.

"You're so busy," I say, laying on the whole innocent act, although I don't think anyone in this room will fall for it. They've been around me enough to know better, even Percy. "I wouldn't want to take you away from anything important."

As soon as I say it, I know I'm toast.

He shakes his head, grinning broadly. "Oh, no, Noah. Nothing is more important than you right now. I'll happily sacrifice my free time to help you."

I think about arguing, but is there really any point? Instead, I manage a grimace-slash-smile. "Great. Thanks. Really looking forward to it."

Sam coughs, and David clears his throat, lips pressed together like he's trying not to smile.

Andrew, the asshole, claps his hands. "Great! Can't wait to get started. In fact, we can start today!"

"You're such a dickbag," Alistair tells him, then turns to me. "If you accidentally maim him, that's okay."

"Good to know." Yeah, I definitely like Alistair.

"*Not* good to know," Sam chides. "Holy crap, it's hard enough riding herd on this lot. Don't make it worse, Noah." He's smiling at me, though, and I get the feeling that he likes seeing me comfortable with the team. Like I said, Sam's appointed himself as my mentor-slash-father figure. He wants me to be happy and goes out of his way to make it happen.

I honestly don't get it.

Percy clears his throat. "We might leave it there, then. Noah, we'll give this theory some time, but if it turns out to not be valid, I have some other ideas about why the magic likes you so much."

I nod. "Thank you." I mean that. Percy's been great —at first, when they brought me to meet him and said they'd know what to do with me after, I was shit scared. But he's been nothing but kind and patient, and after he said the magic vouched for my story, everyone else got on board too. This may be a completely unfamiliar world to me, but these total strangers have been nicer to me than my supposed parents ever were.

The meeting breaks up then, and as everyone's getting up and gathering their things and chatting, I sidle toward the door. Maybe I can sneak out while they're all distracted and avoid Andrew—

The hand clamping on my shoulder kills all hope.

"Trying to get away?" a feminine voice murmurs in my ear, and I turn to see Elinor's grinning face.

"I could learn to hate you," I tell her, and she laughs.

"It won't be that bad. And you never know, you might like it."

Like spending time with Andrew? Is she—

Oh. She means the exercises themselves. Yeah, sure, maybe.

"Ready, Noah?" The dickbag himself—*thanks for that word, Alistair*—comes up beside me, Percy with him. I stretch my mouth into something that could probably pass for a smile.

"Sure. Can't wait."

Elinor laughs again and pats my shoulder before leaving. Percy smiles at me and follows her out. But before I can even think of maybe making a break for it, Sam and Gideon join us.

"Where are you going to do this?" Sam asks, and Andrew shrugs.

"Not sure, actually. I was thinking the gym, but it's probably better to keep it private to start. My place, maybe? Or Noah's."

Oh, hell no.

"What about a meeting room?" I suggest, somewhat desperately. "How much room do we really need, anyway? My place isn't big."

Andrew smirks, like he knows I don't want to leave the office with him. "Probably not that much room, but the meeting rooms are a little small." He gestures around, and he's right. With the table and chairs, there's not a lot of space to move around in.

Not that I know how much space we'll need.

"The main conference room?" Gideon suggests, and

I jump slightly. He doesn't talk a lot—not to me, anyway —so when he does, it always surprises me.

Andrew tilts his head and purses his lips like he's thinking about it, and he looks so stupid, I snort.

Which means they all look at me.

So I fake a cough. "Sorry. Something in my throat."

Sam sighs, and Gideon raises an eyebrow. I don't think any of them believe me.

"That could work," Andrew says. "Especially if we shove the table over a bit. Come on, Noah." He turns and walks out, and my jaw drops. Does he just expect me to follow him like a puppy?

Since he's well and truly gone, I guess so.

"Noah?" Sam puts a hand on my arm, and I look down at him. I'm not super tall, but he's short. "Try to be patient. I know Andrew can be... exhausting sometimes, but he's trying to help you."

Guilt stabs me in the chest. "Yeah, sorry, I know. It's just..." That he's a giant douche monkey? He is actually going out of his way to help me. "I'll try harder."

Sam smiles—

"Come *on*, puny human! You don't have that many years left in your life that you can waste them like this!" The shout echoes down the hallway and into the room, and I'm pretty sure everyone on the floor—or at least in the immediate area—heard it.

Sam closes his eyes.

I don't think I have enough fucks left to waste on that guy.

# CHAPTER TWO

## Andrew

I LEAN against the wall in the hallway and smile at the sorcerer passing by. I'm pretty sure he works in HR and is about to race back to his office to file a complaint about me. Something about noise, maybe, or that it's inappropriate to point out to human colleagues how short their lifespans are.

Not that we have many human colleagues. Noah's it, in fact. We used to have Sam, but then his shifter blood bred true. It's a long story. Anyway, Noah's the only human at CSG.

And he's so fun to tease.

Yeah, I know I piss him off, and yes, most of the time I do it deliberately. Do I feel bad about that? Not really. Noah's not the shy, retiring type. At first I was worried that he'd never retaliate in case it affected his status with us. Then I saw him in action, and that worry disappeared. Man, Noah can be an ass.

It's adorable.

I might actually tell him that. It's guaranteed to get his hackles up.

Anyway, the point is, Noah has no qualms about dishing it back. The only time he really restrains himself is around Percy—and he seems wary around Gideon, which is weird, because Sam dotes on Noah, and Gideon's main purpose in life now is to make Sam happy. In fact, if you look up "sickening" in the dictionary, you'll see that it's defined as "Gideon and Sam's relationship."

I'm starting to lose patience and just on the verge of shouting again when Noah comes out of the meeting room and glares at me. He stalks down the hall toward me, and if looks could kill—or if he had a weapon in his hand—I'd actually be concerned. Instead, I straighten and give him my biggest, most infuriating grin.

"There you are! I was starting to wonder if you'd succumbed to your lifespan earlier than we expected." Sure, it's dumb, but I've noticed that humans have a preoccupation with aging.

He keeps going, right past me, muttering to himself about geriatric fucking vampires who don't have the grace to stay dead. That throws me for a second until I remember the human myth about vampires being undead.

What does that mean, anyway? *Un*dead. Dead is dead. And if you come back to life after death… you're alive. Right?

Humans are weird. They make up this whole ridiculous culture to help them ignore the reality of our existence, and then don't believe that either.

I catch up to him at the elevator and clear my throat.

"It's cool for you to call me undead," I say softly, staring straight ahead, "because I don't give a shit *and I* deliberately insult you. But make sure nobody else ever hears it. Most vampires don't like it."

For a second, I think he's going to ignore me, but then his head jerks in a nod. "Sorry." He doesn't turn his head to look at me, so he doesn't see my grin come back.

"That's okay," I tell him magnanimously. "I understand that the human brain doesn't have as long to develop as everyone else's."

He slams his fist against the elevator call button.

Score for me.

We ride the elevator in silence, and he doesn't say a word until we get to the conference room. Seriously, not a single word, not even when people say hello in the hallway. He does nod at them, but still. Would it kill him to say hi? No wonder people think he's an ass.

Not that we don't have a large percentage of assholes here at CSG—Gideon is their king—but the difference between Noah and the rest of them is that they're not baby humans. Nobody would ever consider taking Gideon to task for being rude. They'd be too busy apologizing for existing and trying to get out of his way. But Noah is vulnerable, and if he pisses off the wrong person, his spitting kitten act is not going to protect him.

Hence the reason I suggested this training to Percy.

We've been concerned for a while about the way the magic clings to Noah. Existential magic just doesn't do that. The only person it seems to "spend time with" is Percy, and that's because he's the lucifer, the leader of our community here on the physical plane. The magic chose him for the job, and it will support him in it for as long as it chooses.

But everyone else... we're all just random beings to the magic. So the fact that it hovers around Noah to the point that he can actually *feel* it is a little disturbing. Hopefully it's just trying to get our attention and show us something Noah needs from us—hence the plan to work with him and see if he has any abilities from his forebears.

In the conference room, I look around, judging the best way to move the furniture to give us some space. We shouldn't really need too much, but if Noah does have some vampire senses and they kick in, I don't want him feeling confined. That would just cause panic.

"Okay, let me just shove the table over, and we can get started." I go to the middle of the table and brace my hands against it.

"Wait, that's not going to work." Noah sounds exasperated. "Go to the other end. I've got this end."

*Oh, puny human.*

Shooting him a mocking grin over my shoulder, I give the table—a fifteen-foot oak monstrosity—a light shove, and it slides across the carpet and comes to rest against the wall. "Vampire strength," I explain, though I can see from his chagrined expression that he knows. "And look, it took all the chairs on that side with it! We only have to move a few." More like seven, but there's an easy way around that.

I plant myself in one of the chairs and shove off. It's on castors, so I roll across the room, shouting "Wheeeeeee," and grab two more chairs as I pass them. By the time I reach the corner I was aiming for, the job is nearly half done—actually, it's more than half done, since we'll need two of the chairs to sit on.

Fuck, I'm good.

Noah is back to glaring at me, though, so clearly he doesn't agree. I'm not sure what his problem is this time.

Sighing, I get up and grab two more of the chairs, slinging them toward the corner and ignoring the noise as they crash into their friends. Then I sit in one of the remaining ones and gesture to the other.

"Come on, let's get started."

He sits, scooting a few inches farther away, though we weren't that close to begin with. That's starting to bug me now—what does he think, that I have lice or something? Please. I was bathing fastidiously while his ancestors still thought dirt insulated them against disease.

Except... he has vampire ancestors, so that's probably not true. Not entirely, anyway.

"Do you know much about vampire abilities?" I ask, mostly in the hope of getting him to loosen up a little. If he's too tense, this is doomed to fail.

He shrugs. "Only what I've learned since coming here. Most of it has been unlearning what I thought I knew."

I nod. "Humans have vivid imaginations. So you know we're not actually *dead*"—couldn't help myself—"have no issues with sun, religious artifacts, garlic, all that?"

"Yeah. Uh, do you mind if... I mean, I have some questions, but I didn't want to offend anyone."

I laugh outright. "But you don't care if you offend me?"

For a second, I see agreement on his face. "No, that's not what I meant," he says quickly, but there's no mistaking the fact that his tone is just *too* polite for it to be true.

"It's okay; you can ask me anything." I wave a hand

dismissively. "There's no point in me trying to help you if you can't ask questions."

He hesitates for a second longer, then ventures, "Human myths all talk about wooden stakes and beheadings for killing vampires."

"Ah. Well, if you shove a sharpened stake into any living being's heart, it's not going to be pretty. But most of those myths say we turn to ash when stabbed in the heart, right? That doesn't happen. In fact, due to our accelerated healing, if the stake is removed and there's access to blood and medical care, it may not even be fatal. Beheading is, though. I don't know of any living creature that can survive without its head. Maybe an earthworm? And hey, I had a lover once who called me a worm, so I guess I have a chance of surviving a beheading."

He blinks at me, obviously overcome by my wit. "So... you don't instantly turn to ash when you die?"

"Nope."

For a second, he says nothing, then takes a deep breath. "Uh, I get that vampires don't need to drain a body of all blood when they—you—feed. Is that the right word? I don't..."

For the first time, I realize he really is unsure about asking these questions, and I lean forward. "Noah, I know we don't always get along, but I meant it when I said you can ask me anything. I'm your on-call vampire expert, and I won't be offended if you ask something out of ignorance. Yeah?"

He nods slowly. "Yeah. Okay. Thanks."

"Good. So, yes, we do call it feeding. No, we definitely don't need to drain a body of all blood. I doubt there's ever been a vampire who actually *can* in one feeding. That's a lot of blood. Most of us don't feed from a live body anymore, anyway. The advent of blood banks has changed a lot of things about feeding." I have mixed feelings about that, to be honest. Sure, I love the convenience of being able to grab blood from the fridge when I need it instead of having to go out and find a donor or pay for and house a long-term donor, but there's nothing quite like fresh, warm blood from a willing being. It's like e-books. They're cheaper, easier to store, and more convenient to buy, but sometimes you just can't resist the lure of a paperback.

Now he looks intrigued. "So you don't need to actually drink from people?"

"Yes, we do," I correct, "in the sense that animal blood is lacking the enzymes we need. But the blood doesn't have to be drunk from the vein, no. These days, most don't."

"I didn't know that," he says. "Sam gave me links to archive sites about the different species, but I'm still wading through the history parts. It talks a lot about the contractual obligations of vampires to their donors. Does that still exist?"

I quirk a brow. "Interested in becoming a donor? You'd live a *very* cushy life." I'm laughing even before he recoils, pushing his chair even farther back from me. "I'm kidding. Yes, some vampires still keep donors. The contracts you're talking about are only for long-term donors. So if a vampire went out and picked someone up for just a single feeding, there are no obligations—other than to ensure they're safe and healthy afterward. But if a single donor is providing blood repeatedly, a contract is put in place to protect both parties. We don't require a lot of blood—maybe half a pint a week for a mature adult, more for young adults and children—but that does have an effect. It's up to a vampire to ensure their donor is receiving sufficient nutrients, medical care, and is comfortably housed. There's usually also a stipend. Depending on the vampire, their donor might be able to give up work entirely for the duration of the contract."

"So poor vampires just go with the… uh, the single-use donor option?" He winces, but this time I laugh so hard I'm gasping for air.

"Single-use donor option? Shit, I have to write that down. We have to put that in an official document somewhere."

He doesn't seem to find it as funny as I do—not sure why, since he came up with it.

I swipe away a tear and blow out a breath. "Where were we?"

Noah has a unique talent for conveying entire monologues with a single glance. Right now, for instance, his scathing look tells me that I'm an abject disappointment to my species and life everywhere.

"Poor vampires," he reminds me.

"That's right. Yes, vampires without the means to support a long-term donor would just find a… single-use donor"—my voice *barely* quivers with laughter. I'm so proud of myself—"each time they needed to feed. Obviously, they've benefited the most from modern practices. There's much less risk associated with a bag of blood from the fridge, or blood-infused food products, than there is with finding a donor and feeding from the vein."

He leans forward. "Risk? You mean risk of the human being hurt?" There's an edge to his voice now.

"Not even close. The chances of a human being

accidentally hurt during a feeding are incredibly low. Mostly because vampires will only feed on humans as a last resort. We prefer to feed on any other species, including other vampires. The risk is usually of exposing our existence to humans. Let's say, for example, that I was a vampire living in the eighteenth century—"

"Which you were," he mutters.

"—and I needed to feed. I don't have enough money to support a donor, so every week, I need to go out and find someone who can help. In most large cities, there was a network in place within the community to help, but if the city was smaller, options were limited."

"And even more so in rural areas?" There's a hint of fascination in the question.

"Exactly. Let's say, though, that I lived in a decent-sized city. I probably had a group of contacts I could reach out to who would let me feed from them. One of the benefits of the community and CSG is that the species tend to support each other. But maybe one week, nobody is available—they're out of town, or sick, or someone else fed on them already this week. So I go to a bar or somewhere people congregate, and I find someone who's willing to help me out."

"A human?"

I shake my head. "No. It's another member of the community—for a human to be willing to help, they'd have to know I'm a vampire, and that would endanger the whole community. Especially back then."

He frowns, and I can see he's about to ask more questions, so I hold up a hand. "Let me finish, and it will all come clear, young grasshopper."

Huffing and rolling his eyes, he slouches back in his chair. "Fine."

"So I have a volunteer—let's say it's a shifter. But this shifter, as kind as they are to agree to let me feed from them, is a stranger. I don't want to bring them back to my home, and truthfully, they probably don't want to go. They're already offering to put themselves in a vulnerable position; why would they also voluntarily go to a secondary location with a stranger?"

He's nodding slowly. "Okay, so, what? Is it like sex at a gay nightclub? You find a corner or a bathroom stall?"

I tilt my head and study him. "Are you even old enough to be going to nightclubs?"

"Oh my god," he mutters, and I make a mental note to tell him Malia, the current god of the spiritual plane, doesn't want his obeisance… but another time. I need to save the digs up and spread them out, not use them all at once. "Why are you like this?"

"Like what?" I bat my eyelashes innocently. "Do I need to tell Sam you're having dirty sex with strangers while illegally at a nightclub? Just imagine what he'll have to say… you'll probably get hours of lecturing about safe sex and underage drinking and recreational drug use."

Noah shudders hard, his face going blank, and I know something I said crossed a line.

"I'm sorry." I get up and go to kneel beside his chair. "What is it?"

He shakes his head and pushes away slightly. "Nothing. It's… nothing. I'm fine. You—you don't need to apologize." He sounds like he's choking on that last sentence, but I think it might be because he doesn't like letting me off the hook rather than because he's upset. I inspect his face carefully, but he seems to be back to normal, so I return to my chair and sprawl in it like

I'm at the beach rather than in a conference room at work.

"Where was I?"

"You found a stranger in a bar," he prompts.

"That's right—you were comparing the act of a species taking sustenance in order to survive to anonymous blow jobs in public toilets."

He winces. "Uhhh… that's not what—"

"Don't worry, that's pretty close to how it was sometimes. Depending on the people involved, there could even be orgasms. But bathrooms back then weren't like they are now, if there even were any, and since you're so familiar with sex in nightclubs, you know that there's a really high chance of being seen." I pause for him to respond to the jab, but he keeps his jaw locked. How disappointing. "And if a human happened to be the one who saw a vampire feeding… well, usually it didn't end well."

He opens his mouth, then closes it again.

"Go on, ask," I encourage.

"Couldn't you just… use charisma to compel the human not to say anything?"

"Theoretically, yes. But that assumes the human doesn't just sneak out and raise an alarm without us having seen them. Plus, the kind of charisma you're talking about is really unpleasant to do—and complicated. If I were to use charisma to compel the human to not tell anyone what they saw, they could still write it down. They might not be able to say, 'There was a vampire drinking someone's blood in the storeroom,' but they could find another way or combination of words. They could even say they saw something terrible and play a guessing game with a friend until the right answer came up. It would be next to impossible to cover all bases to prevent them from revealing what they'd seen—especially for a young vampire, or one who didn't have strong charisma."

"So just making them not say anything is out—but what about making them forget?" He's leaning forward again now, that reluctant fascination back.

"That's the other option," I agree. "But it's not one we like. We can't make people forget—we actually have to remove the memory from their brain. It's a horrible violation, and one of the reasons why vampires only feed from humans as a last resort."

"Because if they knew about vampires, that would put the whole community at risk. So every time a vampire feeds from a human, they have to take a memory from them." The horror of it reflects on his face. "And if that happened to a particular human more than once, the gaps in memory would be a giveaway anyway."

"Yes. People who believe in vampires have widely been discredited throughout the centuries due to the way the magic protects us, but there have always been enough who knew to cause trouble for us. Mostly in rural areas in highly religious countries. At one point, village priests were responsible for more deaths than soldiers—and usually of innocent humans."

"How does charisma work?" He furrows his brow. "And what's the point of it, if you only feed on volunteers?"

"As far as we've been able to ascertain, its primary purpose is to make feeding pleasant for the donor. Light charisma numbs the pain of being bitten and having blood drawn. It also stimulates production of blood cells to help the donor replace what's taken. We believe the ability then evolved over time to also become a form of defense—a way to confuse and distract attackers. And then after the species wars, when humans were no longer our allies, there came times when it was used to remove memories." I really don't like talking about this. There have been times when I was forced to redact human memories in order to protect the community, and even knowing I prevented the potential slaughter of many, it haunts me.

"But because vampires don't like doing that, they only feed from humans as a last resort." He sounds thoughtful now, and I wonder what's going through his head. If Percy—and by extension, the magic—weren't so utterly convinced he could be trusted, I'd be a little concerned about the way he's digging out information that could aid humans in wiping out my species.

"I've known vampires who held out for assistance and nearly died because they wouldn't feed from a human and violate them that way. And I've heard of others who did die. That kind of brain rape is not some-thing any decent vampire takes lightly."

Noah goes still. "Is that why you were so mad this afternoon when…?"

Adrenaline pumps through me as I remember walking into his part of the office and seeing that succubus looming over him. "Yes. Consent is sexy, Noah. More to the point, in our community, consent is essen-tial, and lack of it is a crime. The only exception is to prevent harm to oneself or others. Did she enthrall you?"

He hesitates, and my blood surges. How dare an employee of CSG, someone who is supposed to stand for the law and what's right, use their power in a personal squabble? In the office! Poor Noah—like he hasn't been through enough, he's now had to deal with a colleague abusing him in what's supposed to be a safe pla—

"I'm not actually sure," he says finally, cutting off the tirade in my head.

He's not sure...?

"How so?" It's really not that complicated. Succubae don't have the ability to remove or replace memories— they just leave their conquests in a sexual fog that usually gets written off to exhaustion.

"Well... she did something, because I've never gotten hard for a woman before. But there was no brain haze or anything—I was thinking clearly, and I knew I didn't want to have sex with her."

I blink. "That's... interesting." Fuck. Could this be because of the way the magic clings to him? I'm not aware of any species having immunity to enthrallment. The closest would be another succubus or incubus, or a vampire, and even then, it's not so much immunity as it is a diffusion. If the succubus had tried anything with me, for example, I would still have become aroused and experienced the sexual fog, but with awareness of what it was and potentially the ability to maintain rational thought.

Which just gives weight to the idea that Noah does have latent vampire abilities.

Tapping my fingers repeatedly against the chair arm because I know it pisses him off and I don't want him getting tense over my next question, I ask, "When you say you were thinking clearly, what do you mean exactly? Was there any kind of haziness or sexual aware-ness, but you were able to ignore it?"

He shakes his head, his eyes dropping to my fingers. "No, nothing like that. I wondered about that, though—isn't there supposed to be? Like, my research so far all says I should have been unable to think because of the out-of-control lust." His eye twitches. "Uh, can you stop that, please?"

I smirk but inject an innocent note to my voice. "Stop what?"

"You're, like, a bajillion years old. Aren't you sick of tormenting people? How old do you have to be to finally grow up?"

My hands involuntarily curl into fists before I force them to relax. "Age is relative, Noah. You have to find the fun in life or it's not worth living." Before he can reply, I stand. "Now, we've gotten off target. We're supposed to be trying to bring out latent vampire abilities."

He stands too, although a lot more reluctantly. "Yeah. So... it was meditation and some exercises, right?"

"We'll get to that. First, since we've been talking about feeding, let's see if you're reactive to blood."

He shakes his head—more forcefully than necessary, I note with interest. "I'm not. They took blood all the time in the labs. And when I was thirteen, my friend came off his skateboard and gashed his leg open. It was bleeding like crazy, but I had no reaction."

"That's because your friend was human, and so is your blood. Plus, we don't go into a frenzy at the sight of blood unless we are starving and beyond control." I unbutton my shirt cuff and begin rolling it up. He watches me warily.

"Why does it make a difference that it was human blood? What kind of reaction are you talking about, if not some kind of frenzy? And what are you doing?"

I look around and spot a box of tissues in the middle of the conference table. Perfect. Noah looks a little alarmed when I get the box and then tuck some tissues in around the edge of my rolled-up sleeve. It's a white shirt, one of my favorites, and I don't want to risk getting blood on it.

"The reaction could have been anything from a slight interest to sore gums to an itchy nose, to a sensation of hunger—general hunger, not necessarily for blood."

He shakes his head. "I don't remember feeling anything like that. What are you doing?"

"And the fact that it was human blood makes a difference because a vampire's ability to process blood is triggered by ingesting vampire blood."

He freezes. "Whoa. So if a vampire never drinks vampire blood, they won't need to ever drink blood?" I can see him wondering why we feed at all if that's the case, and I smile sadly.

"No. If a young vampire isn't permitted to feed from another vampire when the time comes, they'll die of starvation. We *need* the enzymes in blood to survive, but through some evolutionary oddity, our systems can't process any other species' blood until we've ingested vampire blood."

A slow blink while he thinks about that. "How old? Is it like shifters not shifting until puberty?"

"It would be better if it was. Charisma abilities don't

begin to develop until puberty, but we need to begin feeding at the same time we are weaned. Sometimes a little earlier—it seems to go hand in hand with solid food."

He goes utterly white and sways. "Babies?" he chokes out, and I nod.

"Vampire children are utterly dependent on their parents—either for them to supply blood, or to compel donors for them. Obviously things are much easier in modern times. Now, if you will stop distracting me…" I lift my wrist to my mouth, and Noah stumbles back a few steps, hands up.

"Oh my god, what are you *doing*?"

Sighing, I lower my hand a few inches. "Come on, Noah. We need to see if you're reactive to blood. How did you think we would do it?"

His panicked, wide-eyed gaze is fixed to my wrist. "Can't you just wave a bag of blood under my nose or something? Or I could eat some of that blood-infused chocolate in the break room vending machine."

Should I be offended that my blood isn't good enough for him? Mildly irritated, I point out, "We can't be sure that the blood in those commercial products is vampire blood. I could track some down, but it would take more effort than just doing this." I let my fangs descend and neatly bite into my wrist.

Noah makes a choking sound.

Raising my head, I watch the blood begin to well with a sense of satisfaction. It's a clean wound that will heal easily, but there's enough blood to stir any hunger for it that Noah might have. I really am good at this. Maybe I should add it to my special skills on my résumé.

"Come on, come and smell this." I wave the arm

gently, careful not to send blood flying. Don't want to mess up the carpet.

Dragging his feet, he edges closer, gaze locked on my wrist—though from the expression on his face, he's not feeling any attraction to the blood. When he's within reach, I grab his arm and tug him closer, bringing my bleeding wrist up under his nose.

He recoils.

Hmm. Not the reaction of a latent vampire.

"Anything?" I ask. "Hungry? Itchy? Maybe horny?"

He shakes his head violently, leaning back from my wrist as much as my grip will allow. "No, nothing!"

Sighing, I let go. "Then you're probably going to hate this next bit."

Taking two steps back, he eyes me warily. "Why?"

"Because you need to taste it."

# CHAPTER THREE

## Noah

OH, *hell* no.

And yes, I know now that hell doesn't actually exist. It's still a word that sums up what I'm feeling right now. So does fuck.

In fact…

"You're *fucking* out of your mind if you think there's any way in *hell* I'm drinking blood."

There. That's pretty clear.

He sighs and shakes his head, and for once, I'm pretty sure he's not doing this to torment me.

"Look, it really seems like you're not reactive to blood, but because of… everything, we can't be sure if your sensitivity is just lower. Please, Noah—just a taste."

Fucking Tish and his fucking need to fuck around with people's lives. If it wasn't for his god complex, I wouldn't be in this situation right now.

I also would never have been born, but nothing in the universe will ever make me thankful to him for that.

Eyeing Andrew's wrist, I swallow hard. I really don't want to taste his blood. Or any blood. But I do want to know sooner rather than later if there's any chance I might one day need to feed. The idea of starving to death because I don't even know I need blood is terrifying.

"Could you… smear it on a cracker or something? I don't want to lick your wrist." It's too personal. I can't stand the guy, but I'm going to suck on his arm? No.

"Smear it on a cracker?" For some reason, he looks offended. "Do you see any crackers around here?" He throws his non-bleeding arm out in a dramatic gesture. "Am I supposed to wander the halls looking for a buffet that will meet your standards while dripping blood everywhere and ruining my shirt?"

Ruining his shirt?

The dude is bleeding from a self-inflicted bite wound that he wants me, someone he barely knows, to suck, but he's worried about his shirt?

I roll my eyes. "If blood gets on your shirt, I'll wash it for you. I'm doing a load of whites tonight, and I'm good at getting stains out." I go heavy on the sarcasm so he can tell how ridiculous I think he is, but his gasp seems entirely real.

"This is a handmade couture garment," he declares, like I care. "It cost more than everything you're wearing combined." His gaze skims over my clothes. "A lot more."

Dick.

"You can't just shove it in a washing machine." The very idea seems to scandalize him, and I wonder if it would be really wrong of me to "accidentally" spill raspberry soda or something on him one day.

Probably.

I'll keep it in reserve anyway. If nothing else, it may get me a reprieve from his company.

"Fine, I'll pay for it to be cleaned," I concede patronizingly. "But I really don't think I can suck your arm, Andrew. It's too weird."

He studies me for a long moment, then sighs. "Maybe this can wait until we can find a cracker to smear the blood on," he mutters. His gaze catches on his arm, where a trail of blood is slowly rolling toward his cuff—which he's protected with enough tissues to outlast a flu epidemic. "Oh no, you don't." He bends his head and licks his arm, catching the blood. Part of me is utterly revolted, but the other part...

Well.

I've already said he's hot, right? Even for a dickbag? So picture this: hot guy slowly licking his arm, his pink tongue tracing along the smooth flesh.

I've never been disgusted and aroused at the same time before.

I must make a sound—or maybe my breathing changes or something, because he's got vampire senses and can probably tell that I've started to sweat—because he looks up, tongue still on his wrist.

It should not be as sexy as it is.

"Oh," he says, raising his head. There's a sudden wicked gleam in his gaze that worries me. "I have an idea."

"Planning a move to the arctic?" I suggest. "Want to take up wrestling with polar bears? I can help you pack."

He shakes his head slowly, a smirk stretching his mouth... the same mouth that was just sliding along his arm.

"Nothing so interesting," he advises. "This is just a little trick that might allow us to get this done and move on to seeing if you have any charisma ability."

I wait nervously. As much as I'd love to be able to compel people with my mind, I really don't think this "little trick" to help me taste blood is going to be fun.

"You don't want to take the blood directly from the vein." He gestures to the still-bleeding bite on his arm. "But you seemed okay with the idea of a transfer— blood on a cracker."

"Yeeees…." Where's he going with this?

He shrugs. "So, let's transfer. I'll take a mouthful of blood. A simple kiss, and enough of the blood will transfer for us to tell if you're reactive at all."

I'm so, so ashamed of how long it takes me to understand what he's suggesting. A simple kiss… between him and me?

He's going to kiss me?

My heart rate picks up, and it's not from revulsion. In fact, there's altogether too much interest from my body.

"Fine." The word bursts from me, and Andrew's jaw drops.

"What?"

"Fine, do it. Kiss me. If it will get this over and done with, I can kiss an old man." That last bit is pure bravado, because even though I know Andrew is literally old—by human *and* community standards—the last thing I think when I look at him is "old man."

He blinks a few times, then says, "Okay."

I think I've broken him. He must have expected me to kick up a huge fuss. Which, to be honest, I want to. But I also want to move the fuck on from all this blood stuff and focus on the possibility that maybe I can use charisma.

Andrew comes closer, once again lifting his wrist to his mouth, and knowing he's sucking out some of his own blood is squicky. Then he pulls his arm away and leans in toward me, and I swear, my heart is going so fast, it might explode.

His lips touch mine, the pressure light but insistent, and I open for him. A tiny shiver runs down my spine. It's a good first kiss, exploring but not devouring, and—

The metallic tang of blood hits my tongue, and I gag, jerking back and slapping a hand over my mouth.

"Well," Andrew says, wide-eyed as he watches me gag again and try not to retch, "I've never had that response to a kiss."

I flip him the bird and focus on getting myself under control. Unfortunately, all I can taste is blood.

"Would you like some water?" he offers solicitously, and I nod, afraid that if I take my hand away, I'll actually vomit.

He goes over to a cabinet and opens it to reveal a hidden bar fridge stocked with bottled water. A moment later, he hands me a bottle, and I risk vomit long enough to twist the cap off and take a gulp.

Except, there's nowhere to spit it out.

Fuck.

I could run for the bathroom, but chances are someone's going to see me and want to know what's going on. I'm already the oddity around here—no reason to add to it.

And I'm not going to spit bloody water all over the carpet.

Which leaves… swallowing it.

Gross.

Admittedly, there's not a lot of actual blood. Maybe half a teaspoon's worth. So it's mostly water... and I really just want to wash the taste away.

Giving in, I swallow. Then follow up with another huge mouthful of water. I definitely do not like the taste of blood.

Andrew's watching me with a combination of fascination and disbelief. "It's really not that bad," he chides. "I quite like it." Once more, he licks the punctures on his wrist, but this time when he pulls it away, I can see that the bite is closed. That's some heavy mojo. I wonder if it works on all wounds or only vampire-inflicted ones.

While he plucks tissues from his cuff and rolls down his sleeve, I finish off the water.

The water.

Fuck me. We could have just put a few drops of his blood into some of the water. Andrew didn't have to kiss me.

Or I could have touched the wound and then licked my own finger.

As I stand there, dumbstruck by my own idiocy, Andrew plucks the water bottle from my hand and strolls over to deposit it in a recycling basket by the door.

"It's pretty clear you don't have a need to consume blood," he says cheerfully, and my eyes fix on his mouth as it moves.

The mouth that kissed me.

Because I was too stupid to realize there were other options.

Unless... was I being sabotaged by my subconscious? On some level, did I actually *want* to kiss Andrew?

Probably. I mean, who doesn't want to kiss a sexy guy, right? And now I've indulged myself.

It's done.

"What's next?" I ask, pushing the whole kiss debacle into a titanium-strength mental safe, never to be thought of again, even if part of me is whining about how it felt good and would make a great starting point for a spank-bank fantasy.

*Down, boy.*

"We'll see if you have any ability at all for charisma. Even if you can only cause a moment of distraction, that would be enough to give you an advantage in a bad situation. A few seconds can make a big difference."

I nod. "Okay. So… what first?"

His smile is altogether *too* innocent. "How are your meditation skills? Ever done yoga?"

"A few times. I'm okay at meditation." Not really. Either I'm unable to clear my mind, or I fall asleep. There's been no happy medium for me. But I'm not telling him that. This will be the time I master meditation, because there is no way I'm letting Andrew Turner win.

Not after he made me taste his blood. Even if I did agree.

"Great! Charisma is like meditation in no way."

I wish I was still holding that water bottle, because I'd really like to throw it at him.

"Meditation focuses inward. It's about the self. Charisma is about other people. You need to project outward."

That… actually makes sense.

I'm not telling *him* that.

"Now, obviously when using charisma for feeding, you want your donor to feel no pain and be comfortable. That's a specific skill that you're unlikely to need, since you don't like blood." He shakes his head, his tone disbelieving. "But the starting point, projecting emotion, is the same. So you're going to try influencing my emotions."

I wait, but he appears to be done.

"Is there a how-to manual? This feels like being thrown into the ocean and told to swim." I mean… how the fuck would I even begin influencing his emotions? Other than by staining his shirt, of course.

I narrow my eyes. *There's an idea.*

"Whatever you're thinking, no." He points a finger at me sternly, like I'm a misbehaving pet. "As to how, you need to clear your mind the same as you would with meditation, focus on an emotion, and project it. I know that doesn't seem clear, but it will make sense. *Feel* something and then push it toward me."

Yeah.

The doubt I'm feeling must show on my face, because he laughs.

"Think of it this way. Ever heard the expression 'Fake it 'til you make it'?"

I nod. "Sure. Oh." Huh.

"See? If you're going to a job interview and you're nervous, you don't want the interviewer to know. You fake—or project—being confident. Some people suck at it, but if you're successful, the interviewer reacts to that. What I'm asking you to do is an extension of that."

I've never been for a job interview in my life—my parents insisted my focus should be on school, which is really ironic, since they knew all along I was never going to make it to college—but I get the basic premise.

"Okay, sure, let's give this a shot." I plant myself back in my chair so I can devote all my focus to what I'm doing. "What do we want? What emotion, I mean."

He settles in the other chair and smirks at me. "Something that comes naturally to you. Let's not make this any harder than it has to be. I wonder if it's possible to project snarkiness?"

The look I give him summarizes my feelings about that pretty clearly, but the bastard just laughs again. He's got a point, though. It'll be easier to try to project what I'm actually feeling rather than first trying to feel something different.

I close my eyes and take a deep breath, but that's the only similarity to meditation preparation. Instead of trying to clear my mind, I concentrate on the persistent, vague annoyance Andrew fosters in me—on all the frustrating things he says and his stupid face—and when it's a nagging wound in my brain, I visualize *pushing* it toward him. In my mind's eye, the ugly gray of annoyance flows across the room toward him.

Interestingly, focusing on my own emotions has the same effect as the beginning stages of meditation—an awareness of my breath and the blood rushing through my body. I guess they're kind of the same thing—although no guided meditation I listened to ever suggested focusing on negative emotions.

As it always does when my emotions are strong, the magic tightens around me, caressing against my skin. I wish I understood why.

"Are you doing anything?" Andrew asks, and my annoyance ramps up, stabbing away any self-awareness the deep breathing engendered and causing the magic to whirl faster against me. I *push* harder, willing all my annoyance to rush at him and swamp him.

"Hey!" His surprise cuts through my concentration, and I open my eyes to see him studying me. "That's pretty good, Noah. I definitely felt pissed off for a second." He chuckles, and I don't know why, but for once it doesn't make me want to smack him. "I guess I shouldn't be surprised that irritation was your go-to feeling."

What he's saying sinks in. "Wait… so it worked?" Holy shit. I have vampire powers!

"It worked," he confirms. "Only briefly, but I didn't expect more than that. Let's try it again."

This time, it seems easier—or maybe that's just because I'm buoyed up by success. I'm not annoyed anymore, and I don't bother trying to build it up again. Instead, I just close my eyes and *push* all my elation at finally having something go right toward him.

I don't think it's working, though, because he says nothing. So I take a few more deep breaths, feeling the magic brushing against me with each one, and really focus.

Andrews laughs, a triumphant, almost giddy sound. "Yes! Excellent, Noah. Wow, that's some head rush."

I open my eyes again, grinning so widely it hurts my face.

"This is great work. How does it feel from your end?"

I make myself consider it rather than just tossing off an answer. "I'm not sure how easy it would be to do under pressure. Like, if I was stressed or afraid, I don't know that I'd be able to project any other emotion."

He nods slowly. "That's not unusual. Most vampires can't project emotions they're not feeling unless they've been specifically trained to do so. In your case, since we're looking at this as a defense tool, sending a burst of fear into an attacker would probably be effective as a distraction." He frowns. "What concerns me more is how long it takes you. I know you've just started, but you really seem to need time to concentrate before there's a result."

"Won't that get better with practice?"

He shrugs. "Hopefully. Can we try something different? I want to see if you're able to replicate the outcome without closing your eyes and having quiet."

Uh-oh.

"So… keep my eyes open?"

"And I won't wait silently," he adds. "In an emergency situation, you'd need a split-second response with potential stressors all around you. Your enemy is unlikely to let you take deep breaths and concentrate."

Yeah, I knew I wouldn't like this idea. He wants me to give him *permission* to annoy me. I sigh. "Sure. I can try."

The next thing I know, Andrew is doing his level best to piss me off.

And succeeding.

As he chatters inanely about the evolution of men's handkerchief styles over the centuries, he rolls his chair back and forth, pushing off with his legs and occasionally swiveling as fast as he can like a little kid would. There's definitely enough annoyance in me to drown him with, but I can't concentrate for long enough to shove it at him.

I think it's the visual aspect that's the hardest to

ignore. I could maybe block out the white noise of his voice, but his constant rolling around breaks my focus every time.

I try fixing my gaze on one particular spot, well above the level of his head, and for a second, it seems to be working. My mind seems to be dropping into a groove, and I gather all my frustration and anger together—

His face pops into my field of vision. "Nope! No cheating. You need to be able to do this with visual distractions, Noah."

I blink, my concentration shattered. How...? I mean, he's a tall man, but not *that* tall.

"Do you know how dangerous it is to stand on a chair that rolls and swivels?" I ask. "If HR catch you doing that, you're in big trouble." Am I tempted to give the chair a shove and see if he can ride it? Sure. But I'm not going to. That would be irresponsible and unsafe.

My fingers itch.

No! I'm going to be the better man here. No matter how much I want to see him fly through the air and go sprawling over the conference table.

He snorts and steps gracefully down to solid ground. Yes, *steps*, as though he's only inches off the ground and not a foot and a half. "I have excellent balance and reflexes, Noah. Now, let's try again. It's hard, but you need to be able to do this as a reflex, without needing prep time or specific conditions."

I don't bother reminding him that I've just started, that repetition and conditioning can make almost any action a reflex, but it takes time. Even pro sports players started somewhere.

Instead, I try to ignore his resumed chatter about...

is he seriously giving me a recipe for blood-infused chocolate pudding?

My stomach lurches.

Sighing, I give up. I'm not going to master this today, but I'll practice when he's not around to distract me. Once I have a better grip on it, then I can introduce the distractions.

In the meantime… what the fuck is he doing?

"What are you doing?" The question falls from my lips involuntarily. He's wheeled his chair over to the far end of the room and swiveled to brace his feet against the wall.

"I want to see if I can make it from one end to the other without stopping or touching the floor," he declares with all the enthusiasm of a seven-year-old.

I pick my jaw up off the floor. I shouldn't be surprised. This fits in perfectly with his usual behavior. I don't know why I was expecting different just because he's an ancient vampire, widely considered to be amongst the oldest and most knowledgeable of his kind.

He bends his knees and pulls the chair closer to the wall, presumably to give himself a better push-off, and then suddenly he's whooshing across the room, wheeeee-ing like a kid.

Turns out, I'm not the better man. I can't even say I'm ashamed of myself. It's an instinct, a reflex action.

I stick my foot out, and it tangles with the chair's castors.

Andrew goes flying. Like, literally sails through the air. It's *epic*. I wish I had a camera with me to record it, because this is something I'm going to want to relive over and over.

He crashes to the ground, and I swear, his head is

only *inches* from the wall. If he'd had a little more momentum, he would have smashed right into it —headfirst.

"Ohhhhhh," I groan sympathetically. "You were so *close*." What a shame he didn't achieve his goal.

Muttering, he rolls onto his back and glares at me. His nose is bleeding and crooked, I guess from when he hit the floor, and he looks macabre and dangerous, not at all like his usual self.

For a second, I wonder if I need to run.

Then he starts to laugh, and my whole body relaxes, relief almost tangible.

"Did that look as awesome as it felt?" he asks, levering himself into a sitting position and flowing to his feet. It's really not fair how graceful he is.

"That depends on how awesome it felt. It looked like a movie stunt." I decide to be a good person—however belatedly—and get up to bring him some tissues. If any of that blood dripping from his nose gets on his shirt, he may not be such a good sport about this after all.

Because, you know, *a shirt* is more important than his nose.

"Thanks," he says as he takes them, presses them to his face, and straightens his nose with an audible grating sound. As I take a step back and wince, he adds sharply, "What's wrong?"

"Nothing!"

His eyes narrow and he looms forward, so I tack on, "Really, it's nothing. I think my foot might be a bit bruised from where I— Uh, from where your chair hit it." I try to make it sound like it was an accident, maybe even one he caused with his reckless and unprofessional behavior, rather than me deliberately sabotaging him.

It doesn't work.

"Oh, from where *my chair* hit it, hmm?" He raises an eyebrow superciliously. I wonder if I can yank it off his face and make him eat it. "Sit down and let's have a look."

What?

"Uh, what?"

He gestures to my chair while bending over to right his, which is lying on its side, castors still spinning. "Sit. Down. I want to check your foot."

"It's fine," I protest. "Maybe a little bruised. That's all."

He plants himself in his chair and rolls over to where mine is waiting. "Then it won't hurt for me to look."

I'm not going to win this fight, am I?

I begin to wonder whether the whole Andrew-flying-through-the-air thing is going to come back to bite me.

Sighing, I shuffle over and slump into my chair, then bend over to take off my shoe and sock. No sooner have I straightened and started to wonder how exactly we're going to do this, than Andrew grabs my leg and yanks my ankle up to rest on his knee—completely unbalancing me. I yelp and grab the arms of my chair to keep from falling off.

"Hey!"

"I thought you did yoga," he mutters, turning my foot carefully in his hands. "You should have better balance."

There is absolutely no good response to that. Asshole.

I suffer the indignity of having him examine my foot, twisting my leg this way and that, ostensibly so he can see everything properly, but I'm sure he's just tormenting me. Finally, he lets it go—without warning, of course, so it drops sharply and I'm thrown off balance again.

"It doesn't seem to be broken, but there are a lot of small bones in feet. If it's still bothering you after a while, we'll arrange an X-ray."

"We?" I say snidely, putting my sock and shoe back on. "I think I can manage that myself, thanks. There's a radiology clinic down the street from my apartment."

The look he gives me is so patient and long-suffering, I feel like a kid having a tantrum. "I mean 'we' as in CSG," he says. "I'm sure Percy has told you it's better if you don't visit human doctors. Your bloods and scans all appear fully human now, but we don't—"

"Yeah, I know, sorry," I interrupt, face hot with embarrassment. "I wouldn't have... I don't intend to give you guys away. This might not be what I always pictured for my life, but I *am* grateful." Ugh, I nearly choked on those words. Why is it so much easier to say thank you to Percy than to Andrew? Even knowing that Andrew was part of the group that raided the compound and freed me?

He pats my knee. "I know. So... I'm guessing you weren't able to concentrate while I was moving around."

I don't even bother to reply, and he laughs.

"Well, at least we know it's something you can do and an area to work on. Why don't we check out your reflexes and spatial awareness now? We can come back to charisma another time."

"Spatial awareness?" The wary feeling is back. I'm pretty sure I'm not going to like this much. And after everything else we've done today, that's really saying something.

He nods and stands, pushing his chair so it rolls to the side. "Up. Your job is really easy this time. All you need to do is be aware of where I am and dodge me. It's a bit like tag. You're going to stand mostly still, and I'm going to move around you and try to tap you with my hand. Be aware of where I am and try not to let me touch you."

That sounds easy enough—except for the part where he's a vampire with super speed and reflexes and I'm not.

But hey, whatever.

I sigh. "Sure. Let's give it a shot."

He tsks. "Come on, Noah. What's with the defeatist attitude? You never know what you can do until you try." And then he winks.

Have I mentioned how much I hate him? It bears repeating.

Less than five minutes later, my arms are flailing wildly in a desperate attempt to stop him from touching me. There's no way, absolutely no way I'm ever going to be able to beat his reflexes. Right now, I just want to wallop him.

Unfortunately, my tentacle-waving-kraken impression gets a little too enthusiastic. Next thing I know, I've lost my balance and am flat on my back on the floor. Please note that Andrew did *not* use his super speed or reflexes to catch me. Just in case you thought I was exaggerating the asshole bit.

"Ow." I lift my hand to probe the back of my head. There's a sore spot where it smacked the floor. "Happy fucking birthday to me."

"What?"

I glare up at Andrew. "What? Help me up, would you?" It's the least he can do.

He reaches down and hauls me to my feel so fast, I get a little dizzy.

"Did you say it's your birthday?" he demands. I'm so busy trying to regain my balance while simultaneously checking for a lump on my head that it takes me a second to answer.

"What? Oh. Yeah." I think I'm done for the day. We made a little bit of progress amidst a whole pile of nothing, and I'm ready to call it quits. It's close enough to the end of the workday that I won't feel bad about leaving.

But first, I'm going to grab another bottle of water and sit down for a minute.

I've raided the fridge and am cracking open the bottle when I hear Andrew talking. Only it's not to me.

"Sam? I'm either devastated that you didn't invite me or shocked and appalled that you didn't plan anything."

What the fuck? I spin around to see his phone pressed to his ear and his usual smirk on his face.

"I'm talking about the fact that it's Noah's birthday"—oh, no, no, no! I feel my eyes widen with horror—"and yet I've heard nothing about a party. You didn't even bring a cake to the meeting earlier."

"Shut up!" I hiss. "What are you *doing*?"

"I'm with Noah still, and he seems really upset right now." I can tell he's trying to sound serious, but there's no hiding the note of laughter in his voice—especially when I abandon my water and lunge for him. "This is really not what I expected from you, Sam. I thought you were one of those friends who remembered important events and made a fuss." He puts a hand on my chest and extends his arm, and that's it. I can't get any closer.

I give up trying to get his phone away from him and glower. "I hate you."

"What's that, Sam? I couldn't hear you; Noah was saying something... I think about how he hates to be a bother. Isn't that awful? He doesn't even want to trouble us to celebrate his birthday."

If it wasn't my life he was fucking with, I'd probably admire the way he's gone about this. With one phone call, he's managed to torment two people... three if you count Gideon, who doesn't strike me as the birthday party type but will probably be roped into helping Sam organize one. That takes skill. And wrongheadedness, but hey, what else can I expect from him.

Conceding defeat and leaving Andrew to his puppeteer act, I go back to my water bottle and plant myself in my chair. Maybe I'll get lucky and Sam will decide to take me out for lunch tomorrow or something instead of a par—

"No, I really think it has to be a party, Sam," Andrew insists. "We want Noah to feel like part of the group, don't we? He should know he belongs. What better way than with a gathering to show everyone how much we care? A quiet meal somewhere might make him think you're ashamed of knowing him."

I shake my head. "You're the one who should be ashamed." Sam's not really falling for this, is he?

I sigh. Maybe he is. As grateful as I am to Sam, I've been kind of standoffish. It wouldn't be a stretch to convince him it's because I don't feel like I'm part of the group. Especially since I don't—but that's not actually something I'm sad about. Is it terrible that part of me just wants to be an ordinary human? And ordinary humans don't fit in with… whatever this is.

"Sure, I can do that. We have a few more exercises I want to try"—oh, hell no—"but then we'll come to your place. You should ask David to get the cake from that place near his house."

Is it just me, or does Andrew seem really hung up on the idea of cake? That's the second time he's mentioned it to Sam. Could it be that the vampire who is rumored to have witnessed the signing of the Magna Carta (and no, I don't actually believe that, but it *is* a cool story) has the sweet tooth of a small child? I wonder if that's because sugar was so hard to come by in Europe when he was a kid.

Actually… *was* sugar hard to come by back then? I assume it was, because shipping was much slower and more perilous, not to mention processing and refining would have been very different, but I've never really looked into it. I should ask Andrew—if nothing else, it will give me the chance to slip in a few jabs about his advanced age.

He's ended the call now and is grinning at me expectantly. I'm about to start yelling when my phone rings in my pocket, vibrating pleasantly against my leg.

I groan.

"You'd better get that," he says, and this time I actually do get to throw my water bottle at him. Such a shame it's empty. And that he dodges it.

I fish out my phone and glance at the display before answering. "Hi, Sam."

"Happy Birthday! I'm so sorry, I didn't know." He sounds anxious for me to understand that he didn't just forget my birthday, and I wish I still had the bottle so I could throw it again.

"Thank you, Sam. Don't worry about it, there was no way for you to know. I didn't want any fuss, anyway." I tack the last bit on in the hopes of avoiding a party.

"No fuss," Sam assures me, "but we have to mark the occasion. It's not every day you turn twenty." He pauses. "It *is* twenty, right? Math has never been my strong point."

I snort. "Yeah, I'm twenty now." Man, I never really considered it, but I must seem so young to all the people here. Like, I've always thought about it in terms of how old they all are, but I must be a baby to them. Even Sam is nearly twenty years older than me, and he's the youngest one here by far... as much as I can tell. It's not like everyone wears a badge with their age on it. "But we really don't need to mark the occasion. I don't want you to go to any trouble." I wince. Fuck, that was the wrong thing to say.

Sure enough, Sam falls all over himself to assure me that it's no trouble at all, and I find myself agreeing that a small gathering would be great, and yes, I'll come with Andrew later. "Or I could come over now," I offer in a last-ditch effort to escape the dastardly vampire. "I'm sure Andrew's got other things he needs to do. I don't want to take up all his time." Oh my god, what is *wrong* with me? As soon as the words are out, I know they were a mistake. I need to stop with all the polite expressions I don't mean, because Sam is instantly asserting that Andrew's glad to help me and that I'm a priority to them all.

Andrew just laughs, the fucker.

I end the call with Sam feeling both glum and murderous. It's an interesting combination.

"Ready to move on?" Andrew asks in a perky voice best associated with those people who do telemarketing surveys and assure you they have "just a few questions."

"I'm done," I say bluntly. And just so there's no room for misinterpretation... "No more tests or activities or anything. I'm done."

He studies me, then nods. "Fair enough. It's been a busy afternoon. What if we try some meditation?" He holds up his hands when I start to protest. "Just meditation. Something to help your brain process everything you've done today—including your attempt to maim me."

"I did not attempt to maim you." Not that I'll admit to, anyway. "It was an accident. Your chair hit me."

"Sure, sure. An accident. Anyway, meditation?"

Is it wrong of me to be suspicious? "Just meditation? Nothing else?"

"I swear. Just meditation. I know it doesn't seem like it, but we pushed hard today, and you did something with your mind that you've never done before. It's a good idea to let it relax fully."

He seems to be in earnest, and honestly, I really would welcome the opportunity to just sit and be quiet and still for a few minutes. So I grudgingly agree, then close my eyes as he starts with the whole "breathe in through your nose and clear your mind" spiel. My gym teacher at high school was really into meditation and always started class with a five-minute session, so this is nothing new... although I have to admit, when Andrew's not trying to be a dick, his voice is kind of soothing....

# CHAPTER FOUR

## Andrew

I LUNGE FORWARD and catch Noah just as he topples out of his chair. From the way his heartbeat and breathing were settling, I was pretty sure he was either going into a deep meditative state—which isn't impossible but seemed unlikely so quickly—or falling asleep.

Looks like option number two won.

"Huh? What?" He blinks up at me, then jerks himself out of my hands so hard, his chair slides back on its castors. "What the fuck?"

I go back to my chair and calmly seat myself. "You fell asleep."

For a second it looks like he's going to argue with me, but then he huffs. "Fucking meditation. I can't believe I fell asleep sitting up."

Part of me wishes I'd let him tumble out of his chair —and used my phone to record it. That's the part that wants revenge for the "accident" earlier. The responsible part of me that our people's leaders look to for advice and protection is glad I did the right thing.

That's my boring side. Such a buzzkill. Eats vegetables and washes the dishes right away instead of leaving them to soak.

"Do you want to try again?" I suggest. "This time I'll focus more on visualization and less on breathing." He really needs this, I think. Noah is so self-contained and prickly that it's easy to forget he's been through major trauma. Plus, he's only just twenty years old. Sure, he's an adult who's shown more maturity and self-possession than most people gain in a lifetime, but he's still had to deal with a lot in his short life.

Which is why I will definitely be investigating the incident I witnessed this afternoon. If anyone is bullying Noah—or bullying anyone, period—it's going to stop.

And that has nothing to do with the fact that our very short kiss had the same effect on me as a bolt of lightning.

Noah's settled in a relaxed pose again, although his posture is just a tiny bit tense, as usual. "Okay," he says. "Let's do this." He slams his eyes closed.

I bite back a smile and begin taking him through one of my favorite visualization exercises. Sam was really surprised when he found out how huge a part of daily vampire life meditation is, but it's always made sense to me. We stretch and exercise and care for our physical bodies, and it's important to do the same for our minds—especially since we traditionally use mental abilities to survive.

I watch Noah visibly relax throughout the meditation, and by the time I'm done, twenty minutes later, he's much more comfortable in his body. It's worth the dry throat from talking. Leaving him to come back to reality at his own pace, I quietly go get myself some water—and grab another bottle for him, although thinking about it, he's already had two bottles and probably needs to piss.

Sure enough, when he opens his eyes and blinks at me, he says, "I really need the bathroom," in a surprised voice.

"There's one down the hall, remember? Easy getting up... Do you want me to come with you?" That earns me a fulminating glare and obviously clears some of the fog in his brain. He leaves while I congratulate myself on being such a good meditation guide that he didn't even notice he had to use the bathroom until I was done.

I finish my water and have started rearranging the conference table and chairs by the time he gets back.

"Do you need help— Why am I even asking?" he mutters, going to where I've left his water on the credenza.

"Almost done, but thanks," I say cheerfully. "How are you feeling?"

He takes a slug of water and seems to be thinking about it.

"Good. Relaxed." That note of surprise is back in his voice.

"Great. Do you have any guided meditation recordings or...?" I trail off as he shakes his head. "Okay. There's a few apps that are really good. If you're going to be using mental abilities, you need to look after your mental health. Since you should be practicing with charisma daily, it'd be a good idea to start the day with a short meditation and then end it the same way. Just fifteen or twenty minutes when you wake up and before you go to sleep."

He looks less than impressed by the idea, but this is

important, so I inject a note of steel when I add, "It's nonnegotiable. I won't teach you any more if you're not doing all your homework. You wouldn't go for a run without stretching before and after. This is the same." I know he likes to run; David says he's often in the office gym, using the treadmill, and has run with him a few times on nearby tracks.

"Fine." He's not happy about it, but he pulls out his phone and hands it over. "Which apps?"

His phone is a surprisingly basic model, and it takes me a second to work out how to use it. I find the apps and tap to download, then grab his hand when the phone requests a code. His skin is warm, and the flex of muscle in my grip is absurdly arousing. I can't remember the last time I held someone's hand, even platonically like this.

Maybe I am getting old.

I hand his phone back and paste on the smirk that seems to irritate him the most. "Ready? Go get your stuff. Sam and the others will be waiting." I glance out the conference room window. It's fully dark outside, and I'm sure the office will be nearly deserted. I may have gotten a little carried away with this experiment. I'll have to keep a closer eye on the clock next time.

As we leave the conference room, he says, "You don't need to wait for me. I know the way to Sam and Gideon's place."

I laugh in his face. "Nice try. If I turn up there without you, Sam will hurt me."

He shrugs. "So?"

See? The others all fuss over him like he's breakable, and sure, he needs some time and space to recover from his PTSD, but he's not exactly the sweet young man they all think.

"Sam would be sad," I try. "Even if you don't ditch the party, if I turn up without you, he'll worry that you're not going to come. You don't want to make Sam worry, do you?" It's more a taunt than anything else. I think he feels a bit guilty about the fact that Sam frets over him while he really doesn't care that much about Sam's feelings. Or at least that's what he's convinced himself.

He sets his jaw and stays silent, but when we get to the intersection where I need to go right to reach the elevator and he needs to go left, he says, "Fine, but hurry up." There's an implied threat that if I'm not fast enough, he's leaving without me.

I don't bother to answer, just make for the stairs... at vampire speed. I'll be back before he gets back from his desk, even if he runs. Foolish human, challenging me. Doesn't he know yet that I'm a mighty vampire and he's a puny human?

Yeouch. When did I start sounding like a cartoon supervillain?

Regardless, I've grabbed my stuff and am leaning against the wall by the elevator on Noah's floor, looking all casual and bored, when he races into view. He comes to a skidding halt when he sees me, and I smile at him.

"Ready? I'm glad you didn't rush. Although, really, given how short your lifespan is, you probably shouldn't dawdle quite so much."

He ignores me and jabs the elevator call button.

SAM AND GIDEON's place is close to the office—just a fifteen or so minute walk. Noah doesn't say a single word to me the whole way. Not saying I don't deserve it, but given everything we've been through this afternoon—bleeding wounds, blood kiss, maiming, charisma, and anything I've forgotten—he could at least *talk* to me.

By the time we reach their doorstep, I've decided it's funny. I wonder how long he can keep it up? And what should I do to make him crack?

He reaches for the doorbell, and I laugh. "Really? Do you want to make Sam cry?" I grab the doorknob and twist. Sure enough, the door opens. "It's a party, Noah. They're expecting us."

He scowls but follows me in, watching as I close the door behind us. "It's not safe to leave it unlocked," he mutters.

Is he really still so ignorant?

"David's warded this place from top to bottom. Gideon had him bring some friends and do the kind of heavy-duty wards used to protect royalty and sacred cultural treasures. Nobody can get into this building unless they've been coded into the wards *and* have no kind of ill intent toward Sam or Gideon. And when they activate the privacy wards, nobody can get in except them. That *really* bugs Alistair."

Noah just stands there, blinking.

"What really bugs me?" the voice of my favorite nemesis says, and I look over my shoulder to where Alistair is standing in the doorway to the living room.

"The privacy wards," I tell him, and he scowls.

"It's a travesty! Gideon is deliberately trying to keep me out! Everyone knows shifters are supposed to wander wherever they want—no lock can keep us out. It's our destiny to come and go from all places as friends—"

"Wards," Noah whispers, and somehow the sound cuts through Alistair's ridiculous tirade about shifters' destiny to enter homes uninvited. Hellhounds are so hard to get used to.

When I turn back to Noah, he's pale and wide-eyed.

"What?" I ask sharply, taking two steps forward and grabbing his arm. "What's wrong?"

He stares at me blankly for a second, then shakes his head. "Nothing. Sorry. Just… I didn't know about wards. I-I wish I had." Pulling away from me, he turns to look at the front door. "So they're… just there? Invisible? How do they work?"

"Dark sorcery," Alistair mutters dourly, and thankfully, the drama of it all seems to bring Noah back to himself, because he bursts out laughing.

"You should talk to David," I tell him, smiling. "He'll be able to explain exactly how they work. I've never bothered to learn the details myself."

Noah tsks. "That's dangerous. You literally just walked through them, and you don't know how they work?"

"Do you know how your TV works? Or your microwave?" I counter. "You use them every day without knowing the exact details, because you trust the manufacturer." I wave toward the living room, where I can hear conversation. "David wove these wards and the ones at my place, and I trust him."

His jaw sets stubbornly. "I guess," he concedes in that tone he uses when he knows I'm right but doesn't want to admit it.

Which gives me ammunition, of course.

I open my mouth to say something about how he should trust his elders and betters, but Alistair makes an impatient noise and pushes past me to grab Noah in a bear hug. Hellhound hug? Either one makes you feel like your bones are going to crack. I've never seen anyone hug Noah before—he's not exactly the touchy-feely type —and I watch with fascination and concern. I'm ready to pull Alistair off if it looks like Noah is struggling, but he seems to be okay—somewhat flummoxed, with his arms sticking awkwardly out from his body, but okay.

"Happy Birthday!" Alistair shouts, and the voices in the living room go quiet, followed by a rush of footsteps.

Sam bursts into the entryway first, freezes when he sees Alistair squeezing Noah, hesitates for a second, then throws himself at them both in what looks to be a group hug with one unwilling member.

"Happy Birthday!" he exclaims, his voice somewhat muffled because his face is buried against Alistair's arm. "We have cake and presents!"

Gideon comes to a stop beside me, tips his head to the side, and asks, "What the fuck are they doing?"

I shrug. "Celebrating Noah's birthday, it appears. It'd be more interesting if they were naked."

His head whips around, and he glares at me. He's so predictable. I can't even joke about seeing Sam naked without him getting all possessive and protective. It's one of my new favorite ways to tease him.

And speaking of ways to torment Gideon… "Did you have fun planning the party?"

His glare turns into the kind of glower that would cause a lesser being to piss its pants. Lucky for me, I've known Gideon since he was literally in diapers, and it's almost impossible to be afraid of someone when you've heard their nanny coo over their "plumpy-wumpy little tushie-tush."

Just thinking about it makes me grin.

"I know it was your idea," he hisses. "And I will get you for this."

"Aww, but look how happy Sam is." I gesture to the group hug, which has to be setting records for both duration and awkwardness. Maybe I should rescue Noah. I could mention to him how pissed Gideon is about having this party. That should freak him out.

Gideon turns back to look at the love of his life, his love's annoying best friend, and the human Sam's semi-adopted. "It makes him happy," he mutters, and it has the rhythmic quality of a mantra he's been repeating to himself.

Someone taps me on the shoulder, and I turn to see David eyeing Gideon warily. "Did you break him?"

I put on my most indignant expression, but he holds up a hand before I can open my mouth.

"Just… let's untangle Noah before he has a panic attack or something."

I glance back toward the group hug and see that Noah is now very awkwardly patting Alistair and Sam on their backs in a way that signals he's ready to be let go of.

"Sam, can I cut the cake?" I ask loudly, and Sam makes a sound that's somewhere between a shriek and a squeal and instantly wriggles free. He turns on me with an expression that promises instant death if I even go near the cake.

"Leave the cake alone, Andrew! I mean it. That's Noah's to cut. Go eat a mini quiche or one of the bacon-wrapped figs."

Whoa.

"There are bacon-wrapped figs?" I breathe. That's some fancy food for a casual birthday party thrown together at the last minute. I was expecting sandwiches and whatever he could find in the freezer aisle at the local community grocer.

"I called the caterer and offered them five times their usual fee to blow off their client for tonight and give us the food," Gideon says, a note of smug pride in his voice.

"You *what*?" Sam's shriek echoes through the entry hall. I guess he didn't know.

I prop myself against the wall and prepare to enjoy the show along with everyone else. Alistair's let go of Noah and has an expression of utter delight on his face.

Noah just looks stunned.

"Gideon, you've *ruined* someone's party! What if it was a special occasion? What if someone is right now crying hysterically because their birthday or anniversary or engagement party has no food?" Sam sounds on the verge of hysterics himself.

Gideon shrugs. "They could have made a counteroffer."

David, being the responsible (boring) type, lunges forward and grabs Sam before he can throw himself at Gideon and claw his face off. I mean that literally—Sam is one of the rare shifters who can partially shift, and his claws have just sprouted from his fingertips. He must be super mad.

"What's the big deal?" Gideon asks. "You were freaking out about getting food ready in time. I said I'd handle it, and I did."

The snarl that comes from Sam's throat is definitely not human, and David tightens his grip.

"Uh, Gideon," he says, struggling with a furious Sam, "I think Sam would have preferred you not ruin someone else's party while you 'handled' it."

"But I didn't," he protests, meeting Sam's gaze. "The caterer called the client, and they happily accepted for me to pay for them to go out instead. I got them a couple of tables at that fancy new restaurant on the Riverwalk."

I wince, because that place has been booked out since it opened and probably is for months, so Gideon would have had to splash out some serious cash to make that happen. Fortunately, I know for a fact that they keep the tables widely spaced specifically so there's room for last-minute VIP bookings. They just rearrange the tables and add another one. It's ingenious. My designer friend who planned the interior told me so when I suggested it.

Sam stops trying to get away from David and narrows his eyes at Gideon. "You're sure you didn't ruin their night?"

Gideon shakes his head emphatically. "The woman said she was thrilled to be able to show off her new outfit to strangers instead of just at home with her kids and grandkids. And I told them to order whatever they wanted from the bar too." He sounds earnest now. He hates when Sam is mad at him.

Sam humphs. "Okay then. But next time, maybe tell me this stuff upfront instead of just saying you found a caterer." He looks at David. "You can let go now. I've decided not to kill him."

David steps back. "I'm actually not sure if I'm glad

about that or not." He pats Sam on the shoulder, then looks past him toward Noah, who's trying to mask his shell-shocked expression with one of boredom. "Happy Birthday, Noah. Come on in and we'll get you some food."

Sam gasps and spins around. "Noah! I'm sorry, I didn't mean to cause a scene at your party. Come on, I went and bought that avocado and roasted red pepper dip you like." He grabs Noah's arm and leads him past us all and through to the living room. The rest of us follow.

"That was fun," Alistair murmurs to me and Gideon.

Gideon thumps him in the gut.

I ignore them both and make a beeline for the food table. The party Gideon stole the caterer from must have been for vampires—or at least had some vampires attending—because several of the food options are blood-infused. Even without the handy discreet labels, I would be able to tell from the rich, amazing smell. I grab a plate and load it up, then delicately bite into one of the steamed dumplings and sigh in delight.

You haven't experienced true culinary glory unless you've had prawn simmered in O-neg and then wrapped in pastry.

"Does that have blood in it?" Noah sounds a little ill at the thought, and with my mouth full, I point him toward the equivalent dish without the added ingredient. "Thanks." He grabs a couple of dumplings and adds them to his plate.

The next hour is pretty fun. It's definitely a low-key event, with only those of us on the team and a few people from Sam's old team here. Percy couldn't make it

—the downside of being the lucifer and having unlimited access to existential magic is that you also have to spend a lot of time socializing and assuring very wealthy people of how important they are and that as a result, they should be giving their money to good causes. Percy's position isn't an elected one, so he doesn't officially have to campaign, but it makes things easier for everyone at CSG if he's got civilians on his side. Considering the big fuss when we rescued Sam and Noah and dismantled the CCA, he's had his work cut out for him lately.

So I wander around the room with my frequently-replenished plate of food in one hand and a bottle of really good shifter brew in the other (which I put down when I need to eat—I'm not a barbarian), chatting with people I see all the time and basically just unwinding after a long week.

I'm talking to Jim from Sam's old team and his wife, who's also a vampire and is regaling me with the tale of some new protein-blood shake she tried that is supposed to taste like banana but actually tastes like "Jim's dirty socks with some blood mixed in." Apparently she called the company feedback line to ask them how anybody could think it tasted like banana, to which the customer service rep said, "Between you and me, the people in research and development get high a lot."

"What was I supposed to say to that?" she asks me. "I stammered like an idiot for a few seconds, and then the rep offered me my money back, and I took it."

"Good call," I reply. "Although, I wonder if the product would taste better if they put some of whatever they're getting high on in it?"

Jim laughs while his wife, Andrea, just stares at me,

jaw dropped. I've only met her once before, and clearly she doesn't get my sense of humor. That happens sometimes.

The sound of hands being clapped draws our attention to Sam, who's standing in the middle of the room with a pile of shopping bags surrounding him. "Okay, everyone! It's time for presents!"

Andrea gasps. "We didn't bring a present!" she hisses, grabbing Jim's arm—tightly, judging from the way he winces. "You told me we didn't need to!"

Jim pats her shoulder with his free hand. "Sam told me we didn't," he whines, looking at me pleadingly. "Andrew?"

I'm tempted to mess with him, but Andrea looks like she's on the edge, and I don't think Sam would react well to another scene at this party—even if he did cause the first one himself. "He told me the same. Since it was all so last-minute, he said he'd handle the present-giving."

Andrea relaxes and unfurls her grip on Jim's arm. There's a set of neat holes where her claws sliced through his shirt, but no blood, so she must have held back from actually puncturing his skin. Not to sound sexist or anything, but this is why I mostly stick to men. A man is more likely to punch you in the face, but he won't ruin your shirt. Women know how to get you where it really hurts.

I smooth my hands down the sleeves of my shirt, just to make sure it's okay. The fabric is so soft and fine. Thank fuck I didn't get any blood on it today. Can you believe Noah would have just thrown it into the washing machine?

I shake my head in remembered incredulity.

Meanwhile, Sam's drawn a reluctant Noah out of the crowd and sat him down in a chair that's been brought over just for that purpose. Noah doesn't look terribly excited to be on display for all of us to watch as he opens gifts. In fact, I'm pretty sure I can see the moment he decides to tell Sam it's not going to happen... and then his gaze lands on Gideon and he changes his mind. It's kind of pathetic. Maybe I should tell him about Gideon's little tushie-tush. That might help him get over this fear.

But where's the fun in that?

Sam hands Noah the first bag. "I didn't have time to wrap them," he says apologetically, "but I figure taking each one out of a bag is almost as good."

Noah forces a smile that looks more like a grimace. "You really didn't have to," he says, and then with a quick glance at Gideon, "but thank you." He digs into the first bag and comes out with... a brand-new tablet. "Oh, wow. Sam, this is too much!" It's an automatic statement, because his face has lit up in a way I've never seen, and he's running his fingers over the box.

It's like a one-two punch to the chest and the dick. The chest, because how could we have overlooked this? Noah had literally nothing when we rescued him. He'd been wearing the same single set of clothes for *a year*. We bought him clothes and set him up with a job and the basics in an apartment... but obviously we forgot that he might need more than basics to feed his soul. The money he makes at CSG is decent, but certainly not enough to splash out on pricey electronics after only a few months, evidenced by his basic-model smartphone.

As to the punch to the dick... all these months, I

knew he was a good-looking man, but I never noticed how beautiful he really is. That smile… He glows.

So I'm faced with a dilemma. He's a snarky, tough, no-nonsense, budding asshole of a man, and I won't lie, that's usually my type. Inexperienced guy cheats death to escape evil scientists and survives for a year hiding under their noses? That's super hot. But I didn't want to piss off Sam—and thus Gideon—by making a move. Plus, he needed some space to work through his trauma. And Percy would have killed me. Not to mention it's entirely likely *Noah* would have killed me.

But seeing him lit up like this, and after the kiss I've been trying to convince myself was *not* that good (even though it completely was)… maybe death is something I'm willing to risk.

# CHAPTER FIVE

## Andrew

I'M STILL PONDERING whether Noah would actually try to kill me or just maim me, which wouldn't be that bad, when the gift giving winds down and Sam goes to get the cake. Noah is carefully packing his presents back into their bags. Aside from the tablet, Sam got him some new clothes, books, and gift cards to a variety of stores and entertainment sites. Noah's excitement didn't dim at all, not even when he saw the very awful cotton T-shirts. In fact, he even seemed to like them.

Although, thinking about it, that's not really surprising.

Still, it's a new side of Noah—a happy side. I could get used to seeing it, although I wouldn't like him to become nice or anything. There are enough nice people in the world, and let's face it, they're not that interesting.

I join him as he scoops up an armful of bags and pick up those remaining.

"Oh. Thank you." He smiles tentatively at me. It's nice, but a little weird.

"Where do you want to put them?" I ask.

"In the entryway, against the wall? That way they're not in the way, I guess."

I nod and follow him out of the living room, and we stack the bags neatly to one side. "It's a pretty good haul."

His head whips around, and he glares at me. "What's that supposed to mean?"

Ah, there he is! You know what, I think it would be best if we kept sweet, smiling Noah for special occasions. I like the asshole so much better.

I shrug. "Nothing. Just that you made out well tonight. Especially for someone who never wanted a party to begin with."

He narrows his eyes. "You're being a dick on purpose, aren't you? Screw you. I'm going to have cake."

Oh, that's right—there's cake! I half turn back toward the living room, but Noah grabs my arm.

"You know what? I think I'm going to tell Sam you don't get any cake. It's my birthday, and I bet he'll agree if I say that's what I want."

I gasp. "You're a monster." Honestly, I didn't intend for it to come out sounding impressed and admiring, but I've got to give credit where it's due. He knows how to cause maximum pain.

He sneers. "I'm going to enjoy this so much."

*Think quick!* What can I offer in exchange for cake? What does he want?

"Want to learn how to do wards?" I blurt.

He stills.

Fuck. I shouldn't have said that. There's no guarantee he'd be able to learn.

But… cake. It's chocolate with chocolate-raspberry buttercream. I asked.

"What do you mean?" he asks, and I mentally kick myself a few times.

"No promises," I begin, because yeah, I like to tease, but this is clearly important to him. And I can't blame him—I never thought before how vulnerable he must feel. "Wards as we use them in the community are woven by sorcerers with their innate power, but there are humans who have been able to replicate the effects using existential magic."

He frowns and shakes his head. "What? There are humans who can use existential magic? What does that even mean?"

Wait…

"Has nobody mentioned that to you before? That humans who dedicate effort are able to use the magic?" From the stunned stare, I'm going to guess no. "Oh. I guess I assumed someone had told you… although Sam didn't find out for five years, so why would you know after six months? Uh… we should go talk to Sam. And David. David will be able to answer your questions." I might have just put my foot in it.

Noah follows me back into the living room, a confused expression on his face, and I'm about to lead him straight to David and dump this whole mess in *his* lap, when Sam calls out from over by the food table. The cake is there, and Sam's in the process of lighting some candles.

"Cake," I declare. "David can wait."

Noah seems like he's going to protest, but I give him a little shove in the direction of the cake, and he goes along with it. Possibly because Gideon has stepped up to Sam's side with a knife in his hand. I'm guessing that's to cut the cake with, but part of Noah is probably telling him it's actually to chase him down with if he dares to upset Sam.

I take advantage of the distraction and dash over to David.

"I might have done something I shouldn't," I murmur, leaning close to him.

He sighs. "Of course you did. What is it? Maybe I can fix it."

That right there tells you everything you need to know about David. If the community had Boy Scouts, he would have been one—and he'd be the adult still volunteering with the organization. You can always count on David.

"I didn't realize nobody had told Noah humans could use the magic, and I may have let it slip. Accidentally. In a totally unrelated conversation." That had nothing to do with me bartering for cake.

David scoffs, clearly not believing me, and I'd be hurt, except who are we kidding?

"It's fine," he says. "Percy and I have already talked about this. We wanted to make sure he didn't have any dormant vampire traits first, but then I was going to work with him and see if he could master human magic. Given the way the magic reacts to him, I think he's going to find it easier than most. I actually have a theory that he's already used it without knowing."

"What? When? And how?" Is that even possible?

"You forgot where and why," David teases. "In the bunker. You've heard his story—nobody's that lucky, Andrew. The lab tech and guards getting distracted right before it was his turn to get injected? And then seconds later forgetting that they hadn't injected him and not noticing he was still alive? The guards deciding to wait until they'd brought all the bodies down before loading them into the incinerator—and then not realizing one was missing? And then a *year* dodging around an enclosed space and never being discovered? He's precocious, but trained operatives would struggle to do that. I think he was so desperate that he formed some kind of bond with the magic and it helped him."

Hmmm.

"Why are you frowning?" he asks. "I thought you'd be pleased to know you hadn't fucked up."

"I never fuck up," I declare indignantly. "Sometimes my genius just gets distracted."

He snorts, and I open my mouth to ask more questions—because I have many—but the singing starts. We turn toward the cake table, where Noah stands awkwardly holding a knife while Sam beams at him and takes pictures—fuck, nobody had better tell him when my birthday is—and I sedately join in the singing.

Okay, that's a lie. I sing with gusto. When you get to my age, you realize that embarrassment is stupid. There are some things I'd still get embarrassed about, but hamming it up while singing "Happy Birthday" is not one of them. In fact, it's possible that Alistair and I are unofficially competing right now for the title of most annoying singing friend. He has the benefit of being a hellhound—howling really lets you hit that high note on "yooooouuuuu"—but I have many more years of experience in annoying people with song. Ask me one day about my years in Venice as a gondolier.

The two of us are on our third round of the song and have hit a really great rhythm, if I do say so myself, when party-pooper Gideon growls, picks up two of the plates from the stack beside the cake, and frisbees them, one each in our directions. In case you're wondering, they're *not* paper or plastic.

Sam shrieks. He's been doing that a lot tonight. My guess is that he's finding being a host more stressful than he thought. "Those are the plates your grandmother sent! She's going to hate me forever!"

I sigh, and instead of just ducking, I reach up to catch the plate.

It hurts. A lot. I don't know if you've ever caught a bone china plate frisbeed by a supremely strong demon, but there was a lot of force behind it, and the edge smacked into my palm painfully. That's going to take a while to heal, and in the meantime, I won't be using my right hand.

To eat cake, I mean. I'm ambidextrous when it comes to other things I might want to use my right hand for.

Across the room, Alistair howls, and I glance over to see he's caught his plate too. He's not handling it with stoic dignity like me, though. No, he's a pitiful crybaby hellhound, whimpering and letting people fuss over him. I sometimes wonder what went wrong with hellhounds. Any subspecies that thinks it's funny to adopt a slur as their species name has a few screws loose. Or lost completely.

On the other hand, they're great fun at parties. I can pretty much guarantee that Alistair and Elinor and the other two hellhounds here will start a conga line in a while, no matter how low-key Sam thinks he can keep the night.

Speaking of Sam, he smiles gratefully at me while he

scolds Gideon for throwing plates around, and Noah takes advantage of the distraction to put the knife down and edge slowly away from the table. Most of the candles on the cake have given up, but there are still two valiantly burning.

"Speech!" I call, switching my plate—which is soon going to hold cake—to my good hand. The right one is already swelling. "Speeeeeeeech!"

The look Noah gives me could incinerate entire cities. I'm actually proud—he's mastered it.

Sam instantly turns back to Noah—who's only made it a couple of feet away in his attempt to escape—and proves that he's a lot smarter than people think. "Uh, maybe we'll give the speech a miss, but Noah, could you blow out the candles and cut the cake?"

The relief on Noah's face makes me laugh out loud.

"Crap, Andrew, do you *want* him to murder you? Stop being an asshole for five minutes before he spits in your cake," David hisses. If he'd said anything else, I would have ignored him, but there is a very real possibility that Noah *would* spit in my cake, so…

"He tried to maim me today," I confess, and damned if there isn't a note of pride in my voice.

"He what?" David asks, eyes wide. "What did you do?"

"Nothing!" I tell him about the chair and my short-lived experience as a flying vampire. It hurts me a little that responsible, reliable, caring David is almost pissing himself with laughter when I'm done. But not that much, because it's funny. Like I said, embarrassment is for humans and young people. Too bad there's no surveillance in the conference room—I bet I looked awesome soaring through the air.

"I knew I liked him," David finally says, swiping tears from his eyes. "He's a little hard to get to know, but he's definitely our people."

I look over to the table where Noah is cutting and serving cake, wielding the knife like he wishes he could stab someone with it. "He really is." He and Gideon would probably get along like a house on fire if he could get over his fear of... whatever he thinks Gideon would do to him. They're both assholes who don't like people.

"I'm going to grab some of that cake," David says, taking a step forward, and I remember what I wanted to ask him and grab his arm.

"Wait—"

He huffs. "Fine, Andrew, you can go first. There's plenty of cake, though. You won't miss out if I get my piece before you."

Oh. I hadn't thought of that. I glance longingly at the cake table, but David's right. There's plenty, and this is important.

"No, that's not it. Although thanks, I will go first. No, what you were saying before about Noah manipulating the magic..."

He turns around properly and looks at me. "Yeah?"

"He did something today that I thought might be a precursor to charisma, but honestly, it seems odd to me that that's the only vampire ability he'd have. He hated blood—absolutely hated it."

David's brows rise. "He hated blood? Interesting. I know it's not exactly the same, but generally anybody with vampire genes needs blood—or at least has a taste for it. There was a study once that found even those whose bloodline was so diluted after generations that they didn't need blood to survive still enjoyed the taste of it."

I nod. "I remember that study." I'm not usually into the sciences, but that one was fascinating. "Maybe the difference there was that none of the other genes were human? I mean, technically, nobody with any community lineage should have human genes. It's only because of Tish's insane science experiment that it's possible, and Noah's the only survivor—if we don't count Sam." Sam's not human anymore, and he doesn't have any vampire lineage, so he doesn't factor in.

"Sure, but my point is, needing or at least liking blood seems to be the dominant vampire trait. It's highly unlikely that he'd hate the taste of blood but still have the ability, however weak, to use charisma. Charisma only evolved because of the need to feed, after all—and none of the subjects in that study who liked but didn't need blood had any other vampire abilities."

I turn all that over in my mind. "So it's more likely the events of today have something to do with the magic than any dormant vampire ability?" It makes sense... but I'm a little worried that this isn't the best outcome for Noah. He already struggles to feel a part of our community, and having a connection to his vampire lineage, however vague, might have helped him with that. Being the lone human at CSG and also one of the few humans in the world with an ability to wield the magic would basically make him "different" in both worlds.

But that's a problem for another day.

"The only way to really know is to have Noah replicate what happened today while Percy is watching," David suggests. "Percy will be able to see if it's the magic reacting or not. And if it is, then we definitely need to get Noah started with some training, because he shouldn't be able to impact the magic like that. Humans usually need ritual and instruments, even for little things."

I rub my forehead—then wince, because my hand hurts. Of all the nights for Percy not to be here. "Okay, let's get some cake. We don't mention this to Noah for now, and tomorrow we can talk to him and Percy. Would you be able to train him, if it turns out you're right?"

David's grimace is not reassuring. "Theoretically… maybe. There are some basic exercises I can show him, and I can definitely get some notes from a friend of mine who's Wiccan—remember, I called him when we thought Sam might be able to use the magic? But my abilities are different from what humans can do. It'd be like teaching him to speak Italian when I only speak Spanish myself."

Great. "Would it be best to bring in your Wiccan friend, then? You said he was married to a community member, right? So he already knows all about us."

"Maybe." He shrugs. "That's something we should talk to Percy and Noah about. Phil's husband could teach him the principles of using the magic, but Wicca is a religion, so they don't use it to its fullest extent. I haven't done too much research on this, but I have a sneaking suspicion that back before the species wars, humans didn't need so much ritual and spellcasting to use the magic."

Oh, now that's *really* interesting. And it would explain why Noah was able to use it today—if that's what he was doing—just by concentrating. "You think that when humans began rediscovering the ability to use magic, the first few bound it up in fancy words and gestures and the rest and then convinced everyone else it was necessary? Like a placebo of sorts?"

He squints. "I don't think that's the right word, but basically yeah. Like I said, I haven't had the chance to do any research—I never thought it would be important, since so few humans even believe in the possibility of magic. But it's a theory, and trawling through some old histories would probably get us an answer. Which I will do if Noah needs me to."

Too bad there's nobody around who was alive back then. But it's been nearly nine thousand years since the species wars, give or take a few centuries, and the longest-lived being I'm aware of only made it to 1,486 years before slipping away to the spiritual plane.

Still, the benefit of living for hundreds of years is that we've got plenty of time to index and update records—and we desperately appreciate our history. After all, for some of us, the species wars weren't that many generations ago. There's been a dedicated push in the community over the last twenty years to digitalize records and old histories. So it might be easier than I fear to find the information we need. Even if it is about humans, whose history nobody really cares about.

"Cake," I declare. "It's definitely time for cake."

David takes a step toward the cake table, and I grab his arm again.

"Me first, remember?"

He mutters something under his breath about the universe testing him. I ignore it and make a beeline for the cake. The good bit about having gotten distracted is that there's nobody waiting. And fortunately, there's still plenty of cake left.

Sam and Noah are standing there, eating cake and talking quietly, when David and I reach the table.

"Andrew," Sam says, "I thought maybe you'd gotten locked in the bathroom or died or something. It's not like you not to be first in line for cake." He reaches out and takes the frisbee plate from my left hand. "Thanks for this, by the way. I still haven't met any of Gideon's family, and I really don't want that to happen with the shadow of a broken gift hanging over me."

"Consider yourself lucky," I warn him. "Put it off as long as you can."

He pales. "They can't be that bad."

David makes a sound, and Sam's gaze shoots to him.

"Really? Oh, fuck."

He's starting to look panicky, and David's the nice one, remember, so he tries to reassure him. "They like each other, and you're with Gideon now, so that's a point in your favor."

Yeah. David sucks at reassurance. Sam's eyes bug out, and Noah makes a face.

"You'll be fine," I say soothingly, a little concerned that my plate still has no cake on it. And it's in Sam's hand, so I can't even help myself. Would it really be that bad if I just grabbed a handful?

Probably.

"Think of it this way, Sam," I try, wondering where Gideon's got to. This is really a problem he should be dealing with. "They're all the same level of asshole as Gideon, and he adores you. Even before you guys hooked up, you managed him just fine. So it's all good."

The panicky shock turns to a glare, which is an improvement. "I spent five years avoiding Gideon because I was afraid he was going to murder me," he gets out through gritted teeth—but he grabs the knife and viciously cuts into the cake, so it's all good. "The only reason that fear became manageable was because I joined the team and I knew Percy and Lily"—his voice falters slightly, even as I feel the familiar pang in my chest—"would stop him from killing me." He shovels the cake onto the plate in a very unattractive heap, but it'll still taste good.

"And Gideon will keep his family from killing you when you meet them." I reach out to rescue my dessert and whisk it away before he can change his mind about giving it to me. Once it's safely in my hands, I feel inclined to be generous. "Tell you what, Sam, when the time comes, I'll tag along and distract them for you. They all loathe me, so they can only love you in comparison."

From the look he gives me, that's not as comforting as I thought it would be. Just as well. It would have been a huge sacrifice on my part—Gideon's grandmother and I worked together for a few decades a long time ago, and she's really hard to deal with. I believe I once told her she was "an intolerable bitch." Then she tried to kill me. We stopped working together after that.

David leans over and gently takes the knife from Sam's hand. "I wouldn't have let Gideon murder you," he says, a slight note of hurt in his voice as he cuts himself a piece of cake with one hand and accepts the plate Noah silently hands him with the other.

*Way to miss the point, David.*

But Sam smiles at him. "I know, David. Thank you. I can't imagine being in the team without you."

I clear my throat pointedly around a mouthful of

cake. Sam turns his smile on me. "You either, Andrew. But for different reasons."

Was that an insult? I feel like I've been insulted.

"Want more cake?"

Pah, who cares about insults? I nod and extend my still half-full plate for Sam to pile more on.

"Noah was just telling me he had a bit of a break-through this afternoon."

Oh, fuck. I shovel in some more cake and jerk my head toward David, who gives me a look that promises dire vengeance. I'm not worried. David's the nice one, remember?

"Uh, yeah, Andrew told me too. Noah, do you think you'd be able to demonstrate for me and Percy tomorrow? I'll set up a time."

Noah shrugs. "I can try. No guarantees—I haven't had much practice yet."

David just nods along. "Of course, no pressure."

"Sammy!" Alistair bounds up, his injured hand wrapped around a bottle of brew. He's holding a six-pack of it in his other hand. "Time for you to chill so we can get the party started."

"I'm plenty chilled, thanks," Sam says. "Are you using that bottle as an ice pack?"

Alistair plonks the six-pack onto the cake table and pops one out to give to me. "Yep. It's always cold, because I have to keep replacing it."

"Oh no," Sam says faintly. Alistair hands another bottle to David, who's biting his lip in an attempt not to laugh.

"Don't worry, Sam, I'll make sure this party is talked about for weeks."

"Please don't," Sam replies as he accepts a bottle for himself. "I promised Noah a quiet gathering."

"Pshaw," Alistair scoffs. "Quiet is for the dead. What we have here is a select gathering of awesome people who are going to have a wild time! Well, except maybe for David."

"I really resent the way people keep saying that," David says to no one in particular. "I'm fun."

We all ignore him.

"Whadda ya say, Noah? Ready to turn up the music?" Alistair offers him a bottle of brew, a wicked gleam in his eye, and Sam, David, and I shout, "No!"

Sam snatches the bottle away. "Al, that is *not* okay." He turns to Noah. "It's shifter brew. Humans don't react well to it. A few mouthfuls, and you'd pass out drunk." He whirls back to Alistair. "How could you think that was okay, giving him a drink without telling him what it is?"

Alistair rolls his eyes. "Relax. Noah knows what it is. He asked me earlier. I offered him one then, too, but he said no."

I just happen to be looking at Noah when Alistair says that, and I don't think I'm imagining the fleeting expression of distaste and... fear?

"Although," Alistair muses, "if we're looking for dormant vampire genes, seeing how he metabolizes brew would be a pretty easy thing to check."

"No," I snap, while David sputters lame reasons why it would be a bad idea. And that fear flashes across Noah's face again. "Getting drunk to 'check metabolism' is for college kids. If Noah decides he wants to try brew, he can. Otherwise, no way."

"No, Noah *can't.*" Sam sounds exasperated. "He's twenty, not twenty-one."

David, Alistair, and I exchange confused glances.

"Uh… so?" Alistair asks.

"*So,* as a human, he's not legally allowed to drink!"

David frowns. "I thought eighteen was the legal age of adulthood for humans in this country." He shakes his head. "The laws have changed so many times over the decades, it's hard to keep up."

"It is," Sam says through gritted teeth. "For everything except drinking alcohol."

It's my turn to frown. "Is that everywhere? Because—"

"Just in this country!"

Alistair puts his hands up defensively. "Thank you for explaining it to us, Sam." He hesitates. "Although… would we really say Noah is under the jurisdiction of the human government anymore?"

I take a step back. Sam looks like he's going to go on a murder spree.

"It doesn't matter anyway," Noah interrupts, putting a hand on Sam's arm. "I don't want any. But thanks."

Alistair beams at him. "You're welcome! And you know, since it's your birthday and all, you should choose the music!" He turns to Sam. "Drink up, Sammy. You're looking kind of tense, and we all know drunk Sam is fun Sam."

Sam glares at him, then knocks back half the bottle in one go.

"Whoa," David exclaims. "It's not going to affect you like it did when you were human, but it's still going to have an impact."

"Will that impact include making Alistair go away?"

The dumbass hellhound just laughs. "I'm going. Come on, Noah. Let's get the music going."

Noah looks like he wants to protest—based on what I know about him, he was probably planning to slip out and head home soon—but Alistair drags him away.

I go back to my cake.

"Did you notice," David murmurs, leaning in so Sam and I can both hear, "that Noah looked worried about drinking brew?"

I nod, but my mouth is full.

Sam sighs. "Yeah. And when he fell and sprained his foot a couple months back, he refused to take any painkiller stronger than ibuprofen. I think it's some form of PTSD from the way they used to drug him at the bunker."

"Avoiding anything that could possibly affect his awareness or lower his inhibitions?" David sounds thoughtful. "That makes sense. Have you mentioned seeing a therapist?"

"A couple times, but he always changes the subject. I don't think he's ready."

I swallow my cake. It hurts a little, because I'm not done chewing, but I really need to butt into this conversation. "He's not hurting himself with this decision," I say firmly. "Electing not to drink alcohol or take prescription painkillers is not a bad thing. His reasons might not be great, but he's working through this at his own pace. It hasn't been that long, and he's doing great. He knows you're here for him, Sam, so we need to treat him like the adult he is."

Sam bites his lip. "He's just so young."

That makes me laugh. "Tell me, Sammy, what were you doing at his age?" Sam ran away from home at fourteen and lived on the streets for a while. By the time he was twenty, he'd been on his own for years.

A sheepish smile stretches his mouth. "Yeah, you're right. And he's strong—so strong. He's going to be fine, whether he wants our help or not."

That sounds a little like Sam's threatening the universe, but I let it go. Loud nineties pop music blares through the room, accompanied by Alistair shouting, "It's Britney, bitch!"

Time for the fun to begin. As David and Sam exchange terrified glances and sidle toward the door to the kitchen, I scrape up the last of my cake, savor that final bite, set down the plate, and launch into my dance routine.

# CHAPTER SIX

## Noah

I DON'T KNOW WHY, but I feel almost bouncy when I get to work the morning after my birthday.

Okay, that's a lie. I know exactly why. I'm happy. I had fun last night at my birthday party, even when Andrew and Alistair insisted we do the Macarena—which they had to teach me, and seriously, what the fuck, nineties people? Were you high?—and then I went home and *slept*. I only woke twice, and both times I fell back asleep easily. What's not to be happy about?

The party surprised me. I really thought it was going to be awkward, but it was just casual and low-key—until Alistair got into the music with his weird nineties fetish—and I can't believe Sam got me presents. That was... wow. I need to try harder to be patient with his hovering. He really wanted me to enjoy myself and know they care. Well, he cares, anyway.

The tablet is an amazing gift, and I'm not even talking about the monetary value. I don't have any kind of computer at home for personal use, just my phone, and it's a really basic model. It's hard being part of a digital generation with limited access to electronics, you know? I was going to study electrical engineering at college, or maybe software programming and design. Before the kidnapping, I was used to having a device in my hand or being on my computer for a lot of the day.

Anyway, I had a good night, and today's going to be a good day. David sent me a text bright and early to say he'd snuck half an hour out of Percy's calendar for us at nine, so I'm going to get to show off my new skills—hopefully. I followed Andrew's orders and meditated before bed and when I got up, and even though I was hella resentful about doing it, I've gotta admit, it does make me feel more settled and aware.

Not that I'll tell Andrew that.

I dump my stuff at my desk, ignoring the people around me who watched the episode with Nikita yesterday and did nothing about it. Mind you, they also saw me leave with Andrew and not come back, so they're probably curious about that. Like… dying of curiosity. I'm good with that.

I've heard enough stories about Sam's time at CSG to know he slotted right into his team, after some initial gentle hazing. Alistair fondly tells stories about tiny stuffed animals and recordings of hellhounds howling. It hasn't been like that for me. For starters, I'm not actually part of a team. Officially, I'm on a paid internship doing data management. It's boring and mostly solitary work. Add to that the fact that I don't really know if I want to be a part of this community and haven't exactly made any effort with my coworkers, and it's easy to see why they don't greet me cheerfully every morning. Or at all.

But I don't have time to chat this morning. I log in and quickly flick through my emails. There's nothing there that can't wait—a few new tasks. None of my work is really time sensitive. I shoot back acknowledgments that I received them, then lock the screen and head upstairs. It's a little early still, but I want to drop past Sam's desk and thank him again for last night. He was a bit... well, okay, the word is drunk. He was drunk when I left his place last night. I think it was the Kevin Bacon *Footloose* dance-off that pushed him over the edge, because when that started, I saw him drink two brews in about two minutes, and then *he joined in*. I wouldn't have thought Sam could dance, since he's a bit klutzy sometimes (Yep. Who knew graceful, elegant shifters could be klutzy?), but he's got some serious moves. He was unanimously declared the winner (to everyone's relief, because neither Andrew nor Alistair would have lost gracefully to the other), and then he kicked us out of his house so he could "get down and dirty with my snuggle bunny."

Gideon's never going to live that down. And I'll bet Sam's feeling some regret this morning.

Part of me envies the way he just let go last night, completely secure in the knowledge that he would be safe even with his inhibitions lowered and his defensive instincts gone. I can't imagine doing that. I used to drink in high school—not a lot, because getting drunk all the time is dumb, and my parents verged on being overprotective (which I know now was not because they cared about me), but I went to the occasional house party when someone's parents were out of town or bonfire party in someone's uncle's field. I've been drunk. And if you can trust the people you're with, there's an element of freedom to it. You get to stop thinking and worrying and just be. Of course, sometimes that's not a good thing, but I regret that I never got to the point where I learned what my alcohol threshold was—the loose-but-not-lost level.

Instead, I'm now afraid to ever let go of control. In any way.

Pushing aside the gloomy thoughts, I stroll down the hall that leads to Percy's office. Sam and the others are in a shared office about halfway down, and when I duck in, I see Sam with his head on his desk and Gideon petting his hair.

I freeze, but then realize they're not alone. Elinor waves weakly at me.

"Hi, Noah," she whispers pitifully. "We're talking quietly today." She's sallow, with dark circles around her eyes. I guess she partied a little too hearty—which would explain the attempt at Riverdancing.

Sam moans and lifts his head. "Noah? I'm so, so sorry if I was a bad host last night."

I shoot a quick, nervous glance at Gideon, who's smiling faintly. It's kind of unnerving. Is that the expression he wears when he's contemplating how much he'll enjoy gutting someone?

"Ah, you weren't a bad host. You were amazing, and I had a great time."

"Really?" He looks like a hopeful kitten. I tilt my head. Like... what's with his hair? Is that from Gideon stroking it? Because it's standing up like he's been electrocuted. Or... have you seen those pictures of little kids whose hair is always on end?

"Really," I assure him. "It was fun, and I'm so grateful."

That seems to perk him up a little, and the look Gideon gives me is... approving? I'm not exactly sure, but for the first time ever, I'm sure he's not about to murder me.

Unless he's just trying to lull me into a false sense of security....

Someone shoves me gently from behind before I can fall into that rabbit hole of terror, and I look over my shoulder at Alistair, who looks just as perky as always, even though I'm sure he drank just as much as everyone else, if not more.

"Good morning, Noah!" he sings. Oh, boy. This is going to get ugly. I step out of the way and try to make myself invisible.

Sure enough, Elinor and Gideon glare at Alistair, while Sam moans again and puts his head back down.

"If you're not going to share the secret remedy, Alistair, then shut the fuck up. Any sound out of you, and I'll call your mom. No, I'll call Aunt Vivienne," Elinor threatens.

"And tell her what? That you have a hangover? She's not going to take your side." He whistles as he crosses to his desk and thumps his satchel on the surface. Hellhounds are nuts, but this is a death wish.

I take a step back toward the door.

"You have a secret hangover remedy?" Gideon asks, his voice soft and even and deceptively calm. "One that you haven't shared with your best friend, who's clearly suffering?"

I turn around and run, not stopping until I'm outside Percy's office. Gideon and Alistair going head-to-head might be fun to watch, but not when there's a chance one of them (Alistair) might try to use me as a shield.

Besides, I have a meeting I can't be late for.

I knock, and a few seconds later, Percy opens the door, startling me. I was expecting to have him call out for me to enter.

"Hi, Noah." He smiles warmly in that way he has, instantly making me feel settled and welcome, and opens the door wide. "Come in. I hear we have some exciting progress already?"

I step past him, and my answering smile falters a little when I see that David and Andrew are already here, sitting on one of the couches with their heads bent toward each other as they talk quietly. Have they all been talking about me? Obviously they have, but what's been said?

"Ah, yeah," I belatedly answer. "I'm pretty sure I can do it again too." I tried practicing a little after meditating, but when the goal is to make someone else feel your emotions and there's no one else around, it's hard to tell if you've been successful.

Percy closes the door, and I follow him over to the seating area and choose a perch for myself. The plush armchair is way more comfortable than the conference room chair was yesterday. Will that help or hinder?

"Good morning, Noah," David says, smiling at me, and I smile back, but it doesn't feel all that natural. David's been nice, but I've had a chance to think about it, and I'm not really sure why he's here. I know he's been taking the lead on unraveling the genetic alterations Tish made, since he's a sorcerer, but it's already been established that there are no sorcery weaves attached to my DNA. Percy checked carefully, and David helped. I am definitely human.

"You've probably got some questions," he goes on, "but do you mind demonstrating for us first? Percy ordered coffee and muffins, which should be here soon, so if we get the demonstration out of the way first, we can talk over food."

I have no idea how to respond to that. What does it even mean? It sounds like they're expecting something dramatic—or have something big to tell me.

I swallow hard. "Sure."

"Great! Uh, Andrew's going to be your test dummy. The exercise is the same as yesterday—just focus on what you're feeling and project it onto him."

Yeah, not sure that's going to work, since what I'm feeling right now is nervous and insecure. No way in hell am I letting Andrew know how vulnerable I am. Also, how weird is it that he hasn't said anything yet? Since when is Andrew quiet?

But I nod anyway. Maybe I can conjure another emotion.

"Whenever you're ready, Noah," Percy says quietly.

I close my eyes and breathe deeply, using some of the techniques from the guided meditation I did this morning. The magic, which has been clinging to me since Andrew and I meditated yesterday, slides against my skin, an almost comforting presence. I hear a stifled gasp, and while part of me wants to open my eyes and see who it was and what the problem is, the rest of me is sinking into a state of mental awareness, and that seems more important.

I concentrate on my emotions, and the process feels a little different than yesterday. I guess the meditation really does help. It's less chaotic, and it's easier to gather the emotions up. I push them to the side, safely out of the way, and try to conjure something else. Annoyance is my go-to with Andrew, so that should be easy enough.

It's not, though. Even with my emotions penned up in a corner of my mind, they permeate everything else. I try several times to build annoyance, thinking of all the things Andrew says and does that piss me off, but I can't hold it. I do manage to get a little annoyed by the fact that I can't feel annoyance—and doesn't that sound ridiculous—but it's not enough to tamp down everything else.

I take another deep breath, and the magic… warms? I don't know, exactly, but it's reassuring. Maybe I should just use the emotions I'm actually feeling. Andrew's a dick who thinks he's funny, but after seeing the way he reacted yesterday to the bitch succubus and how supportive—kind of—he was while trying to train me, I don't think he'd use my insecurity against me. And if he does, well, I'm not completely defenseless. I broke his nose yesterday, didn't I?

There's a rustle of sound as someone shifts position. They're probably getting restless—I've been sitting here focused on my breathing for a few minutes now. So… time for some action.

Slowly, concentrating, I *push* what I'm feeling toward Andrew.

"Oh," he says. "Wow. Okay, Noah, that worked. Can you… uh, thanks, that'll do."

Is it wrong that I maintain it for a few more seconds? I'm sure Andrew's been insecure at some stage in his looooong life, but he's had a façade of confidence since I met him, so it's probably been a while.

Letting my focus fade, I blow out a breath and open my eyes. All three of them are looking at me, Percy with a vague air of concern, David with… awe? I must be misreading him.

Andrew seems a little shaken. The pang of guilt takes me by surprise.

"So," David begins. "Uh, well done. Like I said before, you probably have questions, and—"

There's a knock. We all look toward the door.

"Coffee," Percy announces. "David, would you...?"

David's brow furrows in concentration, then a moment later he nods. "Done."

"Come in," Percy calls, getting up and walking toward the door.

Was that weird, or just me?

The door opens, and Candice, one of the receptionists, comes in with a cardboard tray of paper cups and a paper sack. "Good morning," she announces. "Do you want this over there?"

Percy takes the items from her. "I've got them, thank you, Candice. We appreciate you bringing them up."

Her smile lights up her face. "Always happy to help, Lucifer." She turns and leaves, closing the door on Percy's request that she not call him that.

He brings the coffee and food over to us, a pained expression on his face. "There's always someone who insists on being formal," he grumbles.

It's... sweet.

As he hands the food around, Andrew leans toward me. "David has the room warded for privacy," he explains. "Nobody outside can hear us, even if we shout. He needed a second to open a gap."

"And now it's closed again," David adds.

Whoa. This is starting to get a little disturbing. "Was that... I mean, we weren't doing anything secret, were we?" Nobody said I should keep this to myself. Andrew and I were training in the conference room yesterday without wards or anything.

"Not secret," Percy assures me, "but we didn't want to be disturbed. It's easier this way—and it gives you control over who you tell. If you want to keep these abilities secret, that's your call." He hesitates. "Andrew mentioned that Nikita from accounting attempted to enthrall you yesterday. That's not permitted, and she's going to face consequences."

Tell me, what am I supposed to say to that? Good? Thank you? Aw, you shouldn't have?

"Okay" is what I settle on, following it up with a sip of coffee.

He raises a brow and gives me a stern look. Yep. Percy can actually be stern. It's even intimidating. "Have there been any similar incidents?"

Fuck.

"Nobody's attempted to use their abilities on me before," I compromise.

"But they have tried to intimidate you?"

So, compromising didn't work.

"If I had felt the situation was out of my control, I would have talked to HR." It's weird—if you had asked me yesterday, or even half an hour ago, I would have said I owed my workmates nothing and they were responsible for any consequences their actions might bring. And yet here I am, doing my best not to snitch on them.

Percy sighs, a sound of disappointment and regret.

"I'll respect that," he agrees. "But if anyone tries to use their abilities, please report it to me immediately. If they feel safe doing that here, then who knows what they're doing to other humans they encounter. It's not okay."

I nod. "I will."

He nods too. "Okay. So, let's talk about your newfound abilities."

"I don't know what to call it," I admit. "It's not really charisma, is it?"

"It's not charisma at all," David says bluntly.

My gaze darts toward Andrew. "It's not?" Fuck. Fuck fuck fuck. Am I developing some kind of freak ability? What did Tish do to me? My breath grates in my chest.

In the next heartbeat, Andrew's sitting on the arm of my chair, his big, warm hand closing over my nape. "It's fine," he declares, looking me right in the eye. "This is a good thing."

The panic lessens a little but doesn't completely disappear. I make myself nod and concentrate on regulating my breathing, the magic twining around me in a noncorporeal hug.

"I'm so sorry," David says. "I should have eased into that. Andrew's right; this is good news." He sounds utterly remorseful, so I paste on a smile.

"It's fine, just a surprise. I guess you'd better tell me all of it." I meet Percy's searching gaze, trying to seem confident despite the fact that I'm still a bit shaken. As long as this isn't something Tish did, I can handle it. And if it is… well, I guess I can still handle it.

Andrew gives my neck a light squeeze, then lets go and goes back to his seat on the couch, collecting a muffin on the way. Which reminds me… coffee. I take a big gulp and let the caffeine settle my nerves.

"Okay," David begins. "Bear with me, because this

gets a little exotic. And some of it is still based on theories. You know how the magic seems to really like you?"

As if it knows we're talking about it—which it might. Nobody seems to know how much sentience the magic has—it dances over my skin. "Yeah. I can feel it most of the time." He knows this. We had some pretty extensive conversations about it when they were trying to get an idea of what was going on with me.

"Andrew mentioned last night that he'd told you humans have the capacity to use the magic…?" He seems to be fishing, and I'm not dumb. Well, not usually, although really, I should have put this together before.

"You think I can feel the magic because I can use it? And that's how I projected feelings at Andrew, not charisma?" That's so fucking cool! Existential magic is part of *everything*. It makes up the fabric of the universe. I wonder if I can learn to fly? Or teleport like demons do?

"Yes and no," Percy says. "It's definitely how you projected emotions just now. I could see it reacting to you and influencing Andrew. But our knowledge of how humans can manipulate the magic is limited, and everything we know indicates it shouldn't work this way."

The coolness factor fades a little. "So we don't know if this is because of what Tish did?" There's a tiny, eensy-weensy tremor in my voice.

Percy hesitates.

"We don't know for absolute sure," Andrew says. "But we don't think so. Let David explain his theory. Whether it turns out to be true or if Tish has influenced this somehow, we'll make sure you're safe."

David and Percy hurry to agree.

"I really don't think this has anything to do with

Tish," David adds. "Not in the sense that he did something to you, anyway. I did a lot of reading last night, and this seems to be within the parameters of how humans use magic. Uh, so... quick recap. All community species have a certain subset of abilities as well as a small amount of personal magic that can be used for glamor and disguise. This was something that came into play after the species wars."

I did not know that. Maybe I need to do some more research myself.

"Wait, let me just make sure I understand. Before the species wars—that was, what, ten thousand years ago?" Holy fucking crap, that's a long time. And these people talk about it almost casually sometimes.

"A little under nine, actually," David corrects. Because that makes a big difference.

"Yeah, so before the species wars, humans knew all about the community? And then after, the magic made it so we... forgot, I guess, and gave the community species what they needed to hide in plain sight?"

"Before the species wars, humans were part of the community. There was no separation between us," Percy says softly. "But yes. That's what happened."

I narrow my eyes, thinking about it. "So all the species had abilities. What did humans have? Magic?"

David grins. "Yes. It's not well known, because most humans don't use it anymore, and many members of the community just don't pay attention to humans anyway. But before the magic intervened and hid us all from humanity, humans used the magic in the same common way that we use our abilities."

"And when the magic made humans forget the community, it also made us forget about the magic?"

That seems kind of unfair... although since we were on the verge of wiping out about half a dozen highly developed sentient species at the time, I can kind of see why the magic thought it might be a good idea. Like taking a hammer away from a toddler.

David spreads his hands. "Yes. We can't be entirely certain why, but the most popular theory is that knowing about the magic would either jog humanity's memory about the rest of us, or make them somewhat more accepting of the idea of 'supernatural' species living among them—which could then lead to our exposure." He shrugs. "I lean toward a combination of both, that having magic would make it seem logical to humans that other species could exist, thus jogging their memories of not only us, but also the wars, and potentially restarting them. I can't be sure—not yet, anyway—but I believe it took several generations before any humans started using the magic again, by which time none of them would have had any suppressed memories of the wars and us that could be triggered."

I follow that theory through from one end to the other, and it makes sense. It's actually kind of interesting. I lean forward, propping my forearms on my thighs. "So humans all have the ability to use the magic, but we just don't know it? And because we've convinced ourselves magic doesn't exist, we don't even stumble upon it by accident?"

"Yes!" David's excitement lights up his face. He really is a geek about this stuff. "More, most human magic practitioners are Wiccan. They've tied their use of the magic to a religion that further restricts what they can use it for. Not that I advocate using the magic to harm others—not that the magic would allow itself to be used that way—"

"Wait, but didn't humans use the magic during the wars? If they weren't weaponizing it, how were things able to get to the point they did?"

"Numbers, mostly, remember? The fertility rate—"

"Yeah, sorry. I forgot. But still…"

He nods. "This is where I have to do some more research. I believe humans were weaponizing the magic, but not directly. As in… if their intent had been 'kill those shifters,' the magic would have refused to respond. But if it was 'hold my attackers in place,' or something like that—"

"The magic would have helped. Which would have allowed humans to pick them off with no risk to themselves." It's a terrible reflection on humanity that the idea doesn't surprise me. I can imagine some human general coming up with such tactics.

"Exactly. But I can't prove that yet."

"It makes sense, though. Especially when you consider that the magic would finally have noticed the dropping numbers among the community species, realized what the humans were doing, and pretty much took away their toy until they learned how to behave responsibly."

Andrew bursts out laughing, and I blink at him in surprise. I'd actually forgotten he and Percy were here. He's lounging back against the couch, his feet kicked up on the coffee table. The overhead lights gleam against his silver hair. It's really unfair that he looks like a GQ model ready for a photo shoot, even though I know he overindulged last night.

Speaking of… "Why aren't you hungover?"

It's his turn to blink. "What?"

"You were drunk last night. Why aren't you hungover? Sam and Elinor are suffering down the hall."

He shrugs. "Natural resilience."

Percy chokes on his coffee, and David laughs out loud. I look at them, then back at Andrew and raise an eyebrow.

"Oh, really?"

He smiles charmingly. "Sort of. Vampires can use charisma on themselves... to a certain extent. That minimizes the effects of the hangover. And I found a really good remedy many years ago. Plus, I wasn't *that* drunk."

"Oh, so Hammertime is something you do sober?" I smirk at him, but the asshole just smirks back.

"I have done. There's nothing I've done drunk that I won't do sober, Noah. I don't need alcohol to fortify me."

I hold back a shiver. That should not have been as sexy as it was. Nothing about Andrew should be sexy. Clearly, I need to get out more if my sex-starved hormones are fixating on Andrew. I never went for older guys before. Of course, with the way Andrew behaves most of the time, it's hard to think of him as "older."

"Can I interject here," Percy says calmly, "and ask why it sounds like most of my senior team was drunk on a weeknight?"

"It was Noah's birthday," Andrew says solemnly. "We were morally obliged to party it up."

Yes. He actually said "party it up."

I'm half expecting Percy to rebuke him, but he just grins at me and says, "Happy Birthday, Noah. I'm sorry I missed it."

"Thanks," I mutter, a bit thrown off stride. "The party was a last-minute thing, so don't worry about it." I turn to David, eager to change the subject. "So... humans gradually began rediscovering magic?"

He nods. "Yes, but those who used it or were suspected to were mostly reviled. The village 'witch' was always the first to get blamed if something went wrong, even if she was just someone who knew herbal lore and had no actual ability. And then there was the Inquisition and the witch trials and the rest. So humans have been indoctrinated over thousands of years to not believe magic or any 'extra' ability exists. Those few who do have tied it to very ritualistic practices, needing spells and charms and other paraphernalia to make it work."

I shake my head, confused. "But you said I used the magic before?"

"You did," Percy confirms. "And I don't think it's the first time. If David's right, you've been using it for a while."

That only confuses me more, but David launches into another explanation.

"Wiccan spellcasting practices are just window dress-ing. Some subsets almost have it right when they talk about will, but they still insist on their rituals—remem-ber, it's part of their religion. If what I think is true—and from some very cursory research, it looks like it might be—humans originally never needed any kind of spells or trappings to use the magic. It was about train-ing, focus, and will, the same as for any of the rest of us with our abilities."

"But I've never had training." It seems fantastic that I could have just stumbled across this ability.

He shrugs. "I'm still looking into it, but we see this in

our kids all the time. They haven't yet been taught to do something, but in moments of high energy, it bursts out of them. It's part of why shifters lock down their children's ability to shift until they're older. Demons do the same. Young demons aren't supposed to be able to teleport, but there used to be instances where a tantrum turned into something a lot scarier. Will is a powerful thing."

I guess it makes sense. "Like… you need training to become an MMA fighter, but anyone can flail wildly and hit someone?"

Andrew coughs, and David pastes on a polite expression. "Well——"

I wave dismissively. "Never mind. Bad analogy. So when do you think I've been using magic?" The answer comes to me almost before the question's out. "In the labs?"

David nods. "What happened to you there, how you survived, is just so incredibly lucky. A series of perfectly timed coincidences that just fit together like a puzzle. It's been playing on my mind for months. Isn't it far more likely that you were inadvertently using the magic to keep yourself alive?"

My chest tightens as images—memories—flash through my mind. "But… but that would mean that the magic knew what was happening to me. What Tish was doing." I can't get my head around that. I know the magic doesn't "speak" directly to Percy, but from what I've been told, it communicates fairly clearly with him about things it's aware of. And if I was using it, it would have been aware of me.

As if it knows what we're saying, the magic tightens

its grip on me, and all I want in that second is for it to be gone.

But David's shaking his head. "Not necessarily. I know it was a while ago, but can you remember what you were thinking at those times of extreme luck?"

What I was thinking? Is he fucking stupid? I was thinking that I didn't want to die!

Except… was I? My thoughts are all jumbled with this new information and an influx of anxiety. I put a hand to my forehead. "Can you… just wait? I need…" Fuck, what do I need?

"It's fine, Noah," Andrew says firmly. "There's no rush. We can leave this for now if you want."

"Absolutely," David agrees. "I didn't mean to stress you out like this. I'm sorry. And as I said, it's just a theory. I could be completely wrong."

My churning gut settles a little. "I just need a minute." I need to think this through. There's something I'm missing.

"Take as long as you need," Percy assures me.

Breathing evenly, I close my eyes, using some of my newly acquired meditation techniques to calm myself. I am never, ever, not ever telling Andrew how grateful I am he insisted I take up meditation. It's been less than a day and already it's saving my ass, but he'll lord it over me until the end of days if he finds out.

Smug bastard.

Oddly, thinking of Andrew's annoying habits helps to clear my mind. Reminding myself that I'm in a safe place now, I think about my moments of "luck" in the labs. The first that I can think of was when the lab assistant and the guards went to see what the noise in the hallway was.

Which, now that I think of it, is weird. There had been other times when there were shouts from other rooms or outside the lab. The guards only left if another guard called for help, and the lab assistants *never* went to see what was happening. Even the sloppy one knew Tish would have his guts if he left us unsupervised. So why did they all go then?

I replay the moment in my head. The memory is well over a year old, but it's been burned into my brain by the sheer terror I felt when I realized something was wrong, and the stillness brought by the meditation techniques throws it into even sharper relief.

The lab assistant and guards came in, and I was curious. It wasn't unheard of for them to give us shots outside the lab—usually when it was something that needed time to kick in before tests—but it wasn't common, either.

Brendan went first, and when he just collapsed seconds after the injection, I was alarmed. Sure, they put us under occasionally, but never like that. Maybe he'd had a bad reaction to whatever it was? But the assistant didn't seem concerned.

Then the same thing happened to Paul, and I panicked. I knew something was wrong. I still thought they were just unconscious, but it still seemed really off, and I didn't want to be injected with whatever it was.

Diego hesitated when it was his turn, and one of the guards stepped forward to hold him in place. There was no chance I could avoid it as long as they were in the room. I needed a distraction. I needed them to be distracted. Dammit, they had to be distracted!

Just as the assistant withdrew the needle from Diego's

arm, there was a noise from the hall. I couldn't tell what, but as if on cue, both guards and the assistant turned to look toward the door, and then went to see what was happening.

Diego met my gaze, then his eyes rolled back and he collapsed. Fuck! I had my distraction, but now what? How could I escape?

Movement by the door was my only warning. I had to act.

I dropped to the floor, letting my limbs sprawl awkwardly, and focused on regulating my breathing, even as I knew it was pointless. Even if they decided they'd lost count—unlikely—there had been four syringes on the assistant's tray.

Still... *don't notice me. You already did me. It's done. It's done. It's all done.*

And then, miraculously, the assistant left and more guards came in to... drag us away? I kept my eyes closed, ignoring the scrapes and bumps from being dragged, pretending with every iota of acting ability in me that I was unconscious. *Don't notice I'm conscious. Don't notice I'm conscious.* Part of me suspected—knew—that the others weren't just unconscious. They'd never treated us so carelessly before.

The incinerator room was hot—

"Noah?" Andrew's voice is gentle but firm. "Noah, if you can hear me, you need to come back. Open your eyes."

The memory breaks apart, and I suck in a deep breath and open my eyes. Andrew is kneeling in front of me, concern on his face. There's something on my cheeks... I lift my hand and swipe, and it comes away wet. I'm... crying?

"There you are," Andrew says, breaking into a relieved smile. "Are you okay?"

I just stare at him.

"Take your time," Percy says quietly. "Do you want some water?"

I don't even have a chance to say yes before Andrew is up and going to get some from the little fridge in one of the cabinets.

"You're safe here, Noah." David hands me some tissues, and I mop up my face. "I know you haven't wanted to talk about it, but it would be normal for you to have some PTSD after what you've been through. Whatever you were just thinking about was obviously difficult for you... and very absorbing. We've been talking to you for a while."

I take the bottle from Andrew and don't utter a peep of protest when he sits on the arm of my chair and puts a hand on my shoulder. Instead, I take a swallow of water, which finally allows me to speak.

"I didn't hear you. I was... remembering. That day at the compound." I meet David's gaze squarely. "I think you're right. That day, I was thinking a lot about how I didn't want them to notice me. Or not to notice I was conscious. That I needed a distraction. I never once thought anything like 'don't inject me with drugs that will k-kill me.'" My voice wavers, but I push on. "Or 'don't load me into the incinerator and burn the evidence of your genetic experiments.' Even after that, while I was hiding, whenever it seemed like someone was going to discover me, my focus was on them not noticing me. So the magic—" I break off, suddenly aware that I can't feel it. It's been with me for months, but now it's gone. "Percy," I gasp, eyes widening, and Andrew leaps to his feet.

"What is it? A telepathic attack?"

"No, I can't feel the magic." I blink, momentarily distracted. "Is a telepathic attack even possible? Who has that ability?"

"Any ability that can affect the mind of another is technically classed as telepathic," Percy says calmly. "Charisma, enthrallment, even some elements of sorcery. Take a breath and focus on the magic, Noah. How does it normally feel? If you want it to come back, you need to invite it."

Does that sound fucked-up to you? The magic's been clinging to me for months, and now I have to invite it?

Even as I think it, though, I'm mentally reaching out for that familiar tingly pressure… and there it is.

Percy smiles, obviously able to tell, and says, "There you go."

Andrew sits back down on the arm of my chair as I take another swallow of water, reassured by the magic twining itself back around me. "Where did it go? And why?"

"I don't know," Percy answers, shrugging. "Maybe it wanted to give you some space while you were upset? Or it sensed that you weren't receptive to it in that moment. There's so much we don't know about existential magic."

I nod slowly. "Well, it's not a definite test, but I think you can safely assume that it reacted to me having strong emotions in the compound."

"So the magic… I'm going to say 'grants spells' because I don't have a better term right now," David says, "based on what you're asking, not your intent. You wanted to be ignored, hidden, so it helped you do that rather than realizing you were in trouble and what was actually happening."

"I... think so." I play those moments where I was feeling most desperate over in my head. "I honestly don't know, though. Even thinking about it now, I can't say I felt any connection with the magic then. I didn't feel it at all until—" I break off, frowning.

"Noah?" Andrew peers down at me.

"I'm okay." Absently, I pat his leg. "I was going to say I never felt it until I met Percy, but I think... maybe before that. When I was waiting for Sam to wake up in the lab. My skin was kind of crawling, but I put it down to the fact that there was nowhere for me to hide in the lab if someone happened to come back, plus it was under attack, and there was this new guy and I didn't know what that meant." I shrug. "It could have been the magic. It wasn't as, as... firm a touch"—I cringe at the word choice, and Andrew snorts—"as what came later, but it's the same basic feeling. And if it was there for Sam and didn't know what to make of me..."

David sighs. "The problem is, we really have no idea how sentient the magic is." He raises his voice. "If you can understand me right now, you're a pain in my ass and we'd really appreciate some input so we know if we're on the right track."

We all wait.

Nothing.

"I guess that would have been too easy," he mutters. "Okay. Noah, are you comfortable with the idea of being able to manipulate the magic?"

"Yes," I say instantly. "Don't get me wrong, it's super

weird and I'm not sure I entirely believe it yet, but I am totally there for having magic powers."

He hesitates, and I don't know him *that* well, but I can still tell he's mentally debating whether he should correct me on the whole "magic powers" thing.

"Then we'll focus on training you," he replies, obviously deciding to let it go. "Andrew said he told you to take up meditation?"

I heave a huge sigh and grumble, "Yeah." No need for Andrew to know I'm now officially a meditation convert. I think Percy might suspect, though, because there's a sudden cheeky twinkle in his eye.

David, on the other hand, seems to have fallen for my act and sounds genuinely sympathetic. "I know it can be a pain, but it really will help in the long term. I'm going to talk to a friend of mine who's Wiccan and see if I can get him to give me some pointers for beginners, but one of the things he suggested when we thought Sam might be able to use magic was to conjure a ball of light. Do you want to try that now?"

Do I want to use magic in a way that will have a tangible result?

"Yeah. Yes. Let's try." I don't even care that I sound like an overeager loser, and David smiles.

"Andrew, can you get the lights and close the blinds? The first time might be a little bit small or faint, so we want to give ourselves the best chance of seeing it."

Andrew goes to do his bidding—that's a neat trick—and David studies my face.

"Are you sure you're feeling up to this?" he asks gently.

"Yes." My voice is firm. "I think you're right about the PTSD, and I should probably do something about that, but I really want to do this." I hesitate, not wanting to sound like a dork, but it's David—he'll get it. "I'm excited about this."

He's still looking closely at me, but he grins. "I'm excited too. I don't want you to feel like a guinea pig or anything, but I've never gotten to help someone discover their abilities before. Well, someone who isn't a sorcerer. And if our theories are right, we're going to redefine what human magic is."

But no pressure, hey.

The room darkens a lot when Andrew closes the blinds over the big windows. I can still see everyone, but mostly just silhouettes and shadows. If I manage to create any light at all, it should be vis—

"Motherfucker!" Andrew's howl of pain makes me glad there's a ward preventing sound from escaping the room.

"Did you trip on something?" David asks, and I'm surprised to hear a little waver of satisfaction in his voice. He's the responsible member of the team, so I would've expected him to be more sympathetic. I guess it just goes to show that Andrew doesn't just annoy me —he's an equal opportunity annoyer. Annoyance?

"I'm going to chop that table up for firewood," he snarls, and I can't help it—I laugh. The image of GQ clotheshorse Andrew chopping wood just does not compute.

"Are you laughing at me, puny human?" he asks, and the silky tone in the darkened room makes me shiver.

"Not exactly. I thought of something funny."

There's a thud, which if I'm interpreting the shadowy movements correctly is Andrew throwing himself onto the couch. "Oh yes?" he asks silkily. "Perhaps you could share it with us."

"Another time," Percy interrupts—thankfully. "I have other meetings this morning."

"Let's get to it, then." David takes back the reins. "Noah, can you feel the magic?"

"Yes." I don't even need to concentrate. It's back to sliding along my skin, making me incredibly aware of my every breath.

"Great. That's where most people struggle, I'm told, and have to spend days practicing. Okay, so I want you to close your eyes and visualize a ball of light in front of you. Not too big—something that could fit in your palm, maybe. Once you've got the image— Fucking shit!"

I open my eyes, but I didn't need to. Even through my closed lids, I saw the light. I also felt the heat.

"Uh, David, weren't you supposed to tell him not to imagine a fireball? I'm sure you did that with Sam." Andrew is leaning away from me and my absolutely fucking badass fireball. That *I* created. With *my* magic powers.

This is so cool!

Although it's actually kind of hot. Who knew a fireball put out so much heat?

"I was getting to it," David says, taking a cautious step closer. "I didn't think he'd get to this point so fast." He leans in, squinting in the light of *my fireball.* Because creating fireballs is just what I do now.

As if the ball can feel my smug satisfaction, it flexes and grows a little. David scrambles back.

"Okay, uh, Noah, tell me how this feels. Do you have control of the ball?" He sounds a little apprehensive.

Oh, fuck me… I've created a fire inside an office building. This is not good.

"I… think so?" I concentrate on the ball, trying to shrink it. It instantly becomes a little smaller, but sweat breaks out on my forehead and my heartbeat picks up. "Uh, yeah, I do, but it's not easy."

"So what you're going to do is extinguish it. Percy's keeping an eye on the magic and will let us know if it looks like you're losing control, and I can always contain it with sorcery, so there's no risk, okay? You're safe. We're all safe. If you start to feel unwell or like you can't manage it yet, that's fine. Just say so."

I want to nod, but it feels like it might be too much effort. "'Kay," I say instead and concentrate on reducing the fireball, making it less, smaller, until it's nothing but a spark that I snuff out.

Whew.

I collapse back in the chair, resting my head against the high back. The room is dark again without my awesome light source, but I'm glad to have a few moments to collect myself.

The blinds go up, flooding the room with daylight. Moment over, I guess.

Andrew glares at David. "Why'd you make me get up before if you could've done it this way?"

David rolls his eyes. "I needed to talk to Noah and wanted you out of the way." He turns to me. "Wow. That was incredible!"

A grin breaks across my face, and I wipe the sweat from my brow with the back of my hand. "It was, wasn't it? My fireball was awesome." I reach for the bottle of water Andrew brought me earlier. There's still about half left, and man, do I need it.

"How are you feeling now?" Percy asks.

"Great," I reply instantly. "I feel amazing."

"Tired?" he persists. "Hungry? Headache?"

I make myself actually think about it. "Not bad tired. Tired like I've been for a run or something. There's adrenaline too, but I'm not sure if that's from what I did or just finding out I actually can do it."

Percy looks at David, who shrugs. "It sounds like the same effects we get when we're learning to use our abilities." He turns to me. "The run analogy is a good one. When you first start working out, you can only do so much before your body gets tired and sore. The more you do it, though, the more you're able to do. The mind works a lot like the body does in that way."

"So next time it will be easier?" I hope so. My fireball was badass, but it existed for less than two minutes. I need to be able to do more than that.

Percy nods. "I believe so."

"Can I try again?" I ask. "Not a fireball this time," I promise hastily.

There's a moment of hesitation, then Andrew says, "Of course. Let him have another shot."

David looks doubtful, but finally Percy nods, so he sighs and capitulates.

"Sure, why not. We know it's not going to be a pinprick, so let's not bother with closing the blinds this time." He winks, and I grin. "Do you want to try with your eyes open?"

I nod. "Yeah. Yesterday, I couldn't manage to… to… *influence* Andrew unless I had them closed, but this feels different."

Andrew shrugs. "Projecting emotions probably uses a different part of your brain," he suggests.

"Exactly," David agrees. "While it's a beginner exercise for vampires learning charisma, it's probably much more advanced for humans using magic. I'll add it to my list of things to research. Now… what we want this time is a cool light. Or rather, something that doesn't have any temperature at all," he adds quickly, probably afraid I'm going to create some kind of ice ball that sucks the heat out of the air.

Huh. That could be a great alternative to air conditioning in the summer.

Pushing aside thoughts of my future empire in the HVAC industry, I concentrate on visualizing a lightball.

And one pops into existence in front of me. It's about three inches in diameter, white, bright, and kind of shimmery at the edges.

"I am a god," I whisper.

"There's only one god, and she can't do this," Andrew points out, getting up and coming closer to peer at my super-fucking-cool lightball. "That's pretty cool, Noah. Can you move it?"

I don't bother to answer, just will the ball to smack him in the forehead.

It does.

He yelps.

"Andrew, sit down and stay out of the way," David says, sounding like a beleaguered parent. "Noah, tell me how it feels."

"Easier than the fireball," I admit. "That was harder. This takes less effort. And moving it was easy too." I make it spin and dance about for a second, admiring how pretty it is.

"It seems to be using less of the magic too," Percy says, that strange unfocused look on his face that he gets when he's watching the magic. "Can you increase the size?"

It only takes the tiniest bit of concentration, not at all like when I was changing the size of the fireball. Percy and David have me play with size and movement for a while, constantly checking in to see if it's wearing me down, but I feel like I could do this for hours.

"All right, I think that's enough for now," David finally says. "This seems like a pretty good exercise to flex your magic muscles, so try to do it a few times a day for a few minutes—maybe right after meditation. Keep notes about how it feels and what you do, in terms of the size of the light and movement. I'm going to talk to my friend and do some research, and we can meet up again in a few days." He levels me with a steady look. "Call me if anything unusual happens. You've got my number, right?"

"Yeah," I assure him. "Sam put everyone's number in my phone."

"Am I allowed to speak yet?" Andrew asks snippily. "Because you're all being very short-sighted."

David rolls his eyes. "Speak, then."

I wish I was as patient as David, because I'm tempted to throw one of the empty coffee cups at Andrew's head.

"Right now, Noah is doing basic data management that's not time sensitive, is that right?" He raises a silver eyebrow at me, and I shrug.

"I guess." *Way to make me feel like my job isn't needed, douchebag.*

"Instead of that, why don't you put him to work on some of this research? Nobody's got more of a vested interest than him, and it would be better than having you die of exhaustion, David. When's the last night you slept for more than a few hours?"

I look sharply at David. He doesn't seem that tired. Can Andrew see something I can't?

"I don't know what you mean," David replies. "I've been sleeping."

Andrew crosses his arms over his chest and says nothing.

We all just sit there in awkward silence until Percy sighs. "David, I'm so sorry. I should have noticed."

"You mean Andrew's right?" The words burst out of me. "He doesn't look tired!" It's so fucking unfair. If David's only sleeping a couple hours a night and can look well-rested and put together, why can't I?

"Well, puny human," Andrew begins, and I shake my head.

"Nope. No. Don't talk."

David snorts with laughter. "Noah, you may just be my favorite person. As much as I hate to say it, though, Andrew might have a point about the research. We'd get more done with another set of eyes. Are you interested?"

Am I interested in researching the ways ancient humans used magic so I can apply that learning to my own magic use?

"Yes! Uh, yeah. That could be cool."

"You can thank me now," Andrew says, and I must have some kind of brain fart that makes me momentarily forget where I am and who I'm with, because I flip him the bird.

Percy clears his throat, and horror smacks into me, but he's smiling. "Andrew, can you please arrange it so Noah's current job is given to someone else?"

Andrew opens his mouth, outrage on his face, but Percy's still talking.

"And I think that in light of the sensitive nature of this research, Noah should be moved up here. Can you find room for him, David? Somewhere secure where people won't be able to look over his shoulder?"

If it weren't for the fact that I'd really like to be moved, I'd point out to Percy that very few people have looked over my shoulder since I started here… and definitely nobody's done it twice. Maybe it is my fault that I don't have any work friends.

"We could probably get another desk into our office," David muses. "But Noah would have to take the super-secret oath to never tell anyone what he learns in there."

"I would never breach CSG security," I say, a little hurt that he thinks I might. Sure, this isn't where I ever wanted to be, but these people literally saved me and gave me a new life. I could never betray them.

"He's not talking about security stuff," Andrew informs me. "He's trying to protect his secret stash of chocolate bars. And probably also save the team's dignity. Alistair can be a bit boisterous sometimes."

David nods. "That's right." The second Andrew looks away, David rolls his eyes and points at him, making a face that clearly tells me Andrew is also bad for the team's reputation.

Percy coughs. "Well, that's settled, then. There's just one more thing."

We all look at him.

"Noah, you are now the only living human being that we're aware of who can manipulate magic at will with no trappings or limits. You're also known to Dr.

Tish, and while we still believe he thinks you're dead, there's a chance that he's been able to access information that would tell him otherwise."

I sit up straight, dread forming a heavy ball in my gut.

"What?" Andrew demands, just as David says,

"When—"

"I planned to tell you and the team later this morning," Percy tells them. "I got some information last night that indicates Tish *may* have a source inside CSG."

The blood rushes from my head in a dizzying wave. Tish can't find me. He can't. I'm not going back there.

A hand clamps on my nape. "Breathe," Andrew demands, and I suck in air. The world spins back into place.

"…begin investigating," David's saying grimly. "I know we definitely shut down his last source. We can take what we learned then and apply it now, hopefully find this leak faster."

Percy nods. "I've already spoken with the head of security and had the magic check him and his team. They're all still loyal and have initiated a search for this *possible* source. It's still not definite that there is one."

I breathe a little easier.

"But," Percy's gaze swings to me, "if there is and news of Noah's survival does reach Tish, we have to assume he'd want to take you back. He's aware now after kidnapping Sam that the work he did on the first generation of his victims breaks down over time. It's highly likely that he'd want to do further research on Sam and you."

I nod, barely able to move my head. I'm not going back there. If I'm not safe here, I'll disappear. I have the magic now, and if it helped me hide before when I knew nothing about it, then it will definitely help me now.

"So we need to make sure you're protected at all times." He turns to David. "His apartment is warded, yes?"

"Ye-es…" David makes a face. "But standard wards only. I didn't think he needed more, since he's officially dead and Tish had no reason to search for him. They'd keep out a casual incursion, but not a determined sorcerer who knows what they're doing. I can beef them up, but—"

"Those kinds of wards take a few days and a lot of effort, neither of which you have to give right now," Andrew says, and the fact that David doesn't argue tells me more clearly than anything else could that he's right.

"Then I'm sorry, Noah, but you can't stay there until we can ensure it's safe. I'll ask Sam and Gideon if you can stay with them. Anybody who gets through their wards—if that's even possible, after Gideon had them reinforced—will have to get through Gideon, and that's no easy task."

While part of me hates the idea of giving up my independence, and another chunk really doesn't want to live under the same roof as scary Gideon—what if he doesn't like the way I breathe in his house?—most of me really doesn't want to be kidnapped by Tish and experimented on, locked in a lab for the rest of my life, so I'm willing to agree to anything.

"I don't think that's the best idea," David says thoughtfully. "It would put Sam and Noah in the same place and make them one single target. It might be better to separate them. That way, if Tish attacks one, we'll have warning to protect the other."

I shudder, and Andrew's hand tightens on my neck. "Besides," he says, a fake jovial note in his voice, "you don't want to live with Sam and Gideon. They have sex all the time. Who can sleep with a constant porn soundtrack?"

David winces. "Actually, yeah. Gideon might not be happy to have someone staying. He beefed up those wards to keep us all out so he and Sam could have more privacy."

"Gideon wouldn't leave Noah at risk just so he and Sam can have more privacy," Percy insists, and David and Andrew immediately agree.

"Never."

"Definitely not."

There's a momentary pause.

"But he wouldn't be happy about it," Andrew adds. "And Gideon's not exactly kind and welcoming even when he is happy. I wouldn't want to be the one who has to live with him when he's in a mood, and I've literally known him since he was a baby."

I whip my head around to stare at him. He has? Wait, Gideon was a baby? I just assumed he was spawned as a murderous adult ready to lay waste to anyone who displeased him. It's hard to imagine him as a baby. Did he do baby stuff?

Oh my god, does that mean Andrew was once a baby? He's talked about young vampires, but I just can't quite picture him as an infant. In my head, he still has silver hair and a smug smirk.

"Noah can stay with me," David volunteers, then turns to smile at me. "It'll be fun."

"No," Percy says before I can even decide if I'm

okay with that idea. "You've only got one bedroom. Noah can stay with Andrew."

"What?"

"With me?"

I jerk away from Andrew in horror. I can't stay with him. In his house. With him there. I'd go bananas. Or I'd try to kill him, and that wouldn't end well for either of us.

"It's the best option," Percy continues. "Andrew can counter any telepathic assault that might get thrown at him and still protect you physically. It's one of the benefits that comes with age and strength. Plus, he has a lovely three-bedroom penthouse with a pool and a roof terrace. The perfect place to practice using the magic in private."

A penthouse with a *pool* and a *roof terrace*? I guess being a million years old has benefits after all—a shitload of time to collect money.

It does sound nice… and I can't deny that Andrew could protect me… but…

I say nothing.

He heaves a huge sigh. "Fine. Noah can stay with me."

"I think Gideon would be more welcoming," I mutter, and David nods solemnly, biting his lip.

"He really would. Honestly, Andrew, you could be a bit more gracious."

Did I mention that I'm really starting to like David?

Andrew stretches his mouth in the widest fake smile I've ever seen and says, "Noah, I would *love* for you to come and stay with me! We can give each other facials and talk about our first sexual experiences."

I blush hotly.

I can't help it. I'm normally not the blushing type—a flush of fury, sure, but an innocent blush? Nope. Not me.

But then, I wasn't expecting him to talk about sexual experiences. Of which I've had my fair share, but I've been in a dry spell for two years now. I got around quite a bit in high school—there's a spot behind the gym that's been blanketed with my DNA—but what with the abduction and being experimented on and all that, sex suddenly wasn't a priority. And since being rescued, the idea of making myself vulnerable with a stranger gives me actual anxiety. Considering I don't really know many people anymore, much less people I could trust like that, my recent sexual escapades are limited to my right hand and internet porn.

Andrew stares at me, obviously noticing the ridiculously red color I've gone and my inability to say a single word. A delighted grin spreads across his face, and he opens his mouth—presumably to say something I'm going to hate.

"Great!" David practically yells, proving himself to be a master of diplomacy. "It's all settled then. Come on, Noah, let's get to work. Why don't you go and pack up your stuff downstairs while I get a desk brought in for you?"

Percy claps his hands and stands. "Excellent plan. David, the wards?"

A minute later, I'm walking down the hall toward the elevator to pack up my desk and move to my new job, researching magic use so I can *use magic*, and wondering how the hell I'm going to stay with Andrew without starting a new species war.

# CHAPTER SEVEN

## Andrew

My life has turned upside down.

Seconds. That's how long it took. Literally only seconds for me to go from having a lovely, well-ordered life to suddenly having a roommate. Do you know the last time I had a platonic roommate? Let's just say the printing press hadn't been invented yet.

This is not good. And not just because I selfishly like my own space.

Did you see the way Noah blushed? Of course you did—that red glow could have lit up a night sky. Now, Noah's not the shy, retiring type. He doesn't like being social, but he's got a smart mouth and biting wit. Safe to say I've never seen him blush and never really thought he was the type to blush over a little sexual innuendo. It makes me wonder how much sexual experience he has. I don't think he's a virgin, but there's a difference between hand jobs and blow jobs and a few fumbled attempts at anal sex while listening to make sure your parents aren't coming home from work early and hours-long no-holds-barred sex marathons every night. And Noah hasn't exactly had a lot of opportunity to explore sex as an adult, what with being kidnapped, experimented on, and traumatized.

Listen to me, talking in circles about all kinds of crap to avoid admitting the truth to myself.

I want to help him explore that side of himself.

No, wait. That sounds far too altruistic.

The dirty truth?

I want to fuck him.

I want to make it so the next time he blushes, it's because he's remembering all the things we've done together.

Fuck, just think what sex could be like between us. It wouldn't be roses and moonlight, that's for sure.

It would be wild. There would be biting. And I'm not talking about me.

The morning after would be awkward, though. Really awkward. Because Noah's never hidden the fact that he doesn't like me. Which is going to make being roommates hard enough even without adding sex to the mix. Plus, he's just discovered he can use magic and has a whole new side of himself—unfortunately, not the sexual side—to focus on.

So… I'll be responsible and not say anything. Or do anything. But should Noah ever decide he needs someone to experiment with, I'm definitely not going to say no.

"What are you grinning at like an idiot?" Gideon demands, shoving my feet off my desk for no reason other than he's a dickhead.

"I was just imagining how glorious it will be when Sam finally ditches you and runs away with me."

Instantly, he's growling and looming over me. It's so easy to push his buttons.

"Gideon, leave Andrew alone," Sam demands exasperatedly from his desk, not even looking up. "You know he's only teasing you. If you didn't take the bait every time, he'd stop."

I don't bother to tell him I wouldn't stop. It would be less fun, though.

Before either Gideon or I can say anything else, David walks into the office, directing two maintenance men who are carrying a smallish sit-stand desk. It doesn't have a lot of surface space but will hold a laptop and a notebook—and most importantly, will fit in our office with the six desks that are already here.

"What's going on?" Elinor asks curiously. She didn't give a damn when Gideon was on the verge of beating me up, but suddenly now she wants to be part of the conversation. Bloody hellhounds.

David looks at me. "You didn't tell them?"

"Tell us what?" Gideon's back to looming over me. I sigh, heave myself to my feet, and shove him out of the way as I go to move a potted palm out of the way.

"No. I've been busy."

"Busy staring into space with a stupid smile on your face?" Elinor demands.

"Okay," David interrupts hastily. "Noah's going to be working in here with us. He's helping me with some research."

"What research?" Elinor pries as the maintenance men set the desk down per David's very fussy instructions. Seriously, it wouldn't be any drama if it was a few inches out of place. It's not a heavy desk, and most of us have enhanced strength anyway.

Neither David nor I answer until the men have gone, because there's no way either of us are going to say the words "human magic" in front of anyone outside the team. The news would rip through the organization faster than ice cream through someone with lactose intolerance—and if we do have a leak, as Percy fears, Tish will hear about it and be certain to come after Noah.

Even if we don't have a leak, information like this is sure to get out. When you spend a lot of time and energy keeping your true self a secret from humanity, the idea of them gaining yet another weapon to use against you is daunting, to say the least.

But as soon as it's just us, David gives the others a quick rundown of what we learned this morning.

"And Noah's happy about this? Being able to use magic, I mean," Sam presses like the overanxious mother hen he's become lately.

"Thrilled," I tell him. "I have no doubt that as soon as he gets the hang of it, he'll be lobbing fireballs at me on a regular basis."

He smiles. Any other time, he would have laughed and quipped something about how I deserve it, but—

"So Tish has a spy," he says heavily, an edge of fear in his voice. Gideon takes his hand.

"We don't know that," Elinor replies, injecting a note of fake positivity. "But if he does, at least this time we're more prepared. It won't be like last time."

Nobody says anything. Last time was… Well, losing Lily broke a little part of all of us.

Noah walks in on the awkward silence and freezes. "Um… I'll come back."

Sam leaps to his feet. "No, it's fine." He smiles again,

this time a little more genuinely, and says, "Your desk is here. And congratulations on your new ability! Although please don't set me on fire."

Blinking, Noah asks, "Why would I set you on fire?"

Is it weird that I suddenly remember I need to renew my porn subscription?

"Never mind." Sam waves dismissively. "Go ahead and get yourself set up. I'm going to go find out where Alistair is and make sure he'll be back before we meet with Percy." He takes two steps, then turns back around. "Oh! Um, until things are… um, more settled, you should probably stay with me and Gideon. It would help me sleep better."

Gideon winces.

"That's a great idea!" I declare enthusiastically, and I swear, it's entirely possible Gideon will manifest the ability to telekinetically liquefy my insides, his glare is that focused.

"Unclench, Gideon," party pooper David says. "Percy's already decided that Noah's staying with Andrew."

"With Andrew?" Elinor's eyes widen. "Poor Noah. Although, the pool is great. It's heated almost like bath-water—you can swim in it year round."

Noah's smile is a weak, twisted thing. "Thanks for the tip."

"We'll go with what Percy wants," Gideon says almost cheerfully. Sam's frowning, though, so he adds, "And we can always visit Noah at Andrew's place. It's great for hanging out. I think Andrew should host us all for dinner this weekend."

Oh, how the tables have turned.

All eyes focus on me. Sam looks like a hopeful puppy. Noah looks like a pissed-off house cat. It's ridiculous.

And I'm definitely not hosting the team for dinner at my beautiful home. My sanctuary. Not after what happened last time.

"Would you, Andrew? That would be so great. I haven't seen your place yet," Sam says with big eyes.

I sigh. "Sure. Sounds good."

---

WHEN WE'RE DONE for the day, Noah and I go to his place so he can grab some stuff to bring back to mine. As a result, it's later than usual when I finally let myself into my sanctuary. I feel the wards brushing over me in their creepy semi-sentient way when Noah tries to follow me in.

He scowls, trapped in the doorway. "What the fuck?"

"It's the wards." I think my most reassuring thoughts about Noah, making it clear he's an invited guest. "They won't let you in without my permission." I can tell the second the wards clear him for entry, because he staggers forward.

"Am I going to have to go through this every day? And what about leaving? Can I leave without your permission, or am I a prisoner here?"

I close the door, waving dismissively. "These wards were designed to keep people out, not in. You can leave whenever you want. But we'll have to get David to tweak the weaves before you can just enter without me. I didn't think of it earlier, sorry." Which was really dumb of us. We were even talking about the benefits of having him behind stronger wards.

He doesn't look happy, and I can't blame him. I

make a mental note to send David a message. He was still at work when we left, and knowing him, will be for a while longer. Maybe he can drop by on his way home. Although, given how much he's taken on lately, it's probably best he get some rest. This isn't critical. Noah's unlikely to go out again tonight.

"Tour?" I ask, not bothering to wait for him to respond before heading into the main living area and pointing everything out. It's mostly open-plan, anyway, so he's not likely to get lost.

"You're welcome to use the pool anytime," I say, gesturing to it through the wall of glass sliders that lead out to the terrace-slash-roof garden. "Just no glassware in the pool enclosure, and remember that those doors are warded too, so make sure I'm home before you go out or you'll be stuck there until I get back."

It's late twilight and hard to see outside, but Noah goes over to the sliders and peers through them. "Wow. That really is a great pool." He seems to have forgotten his pissiness over the wards. "How do you have actual trees and garden beds up here?"

I shrug. "Clever design? I don't know. I bought the place after it was built. Come on, I'll show you your room."

He drags himself away from the windows and follows me into the hallway. The first room is my study-slash-library, and the second is the main bathroom. I open the door to the third room and gesture for him to precede me inside.

He takes two steps in and stops dead. I smirk. I *do* have great interior design skills.

"This is the guest room?" He sounds stunned. "Holy fuck."

I can't blame him for saying that. I got a look at his place when we picked up his stuff, and while it's nice, almost the whole thing would fit in this room. There's a king-size bed with a plush upholstered headboard and oversized nightstands, a separate lounge area with a three-seat sofa, two armchairs, and a coffee table, all angled toward the wall-mounted flat-screen TV, and a wall of closet doors. I could have sacrificed the sitting area for a walk-in-slash-dressing room, but it's a guest room. Even if people are staying for a while, there's plenty of storage for their stuff, and they'll get more use out of a private living space than a walk-in closet.

"I like my guests to be comfortable," I say loftily. It's true, but the real reason the place looks like a luxury hotel suite is because I had fun doing it.

"Uh-huh. Is that a door out to the terrace?" He points to the french windows by the sitting area.

"Yes, but it's warded, so don't go out in the middle of the night unless you want to stay out there until morning." Because even if he yells and wakes me, I'm not getting out of a nice warm bed just because he didn't pay attention. "The bathroom is next door— you'll have it to yourself."

He nods, still taking in the room.

"There's a few streaming services already logged in on the TV, and I'll get you the Wi-Fi password. Help yourself to anything you want in the kitch— Oh."

Finally, he turns his attention to me. "Lots of blood, not much food?"

Crap. I'm going to need to order groceries. "No, there's plenty of food, but most of it is blood-infused, and I think we've established that you don't like blood." Memories of that blood kiss rise unbidden, and I push them back down, ignoring the stirring of interest in my pants. That ball's in his court.

Heh. Balls.

"We'll get takeout tonight," I decide. "Any preferences?"

He shrugs. "Anything's fine, but can it have veggies?"

I don't know why I'm surprised by his request, but I am. "Of course. The restaurant across the street does a great veggie pasta. Are you vegetarian?" I can't remember if I've ever seen him eat meat, but if he doesn't, that's going to impact my shopping list.

"No." He shakes his head. "But I didn't get a lot of veg in the labs, and it's made me a bit of a convert." He snorts. "Teenage me would never have thought I'd actually want vegetables—not unless they were smothered in cheese or something. Which is still great, but now I just really like fresh food."

Ever been kicked in the stomach before? I have, and what I'm feeling now is somewhat reminiscent. I also want to go out and buy him as many vegetables as he can eat.

I make myself smile and say, "Well, there are vegetables and fruit in the fridge, and I'll get some more, but most of my grocery items have blood in them, so we'll get takeout tonight and breakfast on the way to work until we can sort that out."

"I'll get the groceries." There's a stubborn set to his jaw that tells me not to argue. "Since I'm living here rent-free."

I hesitate. Part of me—most of me—really wants to push his buttons and insist on buying the groceries. But... this is a way for him to maintain control of his life, and given how very out of control things have been for him, I'd be a horrible person if I didn't let him have this.

Compromise?

"Fine, but I'll come with you. I'm very particular about what I stock in my kitchen." Points for me for saying that with a straight face. "Make yourself comfortable. I'm going to order dinner and grab a shower." I leave before he can say anything else.

I call the place across the street and sweet-talk them into sending over some food (they don't actually do take-out, but I eat there so often that they bend the rules for me) and then jerk one out in the shower while imagining Noah on his knees before me—and yes, I'm aware that he'd be more likely to bite my dick off than suck it. After, I pull on loose cotton pants and wander out to the living room. It's empty, but I heard the shower running in the main bathroom as I passed.

When Noah emerges in sweatpants and a T-shirt, dinner is just being delivered. We settle in to eat with minimal conversation, although he makes a point of thanking me for the food and saying how good it is. Then he insists on cleaning up. I watch like a hawk, because I'm very fussy about my kitchen, but he does a decent job of it.

I go to turn on the TV, although I'm not sure what I want to watch. Noah comes over and hovers uncertainly next to the couch I'm sitting on. It's not like him to be indecisive, and my curiosity is piqued.

"You can sit, you know. Is there anything you want to watch?" I surf through a bunch of channels, but I'll probably end up switching over to Netflix.

"Actually, I was wondering if you mind, uh, spotting me while I practice with the magic."

I drop the remote. It somehow just slips out of my hand.

"Of course." I rein in my surprise. Noah, asking me for a favor? Has the world ceased to turn? "But since I can't use magic, there's not a lot I can do if—"

"I know. I just think it's safer if someone else is here. Plus, if I end up hurting myself, you can call an ambulance or whatever."

There's a cheery thought. "Try not to hurt yourself. Sam would not be happy, which means Gideon would be unbearable."

There's that tiny wince.

"You know Gideon wouldn't hurt you, right? Despite his demeanor, he's actually one of the good guys." If Noah's going to be working in close proximity with our team, he can't be walking on eggshells around Gideon, no matter how amusing I find it.

"I know that." He hesitates. "Are you sure he doesn't eat live kittens for breakfast?"

I snicker. Gideon would probably find that funny. "Pretty sure. And even if he used to, he'd never do it now. Can you imagine Sam's reaction? Come on, forget Gideon. Show me what you've got." Whoops, I did *not* mean for that to come out sounding suggestive.

Slowly, he crosses to an armchair that's about as far from me as he can get and still be in the seating area— which kills any hint of an erection I might have—and lowers himself into it. I scoop up the remote from where I dropped it and turn the TV off.

A second later, there's a ball of glowing white hovering about a foot in front of Noah. It spins almost gleefully in place, then divides into three smaller balls.

He didn't do that today, so I guess he's playing with his ability.

"Do you want me to talk to you, or do you want to concentrate?"

"Talk," he says, his gaze fixed on the balls, which are bobbing around randomly.

"How does it feel?"

He takes his time answering. "Easier than earlier today. Like, it's the end of the day and I'm tired, but the —the movement? action? I don't know what word to use. It doesn't feel as awkward."

"And the white light doesn't wear you out like the fireball did?"

"No." He shakes his head. "To use a really dumb analogy, this feels like an LED light instead of halogen. It takes less energy to power. The fireball was exhausting."

I make a mental note to talk to David about that. It makes sense, since the lightballs emit just a white glow, whereas the fireball had heat as well—and was probably burning oxygen. But it might impact the kind of exercises he has to do.

The balls begin to move in a smoother, more neatly defined pattern, as though Noah is getting the hang of coordinating them.

"Can you juggle?" I ask, and his gaze flicks to me for an instant.

"Uh, not well. I know the basics, though. But I'm not sure if the lights are solid enough to touch."

Oh, now there's an interesting thought. I file it for later. "Don't touch them, then. You're moving them with telekinesis, so try juggling them that way too."

His brow furrows with concentration, and then a

moment later, the three balls form a wobbly arc. He fumbles a few times, and I can tell this is taking more effort than what he was doing before, but he's doing it—telekinetically juggling three lightballs.

It's amazing.

Does he realize how special he is? To the best of our knowledge—and this is the type of thing we keep track of—no human has done this in nearly nine thousand years. Those who are capable of it don't allow themselves to experience it properly, instead making up rhyming spells and rituals that only hinder them. And yet here's this man refusing to see any limits and seizing every opportunity he can.

I know that Noah's young, even for a human, but there are times when it's so easy to forget that. Unlike many other young people, he never defers to the rest of us or expects us to take control because we're older. He found himself in an untenable situation in Tish's custody, but he never gave up. Sure, he had the magic on his side, even if he didn't know it, but he was still a teenager in hiding with no way out. I've known adults in similar situations—adults who weren't human, who had a better chance of defending themselves—who gave up, unable to cope, and became catatonic.

He's exceptional.

The juggling slows a little, and then the pattern changes. I grin. "I thought you said you weren't good at this?"

He laughs. "Turns out it's easier when you're controlling the balls with your mind and don't have to worry about dumb things like gravity."

He maintains it for another couple of minutes while we talk about the research he started on today, and then

I say, "I noticed that you don't take your eyes off the balls. How about you stop juggling and see if you can keep them active without looking at them?"

Biting his lip, he slows the balls. "I don't think I can."

I say nothing, and he sighs.

"Which is why I should try, I guess."

"You should only do what feels right. Are you tired?" I do *not* want to have to explain to everyone that he has some kind of magic burnout because I pushed him too hard.

"I'm still good. I feel the effort, but I'm not drained like I was with the fireball. Okay, gonna do this." He sets his face in a determined expression: he wants to win this battle. The three balls hover in place before him, and he slowly shifts his gaze over to me. "You'll watch them, right?"

"I'm watching." The right-most ball is already fading—and drooping just a bit. "Can I make a suggestion?"

His eyes narrow. "Since when have you ever asked permission?"

I grin. "I'm trying to keep you on your toes. Why don't you start in easy mode and work your way up?"

He hesitates. "What do you mean?"

"You're trying to balance three balls in the air without looking. Why not just have one ball resting on the coffee table or something to start? Then when you've mastered that, you can move on to something harder."

"They're gone, aren't they?" He sounds so dispirited by the idea.

"No." I shake my head. "Although they are really

struggling, and I think you're going to lose at least one in the next few seconds."

Sighing, he agrees, "Let's start over." In seconds, he's merged the balls—which all brighten considerably as soon as he's looking at them again—and the sole remaining one is resting on the surface of my gorgeous blackwood coffee table.

Hmm.

"Hold on." I get up and go grab a coaster from a drawer in the sideboard. He bursts out laughing when he sees it—full-on belly laughs. I don't think I've ever seen him let go like that, and my lips curve up in a smile.

"It's not going to wreck your furniture," he scoffs when he can breathe again.

"I'm sure it won't," I make sure to sound as condescending as possible, "but just in case, it can't hurt." I hover beside the lightball. "Lift."

Snorting, he raises it an inch, and I slide the coaster underneath. "See? Completely painless. Now let's see what you can do." I return to the couch, but at the other end this time, closer to Noah.

Drawing in a breath, he takes his gaze off the ball and looks at me.

"How does it feel?" I ask, keeping my attention on the lightball, which is flickering a little. "Does it seem the same as when you were looking at it?" I have an idea about what's happening, and I want to lead him in that direction.

"I'm not sure," he says uncertainly. "I never really thought about it. Fuck. I've been focusing too much on what it looks like. Let's start again."

I sit back and let him take charge of the exercise. First he looks at the lightball for a few minutes, seemingly just staring, but I suspect he's performing mental evaluations. Then he makes it disappear and brings it back a few times. Finally, he nods.

"Okay, I'm ready." The ball glows steadily on the coaster, and he turns his attention to me.

I look at the lightball. It hasn't changed.

"Talk to me," I challenge.

"About what?" There's an edge of smugness in his tone, and that more than anything else tells me he's got this whole exercise under control. He's mastered how the lightball should feel in his mind rather than how it should look, and that's given him more confidence.

"Anything. You can recite multiplication tables if you like. Or tell me more about the research you're working on."

"Actually, I have a question you might be able to help me with."

I keep my surprise that he's asking me for help—again—under wraps and stay focused on the lightball… which is still glowing steadily. "I'll listen, but no promises. The last time I said yes with no limitations, I ended up helping to babysit two-year-old hellhound triplets."

Noah's indrawn breath is proof that he understands what a horrific experience that was—although once they fell asleep, they were pretty cute.

"This is nothing that scary," he promises. "I was thinking about how, when I was in the compound, the magic reacted to my needs when I was desperate. Kind of like when little old ladies lift cars to reach their loved ones. Even though I shouldn't have been able to use the magic, when I needed it badly enough, I did. And it takes me a lot of concentration now to do anything even remotely similar—like projecting emotions—because I'm not feeling that level of desperate need."

"Sure. That's not a terrible analogy." But I'm not sure where he's going with this. We already covered it today.

"Right, but yesterday when Nikita used her whammy on me, I really didn't want to lose control of my thoughts. I remember feeling disgusted that she'd violate anyone like that and desperately pleased that I could still think clearly."

For a split second, I take my gaze off the lightball. I have to—I need to make sure he's okay. Thankfully, his expression is more analytical and thoughtful than troubled, but I still make a mental note to ensure what happened hasn't added to his PTSD... and to see if we can't find him someone to talk to about that.

"You think the magic responded then too? Shielded you?" I return my gaze to the lightball, which is still steady. He's really mastered this.

"Maybe? Is it even possible to shield from that?"

I'm nodding before he's even finished speaking. "Yes. Vampires have a natural semi-immunity to enthrallment, a side effect of charisma. And sorcerers weave mental shields all the time. They can even do them for other people—but the risk with that is that you need to allow the sorcerer into your mind, and then once they've woven the shield, you need them or another sorcerer if you want to make changes or remove it."

"So theoretically, I could shield myself from... what did you call it before? Telepathic attack? I just have to work out how and then practice."

"This is something you should definitely talk to David about. Even if his Wiccan friend doesn't have an equivalent option, building mental shields is something he's done a lot of. He might be able to walk you through it." Although I'm not sure how that would work. Sorcerers take energy from within themselves that they were born with and literally weave and knit and braid it in certain ways that allows things to happen. Noah's use of the magic seems to be more of a "flow through me and do what I'm visualizing" thing.

It's frustrating not to be able to help him more.

"I think you need to challenge yourself a little," I suggest. "Can you lift the ball?"

It takes a second, but then the ball rises about half an inch. It's wobbling, but still glowing steadily.

"Good. Maintain it there for a bit, and then try moving it some more."

We spend another twenty minutes playing with the lightball—moving it, splitting it into three, recombining them, splitting them again, and then, finally, juggling them.

That's a little trickier than either of us expected. We thought that since Noah had been doing such a great job picking up the other steps so quickly, this would come naturally too.

"Stop hitting me with them!" I'd swear he's doing it on purpose, except he looks so frustrated and pissed off. At least the balls don't hurt—it's just a tingly sensation brushing against my skin.

"I'm *trying*. Fuck, this is how I remember juggling. The damn balls never went the way I wanted them!"

Ah.

I go to stand behind him—we both leaped to our feet after the first lightball careened out of control—and turn him toward the balls, keeping my hands on his shoulders. "Close your eyes." I need to see them, but he doesn't.

"Andrew—"

"Trust me. Close them. Feel the balls. Is everything right? Do they feel the way they're supposed to?"

He takes a deep breath, his shoulders rising in my hold, and considers it while I keep an eye on the balls. They return to "resting" position, in a line about a foot away.

"Yeah. They're good."

"Stop trying to 'see' them juggle. Feel it instead. Feel them exactly as they are but moving. And the way they're moving is in a smooth arc. One after the other. You're not juggling them; you're moving the energy through space."

The first attempt is a disaster, with all three balls moving at once into the same space. They merge, but I don't tell Noah, instead letting him get the circuit started. The ball has made one full round before he says, "It's wrong. There's only one, isn't there?"

"Is there?"

He hesitates, then nods. "There's only one." A second later, it splits back into three. The first one bobs. Then the second. Then the third. "Okay. Okay," he mutters.

It takes a few minutes, but eventually he has all three balls moving in a more or less regular arc. It's nowhere near as smooth as when he could see them, but they're no longer smacking me in the face.

"Is it working?" he demands.

"Hold on." I duck around him and grab my phone from the coffee table, then record a few seconds of his juggling. "Okay, open your eyes."

They pop open so fast, I have to stop myself from stumbling back. It was like a horror movie moment— you know, with a supposedly dead body in a haunted tomb or something.

Of course, the second he can see the balls, their trajectory smooths out. I hold up my phone. "Put away your toys and come and see." He hesitates, and I raise a brow. "You've been at this for a while now. There's no point wearing yourself out."

Muttering a reluctant "Yeah," he… vanishes? extinguishes? the lightballs, then steps forward to see my phone. I hit Play on the recording but watch him instead of the clip.

The grin that lights up his face is beautiful, and in the next heartbeat I have an armful of Noah as he throws himself against me in a hug.

"I did it! Did you see?" He turns his grinning face up to mine, and something in my expression—unconcealed shock, maybe—must bring home the realization that he's voluntarily touching me, because consternation crosses his face and he lets go so quickly, he almost falls over. "Uh, sorry."

I swallow, trying to push away thoughts of how good he felt against me. "No problem. Heat of the moment. Very exciting. Uh…" What was I saying? "I can send you this, if you like."

He nods almost manically. "Yes. Please. I can probably match what was happening to how it felt in my head and use it as a teaching tool. Or something." He peters off into awkward silence while I'm very busy with my phone, texting him the video. Because that takes a lot of effort and attention, you know.

His phone dings in his pocket, and he pulls it out.

"Got it." He waves the phone. "Uh… I'm kind of tired. Guess that wore me out more than I thought. G-Good night."

"It's been a long day," I agree. "Sleep well." Thank fuck he's taking the initiative here, because I need some time to think without him distracting me.

With an awkward wave, he turns and hightails it to his bedroom, and I sink down to sit on my coffee table, even though that's something I *never* do.

What am I supposed to do now?

# CHAPTER EIGHT

## Noah

IT'S BEEN THREE WEEKS, and I still can't close my eyes without seeing shirtless Andrew in my head and remembering how his bare back felt under my hands when I impulsively—foolishly?—hugged him.

Of course, it doesn't help that he has a habit of walking around the apartment bare chested. For someone who's so into clothes, he doesn't wear them as much as he should. And why is his body so nicely defined, anyway? His stupid expensive clothes hide a *lot*.

I've been thinking about his body way too much. Like, lying awake at night in that gorgeously comfortable huge bed, imagining all the ways he could use that body. It's criminal how long it takes me to fall asleep—because while vampire hearing isn't quite as good as shifter, it's still good enough that he'd hear if I beat one out, and while *he* might not feel embarrassment, I don't know if I could handle looking him in the eye knowing he listened to me masturbate.

Maybe if I invited him to watch? That could be hot. Like... really hot. Whew. Uh, but there's always the possibility that he'd say no, and then I'd be back to dying of embarrassment. Although, what sexually active single guy says no to watching someone jerk it? Even if nothing more is on the table, it's fun to watch.

Holy fuck, how did I go down this rabbit hole? Right, thinking of Andrew while lying in bed and not being able to do anything about it. The real shame of it is the lost sleep, because since I moved in, I've been sleeping better than I have in years. I don't know if it's the bed or the knowledge that Andrew's wards are top-notch or what, but when I *finally* do manage to get to sleep, I don't wake up until morning. If I'm having nightmares, they're polite enough to disperse before I can remember them. It's amazing. Sleep is amazing. I recommend it. Five stars.

Things have been good for me lately. Even with the threat of Tish looming, I feel more secure and confident in my life than I have since before the abduction. Work is no longer tedious—the research David has me doing is fascinating. He showed me some online archives that he needed to get special permission for me to access, then put me in touch with librarians and archivists from all around the world who are seriously hardcore at finding information. I think they're excited that David and I are exploring a "new" avenue of historic research. Nobody's really looked into human magic use before, what with being focused on their own species, but they're all academics and so the fact that I'm doing this makes me worthy of respect in their eyes, if that makes sense.

And I'm finding some pretty cool stuff. We've been able to confirm that human magic use wasn't ritualized until after the species wars, which is a pretty big deal.

Humans back then could likely use magic the way I do —with focus and will. This is, like, *revolutionary* information. It also *appears* that David's theory about the magic not allowing itself to be used to directly cause harm is true, but I'm still struggling to prove that. The easiest way to do it would be for me to try to hurt someone using the magic, but I feel really gross about that idea— not that Percy and David would approve it anyway. Talk about unethical.

There're pictures of a section of carvings from a wall in a crypt somewhere that I'm convinced have more information, but they haven't been translated yet, and David and I are worried that if we try to find a translator and push it up their to-do list, we'll attract too much attention to what we're doing. It's a balance between finding what we need and not terrifying the community by revealing that humans can do magic and a human is researching ways to make it easier.

With that in mind, I've been compiling a lexicon of common pictographs and hieroglyphs for my own reference, so I can at least recognize when something might be relevant. It's a lot cooler than I ever thought it would be, and I'm thinking I might look into taking some language courses. It can't hurt to be multilingual, can it? Although the languages I'm most interested in right now are dead ones, and I think learning those would involve an advanced college degree rather than an evening course at a local community center.

Plus, all my free time right now is being spent on training to use the magic. Which, seriously, you gotta try. It's fucking awesome. I can handle fireballs now without wearing myself out too quickly. That helps in making me safer from any attack by Tish, too—if I can lob a few fireballs at my assailants, I have a better chance of getting away. Or if they do manage to kidnap me, I can just burn the whole place to the ground... once I figure out how to protect myself from the flames, because those fuckers hurt. It's still a work in progress. But hey, I've also discovered I can use the magic to dull pain from minor burns!

I'm getting pretty good at most telekinesis, and I've also got a grip on simple wards. That's a lot tougher, because the way David and other sorcerers do it just doesn't work for me. Anything complex that requires me to "set and forget" seems to fall apart pretty quickly. We've had to rely on the information from David's Wiccan friend for the basics and extrapolate from that, which makes it slow going. But the more I use this ability, the more I find myself able to do, so it's a muscle I'm flexing as often as possible.

Andrew's been helping a lot. Don't get me wrong, he still pisses me off on the regular, but now I *know* he's doing it on purpose, because when I need him to be supportive or focused, he is. I guess I shouldn't be surprised that the centuries-old vampire actually can act like an adult. I mean, he's one of the most highly placed and respected people in the community of species, literally responsible for keeping all species safe from discovery by humans and thus potential obliteration. I guess when you're older than clocks, you get sick of always acting like a mature adult. He's still a dick, but it wouldn't hurt for me to cut him some slack, right?

Okay, fine. Yes, I want to do dirty things to him and I'm trying to rationalize that with the fact that I'm not sure if I like him as a... I was going to say "human being," but he's not human. Oh my god, I want to fuck a vampire. Who's *hundreds* of years older than me. My life has become one of those teen movies the girls at my high school used to get all weird over. All that's left for me to do is get all dramatic and introspect—

Like I'm being right now. Fuck. My. Life. I'm a teenybopper vampire lover.

I stare at the bedroom ceiling and wonder how it came to this.

Yep. Still doing it. Dramatic and introspective. Ugh.

I throw back the covers and haul myself out of bed. I've spent too long this morning trying to decide if it's okay to sexually proposition someone I think I dislike. I feel like there's a moral imperative to say no, I should at least not hate someone I'm going to fuck, but honestly, my sense of morality might be on the fritz, because I don't care that much. It's more that part of me thinks I should care. I don't want to be morally broken.

I freeze halfway across the threshold to the bathroom. Could this be an aftereffect of my abduction? Did being held captive screw with my sense of right and wrong?

Nah. If that was the case, I'd have murdered Andrew months ago. Even though the memory of breaking his nose gives me warm feelings, I don't think I could actually kill him just for being annoying. Hell, even the thought of experimenting on him with my new ability is gross—although that doesn't include "accidentally" hitting him with things while practicing telekinesis. Or the time I created a ward right in front of him while he was walking, and he actually *bounced* off it. Man, that shit was funny. But I couldn't use him as a test subject to see if the magic would allow me to use it to hurt people, no matter whether I hate him or not.

I get in the shower and turn on the water, letting the initial cold blast force me to focus. Because I need to ask myself A Serious Question. Do I really hate Andrew?

I hate Tish. Loathe him with every fiber of my being. Hate him for what he did to me. Hate him for what he did to everyone else he experimented on. Hate him for what he's trying to do to this community and society. What I feel for Andrew, even before lust crept in, is nothing like that.

Andrew… Well, he annoys me. But he annoys a lot of people. He goes out of his way to tease and torment and wind people up until they just want to smack him. But I've never seen him actually hurt anyone, not in a way that caused lasting damage—not like Tish. Andrew will pick at your stupid fears—like when I was terrified Gideon would eat me—but he'll stand between you and the real bullies. And I can't lie, these last few weeks, he's proven himself to be a… friend?

What else do you call it when you share meals and conversation with someone and they help you develop skills?

Can you be friends with someone and still think fondly of breaking their nose?

Can you think fondly of breaking someone's nose and still want to have sex with them?

I stick my head under the stream of hot water. I guess the answer's yes on both counts. Does that make me a freak?

Sighing—and then coughing and spluttering as I end up with a mouthful of water—I push the thought aside and concentrate on what's important: jacking off.

THE PROBLEM with working with other species is that they've all got better senses than me. Hearing, sight, smell… and somehow, that also equals them being more graceful and stealthy.

Which is how Sam manages to walk up behind me and see what's on my computer screen at the one time I'm looking up something that's not work-related.

"Noah?" he gasps, and that's the first indication I get that someone's there. I yelp and leap about three feet in the air. The office was empty! Everyone was out doing fieldwork or in meetings—that was the only reason I succumbed to temptation.

I grab for the mouse, desperate to close the browser window, but somehow in my haste, I fumble and end up clicking one of the search results.

The porn clip starts autoplaying, the voices filling the office.

*"I'm going to fuck you so hard, you'll feel me in your throat. Maybe that will shut you up."*

*"Yeah? Just do it from behind so I don't have to see your damn face."*

I close my eyes and bury my face in my hands. What kind of office doesn't have a filter that blocks porn sites? I want it to end, but I'm too afraid to try stopping it for fear of making it worse somehow. Although, the only way this could be worse would be if Andrew walked in right now.

Fear clutching my gut, I jerk my head up and look toward the doorway. It's empty. Thank sweet baby Jesus and all that's holy.

Sam leans across me, grabs the mouse, and stops the clip. He then hits the back button and returns to the fateful search page.

"Uh, Noah—"

"I wasn't looking for porn, I swear," I choke out. There's not much that's more unprofessional than watching porn on company time and equipment, and I don't want Sam or anyone else to think I'm that irresponsible.

"No, I can see that," he says slowly, still staring at the search bar. The place where I typed *Is hate sex okay?*

Maybe it would be better for the man who thinks of himself as my big brother to believe I'm watching porn on the job. Because I have a sneaking suspicion I'm about to get a Serious Talk that's going to make me want to die.

"Is it consensual?" he asks, and I'm so surprised that I just blink at him like a dummy.

"What?"

"The hate sex. As long as it's consensual and you don't feel bad about yourself after—or made to feel bad by the other person—then there's nothing wrong with it."

A long, awkward silence stretches between us.

"Uh, thanks." I suck in a breath and force myself to meet his gaze.

He smiles casually. "Have fun with it. Oh—do you have any questions—"

"No!"

The smile falters, and I race to soften my shout of denial.

"Thanks, Sam, but I'm not… I mean, I've had sex. I just…" *wanted to make sure I wasn't psychologically damaged.*

He leans against my desk. "Sex can mean a lot of different things," he says. "What's sexy to one person might not be to another. I used to have a friend who was into BDSM, and he told me the most important thing was that sex is safe, sane, and consensual. I think that should apply outside of BDSM as well. For me…" He shrugs. "I've never been into anything fancy, sexually speaking, but consent and respect have always been my hard limits."

I give that a second to sink in. Consent and respect. I figure Sam means respect for each other's wishes and limits, but maybe also respect for the person you're with? Because I might not be sure if I like Andrew, but I know I respect him. I might not want a relationship with him, but I wouldn't feel shame for having fucked him.

"Thanks, Sam." I can hear the confidence back in my voice. "I'm sorry I was looking this up at work. And I swear, I *was not* going to look at the porn clips."

"Who's looking at porn?" Alistair says as he strolls in. "And why wasn't I invited?"

Sam rolls his eyes and straightens, going over to his own desk. "No one's looking at porn," he says. "I swear, I don't know where you come up with these ideas."

Alistair starts to protest, and Sam shoots me a conspiratorial little wink. Which, yay, glad he's keeping my secret, but I really hope he doesn't suspect who I'm thinking of having hate sex with.

Who am I kidding? He totally knows.

"…just saying, people should stop making out like porn is a bad thing," Alistair is saying. "We all watch it. As long as it's produced under safe and nonexploitative conditions with consenting adult participants, there's no reason to consider it anything but wonderful."

It's shockingly unsurprising that Alistair has a porn disclaimer. Although, I can't disagree with him about any of that.

"Alistair, why are you talking about porn?" Elinor asks exasperatedly as she walks in and goes to drop the file she's holding on her desk. Seriously, why is everyone here? They were all supposed to be out for the afternoon. I was supposed to have the office to myself.

I go cold at the thought that someone other than Sam could have walked in first. Sam will keep his mouth shut, I'm pretty sure. Alistair or Elinor would *never* let me forget. I'd be hearing about the day I watched hate porn in the office until I breathed my last.

"I didn't start it," Alistair insists. "Sam and Noah were watching porn when I got here."

"*What?*" Andrew's delighted shout bounces off the walls. I want to crawl under my desk, but instead make myself look toward the doorway again, where he's standing with a huge grin on his dumb/sexy face and David and Gideon slightly behind him.

It could be worse. They could all have turned up five minutes earlier.

"We were not watching porn," I insist huffily as Gideon gives Andrew a shove and pushes past him.

"Why were you watching porn with Noah?" Gideon asks Sam—is he *pouting*? Sure, I've come to terms with the fact that he's not quite as fucking terrifying as I thought, but seeing him pout like a kid whose favorite toy—

Whoa. That analogy is waaay creepy when the topic is porn. I'm backing away from that fast.

So. Gideon pouting equals weird.

"We weren't watching porn," Sam tells him patiently. "Alistair made that up."

"I did *not*." Alistair sounds completely offended. "Okay, maybe you weren't watching it right then, but you were definitely talking about watching porn. If you don't want to invite me, fine"—the injured look he gives me makes it clear that it's anything but fine—"but at least be secure enough to admit that you watched porn instead of gaslighting me."

My jaw drops open. We weren't actually gaslighting him, were we?

Before I have a chance to get my brain in gear, David steps in.

"Regardless of who was watching or talking about porn or not," he says in his sensible, calming way, "this is probably a conversation we can leave for another time."

I love David. I think he might be my best friend. At this moment, I would literally kill someone for him if he wanted me to. Especially if that person is Alistair, who has a mulish look on his face and is opening his mouth to argue.

"Or," Andrew butts in, "we can talk about it now and then again another time. In fact, we should have a porn party!"

Dead. Silence.

"A… what?" Elinor asks, leaning forward in fascination. "I'm not into orgies, if that's what you're getting at. Besides, with this crowd, my share of the action would be really limited, and a girl can only watch for so long before she wants to join in the fun."

Oh. My. God.

"Sweet baby Jesus," I whisper.

Andrew rolls his eyes. "I keep telling you, Noah, he was just some random do-gooder sorcerer. Look him up in the archives—by all accounts, he was a nice guy, but he came really close to outing the community with his insistence on helping humans."

"Forget about history," Alistair insists. "I want to hear more about this porn party. Exactly what does it involve?"

With a shrug, Andrew finally moves away from the door toward his desk. "Well, there are different kinds. The most fun include sex, of course. But since I have no desire to get naked with David—"

"Hey!" David exclaims, then shakes his head. "Why am I complaining about that?"

"—the kind we'd have as a group would include very bad porn and shots every time something cheesy happens."

"Are you high?" Gideon asks, but Sam looks faintly intrigued.

"You could also have shots for every time certain words and phrases are used," he suggests. "Like 'do me harder.'"

All eyes turn to him, and he flushes. "What? I watch porn."

"That's right, you do," Alistair teases. "You watch porn and use the World of Wangs."

I really want to ask, but—

"Okay, someone has to tell me the World of Wangs story," Elinor says. "Because it keeps coming up and I still don't get it."

"Nothing!" Sam insists. "It's nothing. Not important at all."

*Oh, Sam.* It's like he doesn't know them at all. He may as well have just thrown chum to circling sharks.

"Well, El," Andrew starts, a wicked gleam in his eye, "it's like this. Sam—"

"We were talking about porn!" I yell, even as I wonder what the ever-loving hell I'm doing. "It was my fault. I-I-I asked Sam some… questions. Um. About… sex. Porn. Things I'd seen in porn. Because… I've only had vanilla s-sex." *Oh, holy fuck, shut up, Noah!* Across the room, Sam's eyes are as wide as saucers and he's mouthing "thank you," but if I could take the last thirty seconds back, I totally would.

My face is so hot, you could fry eggs on it. And there is no way in hell I could possibly look at anyone right now.

"Well." Surprisingly, it's Gideon who breaks the silence. "That's your business, Noah, and not anyone else's." There's a warning edge to his voice, and when I peek up, he's glaring at the others. Alistair shrugs, though he's grinning, and Elinor holds up her hands in a gesture of surrender. Andrew, though, is staring at me with a weird expression… part shock, part… I don't know.

I clear my throat. "Uh, thanks." *Change the subject. Change the subject.* "Um, what are you all doing back here anyway? I thought you were out for the afternoon."

"Percy called us back," David says, leaning over his desk and waking up his computer. "We have a meeting with him in a few minutes."

"Oh." I desperately want to ask what about, because last-second meetings with all of them aren't common and usually mean something big is happening, but it's really not my business, and I'm already skating on thin ice professionally, what with the porn thing.

Everyone gets busy at their desks, checking email and the like, and I sink back in my chair and thank every imaginary deity I can think of that that's over.

An email notification pops up in the lower right corner of my screen. Dread rises in me.

It's just an email, right? Probably about work. I've been waiting on responses from a few archivists. It would be immature and stupid not to check it.

Besides, what's the worst it could be?

I flip windows to my email. The new one is sitting there at the top. It's from David, who's sitting literally feet away from me, and the subject line says *Just so you know…*

I really don't want to open it, but he's probably watching me and waiting for a response. Can I pretend I haven't seen it?

*Grow up, Noah.*

I click the email and scan it.

*Vanilla sex is not a bad thing, but you can ask me and Sam anything, no jokes, no teasing, and absolute confidentiality. Porn is probably not the best place to learn about kinky sex.*

Kill. Me. Now.

I know he means well, but this is not something I *ever* want to discuss with my work supervisor-slash-friend, no matter how good a guy he is.

Still…

I hit reply.

*Thanks.*

My fingers hover over the keyboard for a few moments more, but I really don't know what else to say. So I send it, then make myself look over at him and smile gratefully.

That smile becomes more natural when they all leave a minute later for their meeting.

---

I'VE MANAGED to push my embarrassment to the back of my mind and am dug into an archive of translations from a tomb that seem to hint about magic use when Elinor sticks her head in.

"Noah? Could you join us, please?"

Instantly I know something is wrong. She's too somber. Don't get me wrong, Elinor is a badass professional—she was scary as fuck during the raid on the compound—but in noncombat situations, there's usually a twinkle in her eye, like life's a big joke and she's in on it. Most hellhounds have it. Andrew told me it's a defect in their biological makeup, but he was smiling fondly at the time.

Also, if everything was good, why would they be asking me to join them in an emergency meeting?

"Sure." I match her serious voice and stand. "Do I need to bring anything?"

She shakes her head, so I lock my computer and follow her down the hall. They're meeting in Percy's office, which is unusual. Most of the time when it's all of them, they book a meeting room. I've never thought to wonder why.

All faces turn toward us as we enter. Elinor closes the door, then there's a pause while everyone looks at David.

"Done," he says, and I realize he was activating the super wards.

"Thanks for coming, Noah," Percy says, managing to convey warmth and welcome even with his somber face and tone. "Please sit."

Elinor takes the empty armchair, which leaves me with either the floor, standing, or the empty spot on the couch beside Andrew. I push all my sexual frustration into a tiny ball, lock it down hard, and sit. The couch is pretty roomy, but I can still feel the heat of his body radiating toward me.

*Concentrate.*

"We've found Tish."

I lean forward quickly. "Where? Is he here?" My hands go clammy. Please let him be far away.

"He's not here. And even if he was, you're safe. We're going to keep you safe," Percy reiterates firmly.

I shake my head. "I know. I'm sorry, I didn't mean to make this about me."

Andrew pats my arm, probably intending it to be a reassuring gesture, and I'm a little freaked by how much I want to lean into his support.

"You're fine, Noah. He's in the last place we ever thought to look for him—a compound in the northwest run by humans. Fundamentalist doomsday types awaiting the second coming."

It takes a few seconds for that to sink in. "He's hiding with religious humans?"

Alistair shakes his head ruefully. "Based on the intelligence report, he's convinced them he's an agent of god and that they need to follow him."

A sick feeling churns in my stomach. Don't people in those compounds stockpile weapons? We do *not* need Tish with an army at his back. "How is that even possible?"

"There's a precedent," Andrew reminds me. "It's not the first time a sorcerer has twisted human religious beliefs—but last time, the intentions were good."

What's he— Oh. Right. The sorcerer who claimed to be the son of god in order to help humans. Depending on how you look at it, it was either an epic failure or a rousing success.

"So he's, what, performing 'miracles'"—I make air quotes—"to convince them he's legit? And then he'll bring them to… fight us? How many of them are there?" This just doesn't make sense. Tish's goal with the genetic experimentation was to increase community numbers to the point that enslavement of humanity was possible. While on the surface it seems like he's found himself a group of humans willing to fulfill his every whim, it's unlikely they'll just docilely serve him forever. Eventually they're going to want to leave their compound with their religious figurehead and shove him down everyone else's throat. And then where will Tish be? A single sorcerer could never stand against the kind of forces the human government could bring, even if the community didn't intervene—which it totally would. So what's Tish's end game here?

"We're not sure yet," David says. "And our goal is to not let it get to the point where we are. The thing about these groups is, the leaders are very rarely truly devout. They use religion to build themselves little dictatorships where the benefits all flow up to them. The information we have shows the leader of this group to be no different, and while he supports the idea of converting others by force, he doesn't seem to be that happy about his position being usurped by Tish. His 'council of advisors' are solidly with him on that, since Tish brought his own 'disciples' with him."

I'm confused by that until I remember the other researchers who escaped with him. For some reason, I'd pushed all thoughts of them out of my head and focused all my angst on Tish.

"So if the leadership isn't supporting him, how…?"

Gideon huffs. "You were right before—he's been

'conducting miracles.' Basically walked up to the gate and began weaving; never even asked to speak to the leader. He has most of the lower ranks in the compound thinking he's a divine messenger, and the leadership can't refuse to follow his lead without explaining that they're not interested in religion so much as accumulating wealth and power for themselves." His grin is vicious. "If we approach them right, they'll sell him out."

I like this idea. "Hand him over to us, you mean? Are you sure? How would they explain it to their people?"

"It gets a little tricky there," Alistair admits. "The easiest way would be to denounce him as an imposter, but there's a risk that doing so would expose us."

David takes over. "The thing about using sorcery to perform so-called miracles is that it's not sustainable long-term. An experienced sorcerer with years of study behind them can create many weaves quickly, even with just a second's thought, but a lot of weaves are complicated, and no matter how good you are, they take time. Some, you can prep ahead of time and just finish when you need them, but it's not like you can keep an endless store. You have to know what you'll need and prep it. Most of the miracles he'll have been performing will be small things, with the occasional big one that he prepped ahead of time."

"So lots of glowing lights and hovering glassware, but not so much with the healing sick people?"

David's smile is not nice. I'm taken aback by it—this is a side of him I've never seen. He's always so caring and calm and focused that I forgot he would also have to be tough as nails and fairly ruthless to have gotten to where he is. "Tish *can't* heal people. That's not one of his skills. Not unless their illness is genetic, and even then, it would take a huge effort with nothing to show immediately. He has the same general sorcery ability that we're all born with, but his specialty is gene manipulation. If someone were to ask him to heal them—or for anything else that couldn't be achieved with a quick, basic weave—he'd be stuck."

"We think the best option at this stage is to get a message to the leaders identifying him as a fake. A con man and a charlatan. They would then—hopefully—seize advantage of this opportunity to denounce him to their followers. The most obvious way would be to ask him to perform a specific miracle," Percy says. "He won't be able to, of course, and even if he comes up with an excuse, it's going to foster doubt."

"What about the people with him?" I ask. "What are their skills? Could any of them do it and pass it off as him?" I was shown pictures of the researchers who fled with Tish, and I recognized them as other higher-ranked doctors from the labs. They would come around with Tish to oversee specific tests, but mostly we only saw the lab assistants and guards.

"No." David shakes his head. "The people who got away with him were all gene research specialists. There's one who might be able to heal small cuts, but that's the extent of it. That doesn't mean they're not dangerous, though. They're not combat trained, but as you know, even basic telekinesis can be weaponized. That's where our risk is. If Tish lashes out against the leaders when they denounce him, he could expose us all."

I don't really see Tish giving up just because a bunch

of humans catch him out, so this plan seems doomed to failure.

Alistair grins at me. "Don't look so disheartened," he says. "You haven't heard it all yet."

"This is starting to seem very convoluted. So far I've heard a lot of ifs—what if the leaders don't take your bait? What if they demand Tish do something that he's capable of? What if the followers don't care?" I hate that my voice is getting high-pitched, but the thing is, I'm still not sure why they've called me in here, and that worries me.

"We have ways of tipping the scales in our favor," Percy assures me calmly. "The human government has an agent inside that compound, and the people who need to know have been informed that we may need to leverage that. They're arranging things behind the scenes to make it happen."

I don't know if that makes me feel better or freaks me out.

"Our major concerns here are ensuring the humans in the compound remain unharmed for their own government to deal with and protecting the community from exposure."

"Which is why," Andrew says smoothly beside me, making me startle, "David and some combat sorcerers will be in place to step in. Their job will be to stifle any weaves Tish and his people might attempt."

"*Stifle* weaves?" I didn't know that was possible. "Like, stop them before they can—" I roll my wrist a few times, trying to think of the word. "—deploy?"

David nods. "Something like that. It's a specialist skill. Most people who have the ability to do it tend to go into enforcement, which is just as well. Our goal will be to have it look like nothing's happening. The last thing we want is a battle between sorcerers."

I can see how that would be bad. On the plus side, if this place is like others I've heard about, they're probably low-tech, which means little chance of someone taking video with their smartphone and uploading it to the internet.

"It sounds like you have a plan all ready to go."

Silence.

I sigh. "What?"

"Even when Tish's 'miracle' fails and he's shown to be a fraud, it's unlikely that the cultists will let us take him. In fact, any hint that we want him is likely to gain him support from them. They're very antigovernment. Our part in this has to remain completely secret and anonymous."

I rub my forehead, giving in to temptation and leaning ever so slightly toward Andrew, just enough to feel his warmth. "So, what are the possibilities? They realize he's a fake and kill him? Or throw him out of the compound?"

"Basically," Gideon says. "If they try to kill him, we'll have a problem. Since his ability to weave will be stifled, responsibility for his well-being will rest with our sorcerers. We absolutely cannot have fugitives murdered by humans while CSG sorcerers are stifling their magic. Especially since Tish and his accomplices haven't been tried and sentenced yet. At that point, our people would need to break cover and step in to retrieve them, and that could turn into a bloodbath—or expose us."

I start to laugh. "Come on, you can't seriously think this is a good plan. There are way too many variables. How are you going to ensure the cultists decide to kick

Tish out instead of killing him? And what happens if they do kick him out? He'll just disappear again." There's a dark sense of panic at the idea that Tish hasn't been tried yet—does that mean he could potentially be acquitted and allowed to go free? I never stopped to think of that, never considered anything beyond him being found and taken into custody. I would never sleep again if he was allowed to live as a free man.

"He'll attempt to disappear again," Percy corrects. "Those same combat sorcerers will take him into custody as soon as he's out of sight of the human compound. And just in case he does evade them, we'd like to circulate some rumors that he won't be able to resist."

It hits me like a lightning bolt, the reason I've been asked to join them.

"You want me to be bait."

"Not exactly," Elinor says. "We don't want you anywhere near him. But we'd like to put out some hints about you and Sam visiting the felid clan that Sam's biological father is part of. Tish doesn't know you're alive at this stage, but he recognized Sam as soon as he saw him, so we can assume he'd recognize you too— your face and your name. If we add a description of a young human man that Sam seemingly 'adopted' a few months back to the rumors, we believe he'll dig deeper to find out more—and once he learns it's you, he won't be able to resist finding out how you survived. But neither you nor Sam will be anywhere near that clan."

Every fiber of my being is screaming to run and hide, but I force myself to be logical... and draw on the magic for help bolstering myself. It twines along my body, a metaphysical shield.

"Won't he suspect a trap? If he's chased out of the cult by combat sorcerers and then suddenly hears rumors about a former research subject?"

"You forget," Sam says gently, speaking for the first time since I came in, "that we suspect there's a leak here and that Tish might already know you're alive." He's a little pale, and I know he's remembering his own experience in the lab. "We'd start the rumors from now to reinforce anything he might already have heard before we move on the cult. We won't be ready to do that for a few weeks."

My heart sinks. "So long?" Why does it need to take so long? How am I going to get through a minimum of *weeks* looking over my shoulder every second?

"The human government needs to get their man inside up to speed," David reminds me. "And before that can happen, our contacts need to come up with a reason for it so other parts of the human government don't get suspicious."

I say nothing. I don't want to let the side down, but I also really don't want Tish to know I exist.

"I know it's not a pleasant thought," Sam says. "Remember that you'll be here the whole time, safe with us. Tish will not get near you. And if you want, we can leave you out of the rumors and hope that he hasn't heard anything about you. But…" He hesitates. "When he was questioning me at the lab, he was very interested to know if I had kids. Obviously by then the second generation of testing had been… Well, once he found out that the weaves attached to my DNA had degraded, I think he regretted that there wasn't anyone from the second generation still around. He might be able to brush off news of my location, but he will definitely not be able to ignore you."

Is that supposed to make me feel better?

"Noah." Andrew grabs my arm, and I turn to look at him. "You're not defenseless anymore."

Oxygen rushes through my body as I suck in a deep breath. He's *right*. Even if Tish somehow was able to find me, I have the magic now. I can slap him with a ward or set him on fire—that really appeals to me, although the magic probably wouldn't let me set him on fire unless I was under direct threat. And I'm not alone, either. It's not me with foster parents who literally sold me. I have friends, and none of them would let Tish take me without a fight.

I look into Andrew's eyes, and I know that Tish would have to step over his dead body to get to me.

A shudder runs down my spine, emotion tackling me hard.

"Okay. Do it."

# CHAPTER NINE

## Andrew

THE DETERMINED EXPRESSION on Noah's face hits me like a brick to the gut. I feel incredibly guilty, because a second ago, he was about to refuse. I can't say I'd blame him for that, either. But then I had to open my mouth and remind him of the power he has now, and it was clearly a catalyst.

Sure, he made the decision himself, but it was pretty obvious he felt pressured by us, and I hate that. At the same time, we don't have the luxury of not pressuring him, and that's what makes me feel guilty. We *must* get Tish in custody and tried. He can't be permitted to set up his lab again. It really concerns me that he's found somewhere so off the grid to hole up in—if this particular cult wasn't infiltrated by the human government, we might never have found him, and given time, he could rebuild his research. This really seems to hint that he had a backup plan, and I'm worried that he might have resources hidden away that we missed.

So I just need to live with the guilt. On the positive side, reminding Noah of his new power might have given him a confidence boost and made him feel more secure.

Once we have Noah's consent, Percy wraps things up fairly quickly. We all have things to do—more now that we're planning an offensive against Tish—and this unplanned meeting has eaten into the day. But I've already written off the rest of the afternoon—some things are more important than work.

I follow Noah back to the office and grab his arm before he can settle into his desk chair.

"Shut down the computer. We're done for the day."

His eyes widen. "Oh, *we* are, are we?"

Smartass. "Yes. I thought you might want to do some training."

It's not hard to see that he's conflicted. He wants to tell me to fuck off, but at the same time, he also wants to play around with his magic. He's able to manage most things on his own now, but some of the bigger stuff he still needs a spotter for—especially when he's playing with fire. I've had to use the fire extinguisher three times and treat his burns at least half a dozen.

"Fine." He concedes as though he's doing me a favor, not the other way around, and I bite back a smile. Admittedly, I love spending this time with him, but he doesn't know that. Well, he knows I'm happy to help him with developing his abilities, and we're a lot more comfortable together—maybe even friendlier—than we used to be, but it would be a stretch for him to know that all I want right now is to get him out of here and help him relax.

I throw some things together that I might look at later while he logs off and shuts down his computer, and we head out of the office. Since Noah started commuting to and from work with me, I've given up walking and taking public transport in favor of driving —it's more secure. Too bad it takes twice as long in traffic.

Noah's quiet today, which is unfortunate. It gives me way too much time to think, and the prominent thought in my head anytime these days is how incredibly sexy Noah is. It doesn't help that he's been showering twice a day lately, and we all know what that means. It's not like he works in a messy, sweaty job that would require him to wash twice a day.

And knowing that he's jerking off with the hot water pounding down on him is all it takes for me to, uh, need a shower too.

Five hundred years ago, I'd have just gone out and picked up some nubile young thing who wanted a good time. But age makes you picky, and I don't see any benefit to fucking a random person just because the object of my desire is beyond my reach. Or worse— constantly within my reach, but not interested.

Although, if he's actually not interested, what's with the constant masturbation? Is it really just because he's young and horny, or is there more to it?

My conscience won't let me make the first move. Noah's in an incredibly vulnerable position, so he has to be the instigator.

Which brings me to my current dilemma: Would it be inappropriate for me to ask him about the porn he and Sam were talking about at the office? And why didn't he ask *me*? I've been around a lot longer than Sam —there's basically nothing I haven't tried at least once.

Well, twice. Because I like to experience things from all angles, if you know what I mean.

And I would gladly let Noah take advantage of my wealth of expertise, even if it's only theoretical and not practical. In fact, just thinking about such a discussion makes me hard... although not quite as hard as I was earlier, picturing him watching porn. What kind of porn? Something really kinky? Or just mainstream kinky? Whatever, I'm happy to tell him everything I know. He knows that, right? Maybe I should offer.

"So, ah, if you have any questions I can help you with, you just have to ask. Anytime. Anything. I don't have many limits."

Whoops. That did *not* come out exactly as I planned.

"Oh... kay?"

"What I mean," I begin, determined to rescue this situation, "is that if you're worried about talking about... *stuff* at the office, we can talk about it at home. Private stuff," I add. "Stuff that you may have watched. Or want to watch. Or want to do." *Please want to do it. With me. I will be your willing test subject.*

I sneak a glance his way and see his face is a shade of red so flamingly bright, he could legitimately be confused with a tomato. Damn. Embarrassing him is not my aim here.

Lapsing into silence, I spend the rest of the traffic-clogged drive considering my options. There aren't many my conscience will accept, so I guess backing off and leaving the ball in his court is what I'll have to do.

My poor dick doesn't like that. He was hoping to make a new friend.

Noah doesn't say a word as I park the car in the basement garage. He's silent as we ride up in the elevator. There's not a peep from him as I unlock the door to the penthouse and wave him inside.

As soon as the door closes behind us, he says, "What are your thoughts about sex between people who don't like each other?"

I blink a few times, then calmly take off my satchel and leave it by the door. "You mean casual sex? Between people who aren't in a relationship? There's nothing wrong with that. As long as both—"

He interrupts, looking me boldly in the eye. "No, I mean people who don't *like* each other. Maybe there's attraction, but they don't generally get along."

The breath freezes in my chest. I can't think of any other reason why my lungs are suddenly not working.

He can't mean…? But what else could he mean? Could this be…?

"The same principle applies," I say faintly, then pull myself together. "As long as both parties are consenting adults—fully informed consenting adults—nothing is 'wrong' when it comes to sex." I hesitate for a second. "Just be sure about what you want. Regrets are inevitable in life, but they're worse when you have them because you didn't think things through." I hate myself for giving him that out, but I seriously don't want him to have sex with me and then never be able to look me in the eye again. I like Noah. He's an incredible man. He may think we don't get along, but the truth is, we do. We're just combustible together.

We stand there staring at each other, until finally he says, "Do I need to throw myself at you?"

I open my mouth to say no, then reconsider. "Actually, just this first time… yes."

He looks surprised, then closes the space between us, grabs my head, and yanks it forward to plaster his mouth against mine.

That's all the instigation I need.

I drag him right up against my body, then turn and shove him against the door, pinning him in place so I can feel every inch of him pressed to me while freeing my hands to get under his clothes. It doesn't quite work that way, though, because Noah isn't content to be pinned. He shoves me back, biting my lower lip, then lets me go and rips his shirt open.

Thank goodness. That thing was garbage. Now I can offer to replace it and get him something decent.

"You better not think of doing that to *my* clothes," I warn, pulling my mouth away from his long enough to undo my top two buttons and haul my shirt over my head.

"I will if I want to. I'll rip your clothes to shreds and fuck you on them."

I'm not sure if the shudder that wracks me is from desire or horror. "Try it, and you'll end up begging me for mercy." We both strip off our pants, and then I look up to find Noah's hungry gaze on my chest.

Smiling wickedly, I rub a hand across my torso. I'm not stupid; I know he's been ogling me for weeks. I never used to go shirtless every moment I was home, but teasing him has given me quite the thrill.

His gaze then drops lower, and I have the satisfaction of seeing his eyes bug out.

"What the fuck is going on with your dick?" he exclaims, but not in the awed wow-what-a-beast way I expected. In fact, he seems kind of horrified.

I look down. It all looks norma—

Oh. Right. He's human.

"You mean these?" I brush a finger over my cock

quills. They stir and stiffen in response, but subside when there's no further friction.

"What are they? Are they sharp?" He leans over in fascination.

"No, they're not sharp. You can touch them if you want." *Please touch me.* "They stimulate ovulation in female vampires, but they feel really good against any sensitive tissue." Which I know from extensive experience.

He doesn't touch, though I get the feeling he wants to. "So all vampires have them?" he asks, straightening and dragging his gaze upward again.

"All vampires with a penis." I get a few fleeting seconds to admire his lithe, naked body and hard, leaking cock before he reaches out and pinches my left nipple, then closes the distance between us and bends to suck on it, his hand sliding down to close around my dick, giving an extra little rub over the quills.

And then he bites, and I groan.

"We should—" He tightens his grip on my cock, and I suck in air. "Lube! Going to need it," I choke out. How the fuck did he manage to turn the tables on me this fast?

He pulls off my nipple with a wet pop and straightens, his face smug as he gives me a little shove toward the hallway. "Let's go. We need you nice and slick."

Okay, so he's topping this time. I can live with that.

I lead the way, moving fast—there's no point pretending I'm not eager. I don't hesitate as I pass Noah's bedroom, heading to mine instead. I'm sure he's got lube in there, but he's never been in my room before, and that gives me the home ground advantage—plus, we'll be using my lube. Sexual power games are complicated.

I don't give him time to look around, going straight to the nightstand to grab the bottle of lube there and then stretching out on my back on the bed, slicking up my fingers and making a show of prepping myself. He's on me immediately, taking the bottle and squeezing more lube onto his cock. Then he freezes.

"We don't need a condom, do we?"

I shake my head. "We don't get STIs. We can use one if you're worried about mess—if you've got any—but I can't give you anything, and I can't catch anything from you either."

"A little mess never hurt anyone," he murmurs, his gaze intent on where my fingers disappear into my ass. "Remember that when I come all over you."

I laugh, a low, dirty sound. "Same. I'm going to rub my cum into your skin and make you wear it to work. Everyone will be able to smell you on me, and they'll know your hate can't stand up to how much you want me."

His breath hitches, and his cock seems to swell even harder.

"Are you done, or do you think you're a virgin about to take a Coke can?"

Who knew trading insults during sex could be so fun? I pull my fingers free and quirk a brow at him. "Have at it. Let me know if you need instructions. I'll try not to fall asleep."

The sound he makes is half growl, half chuckle, and as he moves between my legs, he bends forward to bite my pec. He seems to have quite a thing for biting, and

I'd be lying if I said I didn't want to introduce him to age-old vampire sexual habits.

The head of his cock probes against my hole, catching on the rim in a way that makes me twitch all over, and then he's pushing forward, not rough but steady and unrelenting, not giving me time to adjust.

I love it.

He immediately sets up a punishing rhythm, smooth, fast thrusts that stimulate every nerve ending and don't allow me to catch my breath. But I've forgotten more about sex than he can ever learn in his lifetime, and I brace my feet and begin Kegel exercises.

His shout is music to my ears.

In response, he shifts his grip on my hips to one hand and closes the other around my cock, applying firm pressure at the base. I'm not going to be able to come with him holding me like that... is he going to edge me?

He won't last long enough. Not with the tricks I have up my sleeve.

I'm just about to add a special twist to my exercises when he smiles and says, "You're pretty flexible, right?"

In the next instant, he's lifting my left leg off the bed and propping it over his shoulder, changing the angle of my body, and then he adjusts his position slightly and starts thrusting again, his hand still tight around my dick, and my brain explodes. The sound that comes from me is something between a pig's squeal and a hoarse shout.

"Fuck me, how can you feel this good? It's fucking witchcraft," he gasps, sweat rolling down his face. "Are... you... ready... to come?"

"Go harder," I groan, and he leans forward, forcing my leg closer to my torso and changing the angle again.

We both shout, and then he lets go of my cock and thrusts twice more as cum spurts from me all over his stomach and chest before collapsing against me.

"That was fucking incredible," Noah pants. "We're going to do this *all the time*. And not just because your room is even better than mine."

A laugh bursts out of me as I struggle to reengage my brain. "Sure. Yes. Whatever you want. Just as long as you do that again."

He heaves himself off me, pulls out carefully, and rolls onto his side to look at me. "You really piss me off sometimes."

Whoa. That's not what I expected. "You don't have to do it if you really don't want to." I didn't quite manage to hide the injured edge to my voice. "I thought you enjoyed it—you certainly seemed to like my reaction."

He shakes his head, chuckling. "No. I mean, yes, I did enjoy it, and I want to make you make that noise again, but I wasn't talking about that."

Whew. Because I *definitely* want him to do it again. That was fucking hot. "What are you talking about— Oh. You mean in general."

"Yeah. You just… really rub me the wrong way. A lot."

Why does this feel like less of a victory all of a sudden?

"And you do it to everyone. I didn't get why they were all okay with it. Alistair and Elinor are weird anyway, so that kind of makes sense, but why doesn't Gideon ever try to murder you? And David… you're at him all the time, and he just puts up with it. Sure, he's a super calm and patient guy, but nobody's that Zen. The Dalai Lama would smack you in the face if you were even half as annoying to him."

"Uh... thanks?" I know he implied he didn't like me before, but I didn't realize our sex would include a free character assassination. I suddenly really want to put my pants on.

He sits up and jabs a finger at me. "There! That. I knew it. It's deliberate, isn't it? You're not naturally an asshole; you do it on purpose."

I pull up the covers in lieu of putting on pants, taking the opportunity to wipe up some of the mess before it starts to go crusty. "No," I say gently. "If you think it's a persona I cultivate, that's not true. This is me. The difference is, I no longer restrain myself. When I was young, I was a lot more careful about what I said. Now, I don't bother. There are limits, and I would never deliberately hurt anyone, but the people closest to me... David, for example. I do pick on him for being so stable and steady. But David was raised in a very... chaotic environment." I can't think of a better way to describe David's fucked-up family without betraying confidences. "He prides himself on being the way he is—everybody's port in a storm. It's something he's achieved despite early influences. Every time I tell him he's so reliable that it's boring, it's a reminder that there's nobody I'd rather have in my corner." I wince, because somehow it came out sounding all noble, and the truth is that I just don't care what people think of me anymore. "I'm not a monster," I try to explain. "If David was really bothered by what I say, I'd stop. I do know how to behave in public."

For a second, he studies me. "So if I'd gotten upset or offended—"

"I would have stopped," I interrupt. "But admit it, you enjoy sniping back at me."

His chuckle seems to take him by surprise, and he flops back down in the bed and stares at the ceiling. "Yeah. I guess. It's kind of freeing to be able to say whatever, but I couldn't do that with everyone."

"Neither could I. But I've known my teammates for a long time—except Sam, but he fit right in from the beginning."

He rolls his head to the side so he's looking up at me. "You haven't known me for a long time," he points out. "But you were quick to start with the verbal torture."

I hesitate, not sure how he'll take the truth, and his eyes widen. "Jesus Christ, don't tell me it was some kind of bullshit to make me hate you."

"Not exactly. Also, you really need to stop saying Jesus Christ like that. It means nothing."

"But it bugs you," he points out, "and for that reason alone, I'll happily keep doing it."

I let my fangs descend and hiss at him playfully, and instantly his eyes widen and his heartbeat picks up, but rather than fear, the scent of arousal hits my nose.

Oh ho. Now, this could be fun. I reach for him, but he squirms away, rising to a sitting position and pointing at me.

"Hold that thought for a second. I want to finish this conversation before you distract me."

"It's not good that you can think so clearly when I want you like this." My cock, which hardened again at the mere thought of more sex and began throbbing at the possibility of blood sex, is now extremely unhappy about having to wait. To make things worse, my brain is lacking the blood it needs to operate intelligently, since all the blood in my body has rushed to my painfully stiff dick.

Here's the thing about having a relatively low fertility rate: nature compensates by making sure more sex is possible. The more sex you have, the more chances of conceiving. As a result, the refractory period for community species is a lot shorter than for humans.

Which means I'm raring to go. And Noah's twenty, so I doubt it will take him long to get hard again.

He pats me on the arm, a smug little smirk on his face that makes me want to kiss him. "As old as you are, you should know how to be patient. Now… that first snide comment you made to me, was that some kind of deliberate attempt to make me dislike you?"

I've been tortured before, long ago when ignorant villagers hunted vampires and thought they could convince me to give up others. They failed, and I spent several centuries congratulating myself on my resistance to torture. Little did I know, all it would have taken was the promise of sex with Noah to convince me to give in.

"No. You were… unsettled and vulnerable"—fucking terrified—"that day, and I thought it might distract you from being scared for long enough to debrief you. Even if you got upset, at least you'd be thinking of something other than Tish and the fact he escaped. But you got pissed off instead, which was even better." I shrug, a little uncomfortable. My intention that day was pretty selfish—we were focused on getting as much information out of Noah about Tish and the CCA as we could so we could track down any remaining enclaves. We probably didn't think enough about the psychological impact on him of having to relive so much of his captivity right after his rescue.

Sometimes the greater good has shitty side effects.

"Oh," he says, sounding relieved. "That's fine. I thought—" He cuts himself off sharply.

Curiosity rears its head. "What did you think?"

He's shaking his head before I even finish asking the question. "Nothing important. Now, about the fang thing—"

Nope. As much as I want to talk about—and do—the "fang thing" with him, there's not a single fiber of my being that will tolerate an unanswered question. Even my cock is prepared to wait—as long as we eventually get to fun stuff.

"Eight centuries of life has taught me patience," I mock, turning his earlier statement back on him. "Tell me what you thought. Or," I add when he still hesitates, his jaw setting mulishly, "I will devote all my free time from now until eternity to finding out."

He shakes his head. "How can you be as old as you are and still act like a little kid?"

Tilting my head, I say, "You seem really hung up on my age today. Daddy kink, maybe?"

His jaw drops.

"Okay, maybe not. Come on. Share. Or we can role-play instead. I'll be the Daddy, and you can—"

"Whoa." He holds up his hands. "Not sure I'm ready for that." The slightly intrigued gleam in his eyes tells me it might be a conversation for the future, though, and I make a mental note to refresh myself on the whole Daddy/boy thing. It's been a long time since I was last in that kind of relationship, and while it's not a lifestyle choice for me, for bedroom play it's a lot of fun. "I surrender."

I smile innocently at him. From the way his eyes narrow, he takes it as a personal challenge, and for a second I think he's not going to tell me after all. Then he heaves a sigh.

"I thought you were hot," he admits, as reluctantly as if it was a major crime. "It was kind of weird, after being in hiding for so long, suddenly being able to actually talk to people, and then bam, you were there and I was feeling all… lusty."

I bite my lip hard to keep from laughing—c'mon, *lusty*—because he's sharing something personal and I don't want to shit on that. But then he snickers.

"Fuck, that's a dumb word. Horny, then. Anyway, you're right, I was freaked about Tish and the others that day and still getting used to the idea that I was free, and I was also trying really hard not to let you see that I wanted to ride you like a cowboy. So when you went from being distantly polite and professional to making snarky comments, I thought maybe I wasn't as good at hiding it as I thought."

I'm warm all over, and it has nothing to do with the ambient room temperature and everything to do with my emotions. "Okay." I stop and clear my throat. "Even if I had guessed that you wanted to r-ride me like a cowboy"—which we are definitely doing at some point —"I wouldn't have started sniping at you. I would have left and gotten someone else to replace me. And after a decent amount of time, when you were settled into your new home and job and more stable, I would have come to test the waters and see if anything more was still a possibility."

A tiny smile plays over his lips. "Really? You wanted me too?"

"Even when you wanted to strangle me." I laugh. "I wanted you more when you broke my nose, and not because I'm a masochist. Strong, independent people are my turn-on."

His grin is wicked. "I'll be sure to break your nose again in the future, then. Now"—his smile turns seductive—"tell me, do vampires ever bite during sex? Or are fangs just for feeding?"

And whoosh, all the blood drains from my head, my dick once again hard as an iron spike.

"It's called blood sex," I tell him, pushing the covers away and shifting to dot kisses along his neck, pausing to lick where his pulse is strongest. "A bite right at the moment you come transmits the pleasure between both of us, magnifying and sharing the orgasm." I bite down gently. My fangs are retracted, so it's nothing more than blunt pressure against his skin, but he moans wildly. "That usually leads to the vampire coming as well, just a few seconds after."

He's panting as I raise my head, his eyes wide. "Fuck, yes. Do you…" He swallows hard, but it seems to be more from arousal than fear. "Do you take a lot of blood? Like, would I need a cookie and juice after?"

The laugh that bursts from me is involuntary and does nothing to crack the sexual tension around us. "No. How much blood is taken depends entirely on the couple. Sometimes vampires in committed relationships only feed from their partners, usually during sex. It's the bite and accompanying use of charisma in tandem with orgasm that brings the pleasure—theoretically, no blood need be taken at all." I lean down to kiss his puffy pink lips, but he leans back.

"But you'd want to?"

Is this a trick question? What's the best way to answer that will lead to sex? Because while I'd love to have a taste of him, it's not a deal breaker—the sex was good enough without needing to add blood to the equation. I can't even remember the last time I had blood sex.

Oh, wait, yes I can. Because it's fucking *hot*.

"I'd only want to if you wanted to," I prevaricate. "If it's not going to be fun for you, it won't be fun for me."

He hesitates, teeth sinking into that swollen red bottom lip. Jealousy flashes through me—*I* want to be the one biting his lip.

"Would it hurt?"

I shake my head instantly. "No. That's the point of charisma, remember? No pain, and we'd share what each other was feeling, so if you hated it, I'd know to stop even if you didn't say anything."

His gaze wanders over my face. "Show me your fangs."

A shiver runs down my spine as I obediently let them descend. He sucks in a breath.

"Do you have to bite the neck?"

I hiss involuntarily, lust slamming into me with the images that question inspires. His eyes widen, and a gasp escapes those puffy lips.

"It—" I clear my throat. My voice has gone all growly. "No. But if we're having sex, access to other areas might be limited."

He sidles closer and climbs into my lap, straddling

me but keeping careful distance from my dick. "Where else could you bite?" He leans in, staring at my mouth—my fangs?

"Uh…"

He leans back. *Don't do that!*

"Anywhere," I manage. "As long as there's a vein. Places with a strong pulse beat are better, but not necessary." Not for a vampire my age, anyway.

"Just one more question." He's smirking now, the little shit. He knows he's pretty much got me over a barrel.

"Ask," I rasp.

"Can I lick your fangs?"

I surge up, knocking him to his back on the mattress, ignoring his indignant shout as I loom over him.

"Baby, you can lick anything you want."

# CHAPTER TEN

## Noah

ANDREW'S WORDS go straight to my cock. Lick anything I want? I want to lick him all over.

But I'm starting with those fangs.

I lean up and meet his hot mouth. His teeth are ordinary, no fangs to be found, but I'm only disappointed for a second. Last time, I seized control, but now he's in charge, and I'm stunned to realize how much I like the dominating way he takes my mouth.

Pulling back, he looks down at me, and his smile is a dark, wicked thing. "On your hands and knees."

I don't move. "Let me see your fangs," I demand, and he laughs.

"Don't think you're giving the orders here, kitten," he chides, and outrage blooms in me.

"What did you just—"

In an instant, I find myself flipped onto my hands and knees, and I swallow hard, my cock throbbing in time with my racing heartbeat. His strength is a turn-on. Noted.

I look back over my shoulder at where he's flipping

open the cap on the bottle of lube. "I want to see your fangs." I try not to whine, but it's not a complete success.

"Patience," he says, not even looking at me. Well, not at my face, anyway. I shift my weight experimentally, and sure enough, the resulting movement of my ass has *all* his attention. Hmm.

I move again, this time incorporating a little wiggle, and the bastard smacks my ass, a sharp slap that doesn't hurt but makes me tingle all over.

"You——"

He cuts me off this time by grabbing my hip with one hand and tracing a lube-wet finger along my rim. I suck in a huge breath as he sets about stretching me, taking his time and making sure to hit all my most sensitive spots, until I'm squirming in his grip.

Finally, he slides his arm around my waist and pulls me upright, his chest pressed against my back and his cock rubbing against my ass, almost where I want it. And can we just take a second to talk about that cock? I can feel those spiny things getting stiffer the more he rubs, and the added friction is amazing.

"Turn," he whispers, and I twist my torso halfway, raising my eyes to his face.

He's smirking, that smug expression I've always hated so much on his face, but I realize now how badly I've been fooling myself. I never wanted to smack it off... I wanted to fuck it off, to make him want me so much and come so hard that his face is wiped clean of anything except his need for me.

As I grapple with that revelation, his fangs descend, and thoughts of anything else flee my mind. I've seen them before, of course, but never when he was about to bite me.

A shudder rolls through me, and he raises an eyebrow. "Okay?"

"Fuck, yes." I twist a little more so I can reach to kiss him. The scrape of his fangs against my lip and in my mouth is surreal, sexy, and then, as one of them nicks my tongue and I taste my own blood, totally fucking hot in a way I never thought I'd go for. In this moment, I don't hate blood at all.

When we break apart, we're both panting, and there's a wild glitter in Andrew's eyes. "Turn," he orders again, and I do, eyeing the headboard and wondering if it's close enough for me to brace myself against. I like feeling every inch of Andrew against me.

Turns out, I don't need to worry. His preternatural strength comes into play again as he pushes inside me and holds me in position with an arm that feels like a steel band. I grab it with both hands, and the play of muscle under my fingers just adds to the sensory input as he fucks me onto his dick... which is an intense experience. I can feel the friction of his spines against my inner walls—not sharp, not rough, but gently abrasive, maybe like a toothbrush? But a million times better. My channel twitches and convulses in response, eagerly seeking more.

I don't think this position would be possible for anyone with ordinary strength, and that makes me pity my fellow humans. Now that I've been with a vampire, it would take a lot to make me go back to human-on-human sex.

Correction: now that I've been with *this* vampire. Because Andrew has just taken my cock in hand and is stroking me in rhythm with his thrusts. I'm babbling, something about how good it feels and harder, more, and he's licking the side of my neck, muttering about how much he wants to taste me and how incredible it will feel. The pressure inside me is building, my muscles tightening, until he commands, "Now," and I come hard.

There's pressure on my neck and then the most exhilarating euphoria in my mind, an echo of my pleasure bouncing back at me again and again, drawing out my orgasm until I think I'll die from it. I *feel* Andrew come as he draws my blood from my veins, and his pleasure joins mine, twining together and flooding both of us until we topple sideways across the mattress, our overstimulated muscles too tired to hold us up.

I could get addicted to blood sex.

---

I WAKE up feeling pleasantly sore and only a little horny. It's a big difference from every other morning since I moved in here—they all began with a steel-hard cock and an awareness of waking up alone again.

This way is much better.

Especially because Andrew is cuddled up against my back and his morning wood is trying to say hello. If you'd asked me in the past, I would have said I hated cuddling and that overnight guests either needed to stick to their side of the bed or leave—not that I had any experience with overnight guests. More like behind the school gym and ten minutes in the bathroom at a house party. Anyway, turns out I would have been epically wrong, which is just as well, because Andrew is a champion snuggler. Like, the guy's a heat-radiating octopus. I had to get up to take a piss in the middle of the night, and he woke up and hissed at me for trying to get out of bed, then wrapped himself around me like he was a tortilla and I was the meat filling when I got back.

That should annoy me, right? Maybe it will come summertime when I'm dying from heat… although, the air con in this place is awesome, so maybe not. For now, it's nice to know he notices when I disappear. You know, in case I get kidnapped in the middle of the night. At least he'd wake up and be able to chase my abductors.

Wow, that got dark all of a sudden. I guess I'm still a little worried about Tish finding out about me being alive, even if I do have a vampire bodyguard and the ability to set any attacker on fire.

In case you're wondering, I can do other things too. But the fire thing is by far the most painful and destructive, and if someone's trying to kidnap me so they can perform genetic experiments, I kind of want them to suffer. Does that make me a bad person?

Meh.

I never did get around to doing any training last night, so I should probably flex my mental muscles now. I open my mind to the magic, and it's instantly there, a reassuring presence. Even if someone does manage to lock me up again, I won't be alone. That's a huge comfort.

But what to do now… huh, wouldn't it be cool if I could use the magic to make and deliver breakfast in bed? Too bad that's not possible.

Is it?

I wriggle around until I'm lying on my back, ignoring Andrew's sleepy mutter of protest, and stare at the ceiling. Theoretically, it might be doable. I can manipulate and move objects telekinetically, although my "fine motor skills" still need work. But yeah, the concept of making breakfast using magic is sound, even if it might get messy until I'm able to practice more. The problem arises from the fact that I'm not in the kitchen and can't see what I'm doing. It's not like juggling lightballs or fireballs, which were created by me and are tied to me. Inanimate objects have no energetic resonance for me to sense. If I can't see them, I can't move them.

Unless…

I purse my lips and think about it some more as Andrew throws an arm over my stomach and cuddles closer. The magic is an energy that surrounds everything, right? And it has an awareness of things—we established that when we proved it responds to wishes like "protect me." So maybe it is possible for me to use it to manipulate an item I can't see or feel?

No time like the present to test that theory.

Focusing on the ceiling, I think about the remote control for the living room TV. It's on the coffee table, near the left corner closest to the couch, pointing toward the TV in a perfectly straight line. I know this because that's how it always is once the TV is turned off. Andrew has this annoying anal habit of lining up the remote in the exact same place and position. Once I noticed it was always in that spot no matter where I left it, I tried moving it around—one night, I even got up after he'd been in bed for an hour to do it. The next morning, it was back in its place and Andrew was giving me the evil eye.

Heh. I should totally do that again.

So it's one item that I can definitely envision without having to guess. When I have a firm image of it in my mind, I reach out to the magic and show it the visual. Then I imagine the remote rising off the coffee table and floating across the living room.

The magic reacts. I can't tell if it's actually working or not, but *something* is happening, because I'm feeling strain. Sweat breaks out on my forehead as I visualize the remote coming down the hallway. Thank fuck we were too busy getting to the bed to close the bedroom door, because I don't think I could do both at the moment.

I raise my head and glance toward the doorway. This is the moment of truth. If it worked, I should see the remote float into view any second now. And if it didn't, I'm going to have to get up and see what's happening in the other room, because this kind of effort means I've done *something*.

A moment later, a black rectangular object drifts through the doorway and toward the bed.

"Yes!" I grab it out of the air as Andrew bolts upright, fangs out and hissing.

"What? Where?" He scans for danger, only relaxing when he's assured himself that we're alone. "What time is it?" He lies back down, scowling at me, then blinks. "Is that the remote?"

I wave it excitedly. "Yep. I just brought it in here telekinetically!"

That wakes him up, and he sits up again. "Really? Without having to see it?"

"That's right. Because I am *awesome*."

He snorts. "Sure, baby, whatever you say. I wish you hadn't tried something new while I was asleep, though. How are you feeling?"

A rush of emotion I don't want to identify floods

through me. Ignoring my *feelings* and putting on my responsible hat, I think about it before answering. "Fine. It took a little more effort than I expected while I was doing it, but I'm good now."

He studies me carefully, eyes flitting over my face and coming to rest at the base of my throat—where my pulse point is. He's listening for my heart rate, I can tell, and I roll my eyes and hold out my wrist. "Just do it the normal way."

Grinning, he grabs my wrist, fingers pressing to the right spot while he counts off. "All good," he says finally, lifting my wrist to his mouth to lick it—and is that a graze of fang? I shudder in helpless arousal, my heartbeat speeding up. "Whoops, maybe I'm wrong. It seems like you might have overexerted yourself," he teases, and I yank away, making sure to smack his face as I do.

"Dick." To my horror, the word sounds almost affectionate.

Who am I kidding? That rush of emotion before? That was affection. Andrew might piss me off sometimes—okay, a lot of the time, even if it's not as much as before—but it seems I've got some fond feelings for him after all.

Not sure what to do with that.

And I'm kind of disappointed that I'm not going to experience hate sex after all.

"What are you thinking about?" There's a half-fascinated, half-horrified look on his face. "You look like you're about to lay an egg or something."

I grab the remote from where it's fallen to my lap and throw it at his head. He's sitting too close for any sort of momentum to build, but it still hits him, which is satisfying.

"Vicious human," he scolds, rubbing his forehead. "Now I won't rest until you tell me what you were thinking."

"Fine," I concede, because I have more important things to do today—like testing this new skill. "I was thinking that it's a shame we didn't really get to hate fuck." It's part of the truth, at least.

He pulls a slight face and nods. I'm glad he doesn't try to convince me that it *was* hate fucking or tease me about not actually hating him. "We can always pretend," he suggests. "I'll be the conquering warlord, and you can be the village's virgin sacrifice, sent to appease me even though you'd rather stick a knife in my guts."

What.

Just…

"Please don't tell me that's a scenario you've ever lived out in reality." Because let's face it, he lived during a time when conquering warlords and virgin offerings were aplenty.

He sighs. "No." It almost sounds regretful. "It's a great role play fantasy when everyone has a safe word, but the real-life version is just creepy. But," he adds, brightening a little, "a scenario I did live out in reality was when the murdering rapist warlord was forced to bend knee to the heroic vampire liberator. Lots of hate there, but no sex. The role play version would probably benefit from sex."

I can't deny that I'm interested. I want to be the liberator, though.

"Let's put that on the list of things to talk about later," I suggest somewhat regretfully. "It would be better with costumes anyway. And maybe swords. Hey, do you know how to use a sword?" That's something I wouldn't mind having him teach me, purely so I can say I know how. I doubt it's used as a form of self-defense much these days.

He shrugs, and the diffuse light peeking around the edges of the curtains ripples over the sleek muscle of his torso. A man in his ninth century should not look that good naked. Isn't there a rule or something?

"It's been a while, but I know several styles of swordsmanship with several different types of swords. If you want to learn, I can look into finding us a practice space and some equipment."

And there go the feelings again. This could get old fast.

"Sure, that could be fun." I try to sound casual, but he laughs, so… "Anyway"—time to change the subject —"I want to try this blind telekinesis again. What's an object in the other room?"

He purses his lips in thought, and I push away the urge to lean over and kiss his puckered mouth. "It's got to be small and portable, right? Not too heavy, either."

Blinking and looking away from his lips, I shrug. "Portable, definitely. Nothing that would need to be unplugged, either. Not sure about weight. I've been doing okay with moving heavier items over short distances like this, but I guess it might be harder not being able to see it? The remote was. It should probably also be something that's in a set location I can visualize."

"What about the key bowl? That only ever gets moved for cleaning, and it's not heavy. Bonus points if the keys are still in it when it gets here." His trademark smug smirk is just as annoying as always, seeming to challenge me.

"No problem," I boast recklessly. Truthfully, based on the remote, it should be easy. The distance is approximately the same. The weight of the keys might make it a bit heavier, but not too much so. And he's right that we never move it. I can easily see it in my mind's eye.

I plump up a couple of pillows and prop them against the headboard, then wiggle into position and lean back. I'd be more confident if I was lying down and able to focus every bit of concentration on what I was doing, but I'm in the mood to show off and rub this in Andrew's face—which is stupid, because I have no doubt that he wants me to succeed almost as much as I do. Maybe he wants me to flub the first try just so he has something to tease me about, but ultimately, I know he wants me to do it. That doesn't stop me from wanting to flaunt my power a little. And the pillows will support me enough to get it done.

Taking a deep breath, I focus my gaze on the wall above the doorway and let the magic slither over me as I build an image of the key bowl. It's metal—pewter, I think—hammered thin and in a kind of freeform shape. About three inches high and four in diameter, it sits on the corner of the console table closest to the front door.

I *push* the magic toward it, and a second later feel the strain of effort. *Okay. Good.* Next, I imagine the bowl rising—slowly, because it's easier to manipulate a mental image that way—and moving toward the hallway.

There's a crash from the living room, and it's all I can do to hold on to my visual of the bowl.

"What was that?" The bed shifts as Andrew moves, but I don't dare look at him.

"Uh…" It can't be the bowl, because I can still feel the effort of holding it. What— Oh. "I may have forgotten about that freaky metal statue on the console and tried to bring the bowl in a straight line."

"*What?*" His voice hits a pitch I've never heard from him before. "That 'freaky statue' is a priceless artifact!"

My concentration is seriously faltering. I'm not even moving the bowl anymore, just trying to hold it stable while Andrew yammers on about playing dice in some barracks somewhere to win that statue—which is ugly, in case you care. I need him to shut up so I can get the bowl moving again, but he's really hit a rhythm with his story now, and this bowl is starting to feel really heavy, and I just want it here *right now*—

I have just enough time to feel the sudden weight in my lap before the world spins in a dizzying rush and I slide sideways to the sound of Andrew's shout.

---

THIS TIME WHEN I WAKE, the ache isn't pleasant. I hurt all over, the way I imagine being hit by a truck would feel. And my head is throbbing so much, it takes me a few moments to hear the hushed voices. But when I do, I decide they're too loud, so I moan to get their attention.

Talking is definitely too hard. I'd have to move my lips and tongue, maybe take a slightly deeper breath. That's just not happening.

The moan must have been enough, though, because the conversation breaks off and the bed moves.

"Noah?" That's Andrew, and he sounds worried. "Noah, are you awake? Can you hear me?"

I moan again. Why does he have to be so loud? Can't he tell my brain hurts?

"Noah?" This voice is quieter, calmer—David. I must have been out for a while if he's had time to get here. "If you can hear me, moan again, please."

Will it make them go away? I manage another moan.

"Great. Can you talk? Andrew, back off a bit and give him space."

The sound that comes from me this time is closer to a sob than a moan. Just the thought of talking makes me hurt.

"Okay, so I'm guessing you're in a bit of pain." *No shit, Sherlock.* "Can you feel the magic? Use it to ease the pain a bit? Not too much," he adds quickly. "Just enough so you can talk to us."

Huh, that's not a bad idea. The whole burns thing proved that the magic is better for pain relief than ibuprofen will ever be.

Gingerly, I reach out to the magic. It responds as quickly as always, but its touch seems tentative this time. I visualize my need—*less pain*—and within seconds, the sharp ache eases and the pounding in my head stops. It's just a little niggle of a headache now.

Mindful of David's warning, I don't ask for more. He and I had a long chat about this when we first realized the magic was able to act as a painkiller. Our consensus was that I would be manipulating the magic at a low level, so it would be slowly wearing me out. Like a dripping tap. A couple of drops is nothing, but when it's dripping twenty-four seven, every day of the year, it adds up to a lot of wasted water and huge-ass water bill. Since I'm paying said bill with my own energy reserves, I don't want to be careless. Plus, like any painkiller, the magic is just masking the symptoms. I don't want to ignore the message my body is sending me, which seems to be that I fucked up but good.

Slowly, I ease my eyes open. The room is bright, and I squint for a second. Andrew must have opened the curtains.

"You're awake," he gasps with a certain amount of relief, collapsing onto the bed beside me. I wince as I'm jostled slightly.

"Awake," I croak. "What happened?"

"In a minute," David says. He holds a penlight—did he bring that with him? Man, he's a dork—in front of my eyes, temporarily blinding me. "Pupils are reactive," he affirms with satisfaction.

"You couldn't tell that from the way I was squinting when I opened my eyes?" I gripe. "Help me sit up."

"Wait," Andrew insists, picking up my arm with nowhere near the care and tenderness my poor abused muscles need and pressing his fingers to my pulse... again.

"What's the date, Noah?" David asks in what I think is supposed to be a casual tone but misses the mark. But he's trying to make sure I'm okay, and I don't think he'll let me sit up if I don't answer, so I tell him. Then he makes me tell him some other stupid stuff and recite the alphabet. Meanwhile, Andrew is taking about thirty times longer than he really needs to check my pulse, and I am *this close* to dealing with magical burnout or whatever and walloping them both with a couple of metaphysical bats.

"Okay," David concedes finally. "You can sit up— but slowly. Let us help you." Together, they ease me to a sitting position, propping me against the pillows. Gotta admit, I'm grateful for the support. Even with most of the pain dulled, I feel tender and completely wiped out. Andrew holds a glass of water up to my mouth, and I sip gratefully.

"So what happened?" I ask again as the magic curls around me.

Andrew and David exchange a glance. "We're not entirely sure," David admits. "What do you remember?"

I pick through my memories. "I was trying to bring the key bowl here without seeing it," I recall. "But then I accidentally knocked over Andrew's ugly statue and he wouldn't stop whining about it—"

"It is *not* ugly!"

"The Persian piece you keep by the front door?" David asks. "I told you that should be in a cabinet." He turns back to me. "It's not my favorite, either."

"See?" I sneer at Andrew. "David thinks it's ugly too."

"You'd better hope an expert agrees that it's not damaged," Andrew warns, "or you're going to be paying penance for a very long time."

I open my mouth to tell him exactly what I think of that, but David, eternally the peacemaker, intervenes.

"We're getting off topic. What else do you remember, Noah?"

I think about it. "That's pretty much it. Andrew was distracting me, and I was finding it tough to stay focused on the bowl. And then I passed out."

They exchange glances again.

"What?"

David gestures to the nightstand, and I turn my head carefully to see the key bowl sitting there—with the keys still in it. I frown.

"Did you bring it in here? Because I'm sure it was still in the living room when I passed out."

"Actually," Andrew says gently, taking my hand, "it was in here when you passed out. But it didn't come in through the door."

I must look as confused as I feel, because David explains, "Andrew thinks you teleported it."

"*What?*" I surge upright and instantly regret it. "Ow, ow ow ow."

Andrew eases me back against the pillows, and David mutters something about painkillers and disappears into the en suite bathroom. He comes back a minute later with ibuprofen.

Once I've swallowed a couple and am settled into the least painful position, I demand, "Teleported?"

David shrugs. "I wasn't here," he reminds me.

"Yes, teleported," Andrew insists. "It wasn't here, then suddenly it's in your lap and you're flopping over like a dead fish."

A dead fish. Wow. I always wished the man I just had a night of marathon sex with would compare me to a dead fish.

Although right now, my dick feels like a dead fish. I don't think it ever wants to have sex again, and that makes part of me sad. The rest of me just hurts and thinks sex would only be okay if I didn't have to move.

"Is teleportation even possible for non-demons?" I'm fully expecting the answer to be no. There has to be some other explanation, right? Maybe I just moved the bowl super fast, faster than the eye could see, and the effort drained me.

David hesitates.

"Oh my *god*!"

"She doesn't care," Andrew says absently, staring at David. "Wait, it's possible?"

"Well… it's never been proven to be impossible. I've never heard of anyone doing it, though, and it's the kind of thing that would get around."

By "anyone," he means any sorcerers. They'd be the ones most likely to achieve something like this. The other species just don't have those kinds of abilities—except demons, who can teleport already, but only themselves and things they're touching.

A human teleporting an object from another room? I would have noticed that in my research. And David's right. If any sorcerer managed it, they'd be shouting about it from the rooftops.

"What does this mean?" Fuck, this is wild. I want to try again, but honestly, I don't think I could even manifest a lightball right now. And even if I could, my protesting body wouldn't allow me to.

"I don't know. More research for both of us, definitely." David sounds almost dispirited. I can guess why.

"I could try doing it again—not today," I tack on quickly as every atom of my being cries out in protest. "But when I'm feeling better. And if it's more controlled this time, it might not affect me the same way. Plus, my blood sugar would have been low this morning—we didn't even have dinner last night. Maybe next time it won't be like this at all."

David looks about as doubtful as I feel, and Andrew's shaking his head adamantly.

"No. It's not worth the risk, Noah. Not until we know more. Stick to the research for now."

I ease myself a little more upright so he knows I'm serious. Ideally, I'd like to jab a finger in his direction for emphasis, but that kind of sharp movement might be pushing my luck. "This is groundbreaking, Andrew. It could change everything."

"Like?" he challenges. "You're the only person we know who's able to do human magic at this level, Noah. It might possibly end up meaning that you won't have to walk back out to the living room when you forget your phone, or, if you're really lucky, that your commute to work gets really short. But given the amount of effort it took to teleport a small bowl thirty feet, I don't think it's likely you'll be doing that anytime soon."

I open my mouth to protest, but he holds up a hand. "Think about it. It's been literally only weeks since you started using magic. You've been progressing by leaps and bounds, but your 'magic muscles' are still developing. You need to take this slow and steady and make sure you have a solid foundation before you take risky leaps. Back me up here, David."

David sighs. "Sorry, Noah. As much as I'd love to explore this new skill, Andrew's right. We'd never let a young sorcerer leap ahead in their studies like that. And I know the demons are very careful about ensuring all sensory abilities are strong before they allow their young to even consider teleporting. It's just so risky."

I hate that they're right.

"Fine," I grumble. "I'll work on building the other skills first."

"Like telekinetically manipulating items you can't see," Andrew reminds me. "That was the thing you were excited about before."

Fuck, yeah! I forgot about that in all the teleportation excitement. That's super freaking awesome!

"But not today," David orders. "Wait until all the

pain is gone. Did you say you didn't eat dinner last night?"

Oops. "Uh…" I shoot a glance at Andrew, who's looking at the ceiling with a little smile playing over his mouth.

"Is this where I'm not supposed to notice that you're naked in Andrew's bed?" David asks, amusement rife in his voice.

"Am I?" I fake amazement. "Wow, that teleportation thing is even more complicated than we thought! It moved me from my room and stole my clothes."

Laughing, he gets up and backs toward the door. "I'll raid the kitchen and find you something to eat, and then call in and let Percy know we're not going in today."

I blink. "We're not? I mean, I know I'm not"—no way in hell am I getting out of this bed until the muscle aches fade—"but why aren't you two?"

"We're keeping an eye on you," Andrew says with heavy-handed patience. "Someone has to make sure there aren't any more side effects."

"And that takes two of you?" I plan to sleep most of the day away. It doesn't take two people to keep an eye on a sleeping man.

"Well, David's the magic expert, and this is my house, so…" Andrew shrugs as though that makes any kind of sense whatsoever, then turns a dark scowl on David. "And speaking of my house—"

"Relax." David rolls his eyes. "I promise to leave your kitchen exactly as I find it. I'll even make breakfast for you too." He disappears into the hallway, leaving me and Andrew alone.

For the first time since I woke up, I take him in properly. Thankfully, he pulled on some of those cotton lounge pants he likes before David got here—at least, I hope it was before David got here. But his chest and feet are bare, and his usually smooth and tidy silver hair is mussed.

I really hate that I'm too sore to properly appreciate how hot he looks.

Also, what happens now? It's the morning after. David knows. I've pretty much admitted that I don't hate him… and if I'm being honest with myself, what we did last night wasn't casual. In fact, if he told me now that it was fun but done, I'd be… upset.

Okay, I'd go after him with a fireball.

Which makes me feel like an idiot, because yesterday I was genuinely unsure if I could fuck him due to the level of not-liking I felt. This sudden turnaround is weird. Am I the kind of person who can't have sex in a bed without it having to mean something? Is that even a thing? Or maybe it's having sex with someone I know more than just to say hello to… fuck knows I never had a conversation with any of the guys I hooked up with in high school.

"How are you feeling?" he asks, reaching out to push my hair off my forehead—my sweat-stiff hair that needed to be washed even before my exertions this morning. Still, it feels nice to be petted like that, and if he's willing to touch it, who am I to protest?

"Not great." I opt for honesty. "Even with the ibuprofen and the magic, the thought of moving around makes me want to cry."

"Just as well you're not going to be moving around, then." He looks me right in the eye. "I'm sorry David found out"—my heart drops right into my stomach. I swear, it's like my chest is suddenly empty—"without us discussing it first."

Oh. *Way to overreact, Noah.*

"I get the feeling you were worried about other things when you called him," I say dryly.

His eyes close for a second. When they open, the remnants of his worry are clear. "I didn't know what the fuck had happened," he admits. "And then you wouldn't wake up, and your heart slowed right down."

"What?" That's… not good.

He nods. "Right after you passed out. At first it was going like crazy, the way it would after a major exertion, but then it slowed way more than it should have. That's when I called David."

The last remnants of regret about not being able to practice teleporting leaves me. Being dead would not be fun. Although, according to what I've learned since my rescue, I'd move on to the spiritual plane for a while and potentially meet the current god before choosing to be reincarnated. Which sounds like it could be cool, but I want to live this life before I move on to another. There's no guarantee my next life would be any better or even as good, or that I'd meet the same people.

Huh. After all my moaning and whining about wanting to move on from CSG and have a "normal" life again, I guess I'm actually comfortable with what I've got.

Which brings me back to the question of Andrew and whether my current possessiveness is an emotional reflex or if I've just been fooling myself all this time.

"It's fine that David knows. If you don't mind, I mean." I hate that I sound so insecure, but then he smiles, and it's not his usual smug smirk. It's warm and private and says a thousand things I might not have believed if he'd said them out loud.

"I want David to know. And the others. I don't think we should hide what's between us." What exactly that is, is left unspoken.

I nod. "Fine by me. Your bedroom is even better than mine, so I have no issue with that." I'm teasing, of course, but it *is* true.

He laughs, then leans in and kisses me, and even though I'm sore all over and know it can't lead to anything, I want that kiss more than I want anything else. It warms me from head to toe, rushes through me with tingling energy.

I was so fucking dumb to think I hated Andrew. This gentle kiss is everything.

David clears his throat from the doorway. "Breakfast."

We pull apart, and if I had to say, I'd guess the soft, slightly unfocused expression on Andrew's face matches mine. Yeah. Definitely not hate.

David bustles over with two trays floating in front of him, grinning widely. I'm not actually sure which surprises me the most, the grin or the blatant display of his power. I rarely see David actually use his ability— where I'm getting into the habit of turning off lights with the magic, he always does stuff like that manually.

Andrew draws away, settling in beside me, and David nudges one of the trays in his direction. On it is that blood-infused instant porridge he likes, two slices of toast with blood-and-berry jam, a glass of his blood-and-grapefruit juice, and a cup of fragrant hot tea.

I glance down at my tray as it comes to rest in my lap. David's outdone himself. Scrambled eggs with peppers and spinach, two slices of thickly buttered toast, a bowl of freshly cut fruit topped with creamy Greek yogurt, orange juice, and coffee.

My stomach growls loudly. "You're my favorite person in the world, David. Where's yours?"

"In the kitchen. I've already eaten half, but I'll grab the rest in a second. Leave the coffee until last, please. Let's wait and see if there's any improvement before we introduce caffeine to your system."

My mouth is already too full of eggs to reply, so I just nod. I haven't been drinking as much coffee lately anyway—using the magic has made me very aware of the flow of energy within my body, and caffeine seems to alter it. I'm not going to cut it out, but I'm definitely more aware of how much I drink and when.

By the time I've polished off my food, I'm shocked by how much better I feel. I'm still using the magic to dull the pain, but the part it's not helping with is almost gone.

But I'm still hungry.

"So," I begin as David stacks plates and trays to minimize how much needs to be carried back to the kitchen, "I think it's an energy thing."

"What's an energy thing?" Andrew asks absently, looking at something on his phone.

"Teleportation and how I'm feeling now. I think that even though the power is coming from the magic, the heavy lifting involved in… I don't know. Directing a teleport? Steering it? Requesting it? We need to come up with some terminology. Anyway, that comes from me. And since it's not something the human body is supposed to be able to do, it used up my energy stores. Which is why I'm weak and sore and starving."

David looks thunderstruck. "Demons do tend to have more body mass than the other species," he muses. "And they eat almost as much as hellhounds. It would make sense for teleportation to need a greater store of muscle and fat to draw from."

"Which means more food and maybe some protein drinks should make you feel better sooner," Andrew adds. "I'll go make second breakfast. David, do you know of any decent protein shakes that are good for humans? I have a couple, but Noah doesn't like blood."

"Leave it with me." He whips out his phone. "I'll run out and grab them as soon as you're back to sit with Noah. You could probably do with stocking up on groceries too, since we don't know how long Noah's going to be eating extra for."

Whoa, whoa, whoa. "*Sit with me?* I don't need someone to sit with me here in this room. As long as you're in the apartment and check every once in a while that I'm still alive, that's good."

David looks doubtful, and Andrew opens his mouth to protest, but I cut him off. "What are you going to do, watch me sleep like some kind of creeper? No, thanks."

"He has a point," David says reluctantly. "He's awake and aware, and all his vitals are normal. He probably doesn't need to be watched every minute."

Andrew sets his jaw, and I decide that distraction is the key here. "I'm really hungry," I say plaintively. "Could we talk about this later?"

That seems to do it, because he shoots me a warning look and then leaves, grumbling about stubborn puny humans. Is it weird that "puny human" is starting to feel like an endearment?

When I pull my gaze away from the way the soft

cotton drapes over his ass and slides with every step, I see David smiling at me.

"What?" I can't keep from sounding defensive. "He's got a really great butt." Oops. I probably should have kept that to myself. The team is close, but I doubt they're that close.

"I like this." He waves a hand to encompass the apartment and the whole situation. "For both of you. You really fit."

I blink. Is he serious? Here I am struggling to come to terms with what I actually feel, and he thinks we *fit*. What does that even mean, anyway?

"Are you high?" I ask politely, and he laughs.

"No, I mean it. It's taken me a while to see it, but you complement each other really well. And you're a lot more alike than you think."

Now I really wonder if he's high. He must see it on my face, because he pats my arm and says, "Seriously. I know he comes across as immature, but that's just because he's had to be mature for so long. Trust me, Noah. I've known Andrew almost all my life. He loves to tease and kid around, but when the situation warrants it, there's nobody more capable in a crisis. The two of you are the same in that regard. Plus, you have so many interests in common."

I can't argue with that, because it's true. Despite me having convinced myself we don't get along, Andrew and I spent a hell of a lot of time talking over the past month.

"It's just weird," I mutter finally. "I've been so sure I didn't like him, and now…"

David huffs. "Noah, strong emotions can be hard to differentiate sometimes. When you and Andrew were first getting to know each other, he was doing his level best to be an ass for reasons only he could understand"—I don't bother to tell him that I understand them too. It seems so long ago that Andrew and I had that conversation—"and you were dealing with a traumatic event. I imagine feelings of dislike and even hatred were easier for you to grasp and process than anything else." He stands as we hear footsteps coming down the hall. "Don't worry about all of that. The only thing that really matters is if you and Andrew are happy now, even if you bicker like babies."

I make an assenting sound, thinking it over. He passes Andrew just inside the doorway, proclaiming that he'll head out to the store now and to behave ourselves while he's gone.

Andrew settles a new tray on my lap. "What were you talking about?" he asks suspiciously, which leads me to believe he heard at least some of it.

I look down at the tray, which has pancakes this time, plus more fruit and yogurt. "Oh, nothing," I say idly, picking up my fork. "David was just saying I could do better than you and offering to sneak me out of here."

He laughs so hard, I wonder if he's going to hurt himself. "Nice try," he finally wheezes out. "If it was anyone other than David, I might even have had a moment of doubt. But the only time David would get between a couple is if abuse is involved."

I shovel in pancakes and nod sagely, making him wait for an answer while I chew.

"Yeah, he said having to listen to you bitch about the fact that I put your socks in the washer and dryer was akin to torture and that I should get out while I could."

As I expected, he leaps to his feet. "They were *cashmere silk*," he exclaims. "Running them through the washer and dryer *murdered* them. You may as well just have slashed at them with a knife."

"Forgive me," I intone dryly, "for not knowing hand-wash-only socks existed. I mean… they're socks. Most of the time, no one sees them. They just have to be warm and comfortable."

He opens and closes his mouth a few times. "Right. I can see there's only one way to resolve this." He spins and marches through a door that leads into a dressing room—which I discovered when I went looking for his bathroom last night. Lucky I had my eyes open or more of his stupid expensive clothes might have been ruined.

I finish the pancakes and put the fruit aside for later and am just musing over what his reaction would be if I "accidentally" pissed on his shoes—oh, relax. I wouldn't actually do it. But maybe I could make him think I did? —when he storms back out waving… a pair of socks. They flap from his hand like a flag, because these are the kind of socks you can't ball up—apparently it stretches the fibers and ruins them. No, these socks are folded carefully in half and laid in a drawer.

Oh my god, he's going to lecture me about his socks. Again.

He reaches the bed, but instead of sitting down or even pacing alongside as he delivers his lecture, he rips back the covers.

"Hey!" I automatically go to cover my junk before I realize that (a) sudden movements are still uncomfortable and (b) he's the only one here and he's seen everything I've got. Instead, I glare at him. "Not very nice." I give an exaggerated—and entirely fake—shiver.

He doesn't even notice, because he's too busy frowning at my... feet?

"When was the last time you cut your toenails?"

I stare at him. "Are you fucking kidding me with this shit?"

He shakes his head. "Never mind. I'm prepared to make sacrifices to ensure you're educated properly."

Before I have time to wonder if that means he's going to chop off my toenails in some kind of weird vampire sacrificial ritual—he would have mentioned that earlier, wouldn't he?—he seizes one of my ankles and hoists it in the air.

"Ow! Gently, you fucker!" I shriek in a very mature and manly manner as all the sore muscles in my leg and back protest.

"Sorry, forgot," he mutters as he... pulls one of his socks onto my foot.

He carefully lays my poor abused limb back on the mattress and lifts the other—gently this time—while I stare at my newly clothed foot in utter bewilderment.

And yep, there's the other foot. Wearing a fancy black sock.

I blink at my feet. There are several things going through my head right now, and I don't know how to process them all.

First, I'm lying on the bed naked except for a pair of socks that cost about five times as much as the six-pack of Hanes I get at Walmart. Socks should not cost that much money. And when you're trying them on, you should also be wearing underwear. It's gotta be a rule, because this is just too fucking weird.

Second, I have to come up with a way to avoid admitting that these socks are the best damn thing I've ever felt in my life, with the *possible* exception of the orgasms I had last night. I'm not entirely sure. It depends how the socks feel once I put shoes on.

I wriggle my toes. Oh, man. Who knew socks could be warm *and* feel like a cloud on your feet? These things are seriously soft.

"Well?" he demands, smirking. He obviously thinks he's won. I hate that he's right. The worst part is, even if I deny it now, he'll find out later when I start wearing his socks all the time.

"Well, what?" I stall, but the way I rub my socked foot against my calf gives me away, and he laughs.

"You can keep that pair," he says magnanimously. "Do *not* put them in the washer or dryer." Without warning, he grabs the covers and flips them back up over me. "And cover yourself before you catch a cold."

I push the sheet down from where it slapped me in the face—probably by design—and sniff. "Please. The room is hardly cold."

He leans down and kisses me smack on the mouth. "Then cover yourself so I don't have to be tempted by you. You're not up to the kind of shenanigans I've got in mind."

Oh, now that could be interesting. I do a mental assessment of my body. Maybe tomorrow.

"Shenanigans?" I try to sound coy. I think I failed. Coy doesn't mean eager, does it?

His brow quirks. "Those socks are soft, right? Silky. They feel good on your feet. Just imagine how they'd feel in other places."

My dick tries valiantly to stand to attention, but it's indicative of how much of my energy teleportation sucked away when he can't. Like… he twitches, but that's it. I'm so sad for him.

Of course, with the blood still in my head, I'm able to think, and I ask, "You'd seriously risk having your precious socks gunked up with cum?" If he's going to tease me, he should at least make it realistic.

A wicked grin spreads across his face, and anticipation shivers through me. "No. That's why you'll be wearing a cock ring. Maybe a cage. We'll see. I'm going to go shower. I'll leave the door open so you can hear me."

Images… processing… holy fucking wow…

Wait.

"You mean so *you* can hear *me*," I call after him. After all, I'm the one he's supposedly keeping an eye on.

He turns in the doorway to the bathroom and looks back at me. "No."

As the water goes on, I realize what he means. Once more, my dick tries to rally, but to no avail. What else can I do but lie back and enjoy the show?

# CHAPTER ELEVEN

## Andrew

I THINK Noah might just murder Gideon, and I regret that I haven't had a chance to start a betting pool.

It's been ten days since the accidental teleportation discovery, and ever since Gideon found out, he's been hounding Noah for details. Admittedly, we did ask him to walk Noah through the process for demons and for them to compare notes on how it felt—anything so we can gain knowledge that might make it safer for Noah to try again. We had him checked out medically the day after, when he was still achy and sore enough that movement was an issue, and it turned out that he'd lost a small percentage of muscle mass between his last physical, three months after he was rescued, and The Event. (The capital letters were Alistair's idea, and it's not worth arguing with him over it. He was absolutely thrilled to hear about Noah's potential new ability.) So it seems that teleportation does take more energy than a human body can really afford to spend. Between that and dehydration, it was a few days before Noah was in good enough shape to come back to the office.

But now Gideon is showing concern for Noah in his uniquely grouchy way by insisting he eat *all the time* and work out and nitpicking at him for every tiny detail of The Event. They've been over it countless times by now, but Gideon is convinced there's something Noah's overlooked.

"Concentrate," he demands, looming over Noah's desk. "You're not trying hard enough."

I lean back in my chair and watch, wondering if it's too late to at least bet with *one* person. Alistair and Sam are both here. Surely one of them would take my odds?

A quick glance at them disabuses me of that notion. They're both watching as avidly as I am. Alistair is holding his phone in a way that's probably supposed to be surreptitious but makes it obvious that he's recording.

Oooh. That could add fuel to the fire.

"I *did* concentrate," Noah snaps. "I've told you everything I remember. Fuck off and let me do my job!"

I smile proudly. He's gotten over that stupid fear of Gideon, which makes things very interesting sometimes.

"Concentrate harder," Gideon insists. "There has to be something you're forgetting. A feeling or sensation. Teleportation doesn't just happen without a physical warning."

"For demons," Noah says pointedly. "I am not a demon. We don't know how teleportation works for humans."

Gideon's snort is like a red flag to a bull. "It can't be that different. Maybe less effective."

I spot Noah's hand reaching for the heavy stapler on his desk just as Sam shouts, "Alistair, are you *recording* this?"

Damn Sam. He did that on purpose—I'd put money on it.

Gideon swings around to glare at Alistair, whose phone clatters to his desk as he puts his hands up in surrender, the fakest innocent look you've ever seen on his face. Noah's still eyeing the stapler but seems content to hold off on assault for now.

Just when things were getting interesting, too.

Still, Gideon's advancing on Alistair now, so there might still be some entertainm— No. Sam's going in for the block.

"Stop it, both of you," he scolds, and I sigh. "Alistair, delete that video right now and get some work done. You owe me three reports, and you're not leaving today until I have them, even if we're both here all night."

Alistair opens his mouth to argue, a look of horror on his face, but Sam's not done.

"And no, I don't care that you finally have a date with the demon from the convenience store who you've been flirting with for weeks. If you want to go on that date, you'd better get those reports done. Don't test me on this."

A sullen nod is the only response, but when Sam turns toward Gideon—presumably for part two of the lecture—Alistair mutters, "Someone needs to give the World of Wangs a workout."

Sam swings back around so fast, I almost don't see it happen. Fortunately—for Alistair—Gideon grabs the love of his life before he can rain destruction down on his best friend.

"I really have to know," Noah interrupts, probably in an effort to avoid more PTSD, "what's the World of

Wangs? I've heard it mentioned a few times now. Is it some kind of strip club? Or a porn channel?"

We freeze. Sam's made it clear several times that he doesn't want us sharing the story, since we still tease him enough about it even without everyone else knowing, but now would probably be a good time for a distraction.

And since he's already pissed off with everyone else, I may as well add myself to the group.

"It's a collection of different-shaped dildos," I explain. "One for each species."

Noah's eyes bug out. "No fucking way! You mean it's not just vampires that are different? We need to buy that. Can I get it online?" He reaches for his keyboard, then whips his head back to look at me. "What do the others look like?"

Sam starts to laugh. "I'll send you a link," he promises, and I'm not sure if it's a link for Noah to buy the World of Wangs or a link to pictures of community cock.

Alistair tsks. "You two have barely been together a couple of weeks and already Noah needs dildos to get things done." The broad grin on his face belies his mock-sympathetic tone. I flip him the bird. Although, really, Noah might just kill me if we're going to start experimenting with interspecies dildos. Right now, I at least get to rest between rounds.

"Dude," Noah says, "your convenience store demon isn't going to stick around for long if the only positions you know are missionary and doggy. Just think of all the fun we can have with dildos. It'll be like an orgy, only without all the extra arms and legs. We should probably get some butt plugs, too." His face is bright red, but that's the only sign of his previously super-private self.

He's become much more comfortable around the team since discovering his power and coming to work in our space.

"I have some," I tell him, more to tease than because I don't want him to buy more. You can never have enough butt plugs. "But I think you might like anal beads."

"I always walk in at exactly the wrong part of the conversation," David says from the doorway.

"It's okay, David," I commiserate. "I'll explain what anal beads are another time."

His laugh is entirely unexpected and has a dirty edge I'm not used to hearing from him. "Don't worry, I'm covered." He heads for his desk.

Noah, Gideon, Sam, and I look at each other, completely at a loss for words. Alistair is too busy frantically working on his reports to even have noticed that David came in.

"It might interest you to know," David goes on as though he hasn't just flabbergasted us all, "that it looks like Tish has heard the rumor that Sam and Noah are visiting Sam's father's clan. There's been a lot of sudden interest. Which is very helpfully showing us some people we might have missed when we rounded up CCA members."

My attention is focused on Noah. His initial reaction —surprise?—seems to be fading to determination. We've talked about his PTSD and Tish a bit, and he says he feels more in control now. Before, even after we rescued him, he was mostly alone, just like he had been in the compound, and that made him feel vulnerable. Now that he's forming closer bonds with the team and is living with me, he feels more secure—he's confident that if he went missing, we'd know immediately and look for him. And being able to manipulate the magic makes him less vulnerable, which also helps his confidence.

"Something to take care of when Tish is safely in custody," Gideon suggests, the low growl to his voice indicating that he will happily take part in that. "Are our people responding? Feeding the rumor and covering all bases?"

David nods. "Yes. Sam will be safe, Gideon. We've strongly reinforced the news that he's with the clan." He turns his gaze on Sam, then Noah. "It might be an idea for the two of you to lie low for a while. Work from home when you can. The supposed leak here in the office looks to have been nothing, but people still gossip, and the fact that you're here isn't exactly supposed to be confidential information."

"Sure," Sam says. "I can kick all your asses from home just as easily as I can here."

"And I have no problem spending my lunch break in the pool," Noah adds.

I remember the last swim we took together, naked, and wonder if maybe I should work from home too.

"Great," David confirms. "Our people are in place to take Tish back. We're just waiting for a few more things to be handled by the human government, but we should be ready to move in the next few days. I'm leaving tonight for the West Coast so there won't be any delays."

A sudden, sharp prickle of icy foreboding slithers down my spine. I've learned over the years to follow my instincts, so I tune out the conversation and focus on what I'm feeling. Clearly, something in me doesn't like the idea of David leaving… or is it that we're depending on the human government? I don't know. Worse, I don't think we have any alternatives. The government is now deeply involved in this plan, and the plan won't work if David isn't there. He's the most senior combat sorcerer CSG has. One of the rest of us could theoretically run the mission, but none of us are sorcerers, so we couldn't fulfill the duty fully.

Maybe he shouldn't go alone, though.

That idea eases the prickly dread—not completely, but enough that I have to suggest it. I wait for a pause in the conversation.

"Are you taking anyone with you?"

I get surprised stares from everyone.

"Well… no," David says. "The team I'll be working with is based on the West Coast, so they're there already." He seems a bit confused.

"I don't mean for travel, I mean… never mind. I think Elinor should go with you." I don't know why. I really don't. If anything, if I'm really concerned there might be danger, it makes more sense for it to be Gideon —he can teleport. But it has to be Elinor.

Alistair's stopped typing and is watching me with his face set in an uncustomarily serious expression. He gets up and comes around his desk to lean against it.

"Something we need to know?"

That same question is written on all their faces and screaming in the back of my mind, but I shake my head. "I don't know. I just think it would be better if Ellie went with you."

David nods slowly. "Okay. I'll call her and let Percy know. Anything else you can think of?"

It's a testament to how long he and I have worked together and how much he trusts me that he asks that.

My instincts don't always kick in, and they never provide nice, neat directions, but following them has always mitigated disaster in the past.

I shrug helplessly. "I don't know. It… will be better if you take Elinor, but not good. So be careful." I search the recesses of my soul for any niggle that could give us more information. "I'll meditate on it tonight and see if that makes anything clearer."

David's nod this time is sharp, precise. "There are some contingency plans I can put in place. And I have a cache of emergency weaves I can activate and have ready. Whether something goes wrong or not, we'll be ready."

I guess that's all I can ask.

———

TWO DAYS LATER, that low-level dread is still buzzing through my veins and driving me and everyone who comes into contact with me insane. I can barely sit still. David and Elinor have been sending back a steady stream of positive reports, but the danger vibe is so strong, I can almost taste it. I hate waiting. I want to be there with them, but the presence of yet another member of our team on the West Coast would make it hard to hide the fact that we're there. Plus, Noah's here, and despite the fact that our ruse is working, he *is* still at risk. I couldn't just leave him unprotected.

More important, I don't want to leave him. Living together, even when it was platonic, really forged a connection between us. Even if we'd never ended up having sex, eventually we would have morphed into close friends. We complement each other so very well, and I can't deny how much I *like* him just for who he is. More than that, being around him feeds something in me. I've lived a long time, known a lot of people, been in a lot of relationships. With Noah, I can be myself in a way that's so rare—and I want him to be himself. Let all his shields and guards down. Add to that the stupendous sex, and I never want to let him go. Being without him for more than a few hours would make me miserable.

But that sounds selfish when stacked up against the possible mortal danger two of my teammates and close friends could maybe be in. So instead we'll say I'm staying purely to protect him.

If anything's going to happen, it will likely be tonight. Elinor called before to advise that all our people are in place to take down Tish, and the human government has finally lined up all its pieces and is able to support us. By that, I mean strings have been pulled by the few humans who know about us, and their agent on the inside has been fed some bullshit story about who we are and why we're taking Tish out. Whatever. Better that the humans stay ignorant for now.

So tonight is when David and Ellie will be facing down Tish and taking him into custody. It's also when there's the greatest risk of exposing the community to the humans in the fundamentalist cult. Is it any wonder that I'm a mess? Gideon should be ashamed of himself for kicking me out of the office halfway through the afternoon.

He and I, in an attempt to make things seem as normal as possible to anyone who might be observing— including the source of the leak we think we don't have but can't be sure about—have left our better halves safely behind wards at home for the past two days while we made the trek into the office. As I'm sure you can imagine, neither of us have been fun to be around, to the point that Alistair, the only other team member left in the office, went to work in the breakroom and is telling everyone he comes across that we're "churlish boors." (Incidentally, Alistair is only just old enough to have been around when that expression was in use, and I question whether it was ever a part of his vocabulary.) The story circulating around the office is that Sam and Noah both have food poisoning after getting takeout for lunch. Alistair assures us that the excuse works perfectly, as it comes with the implied explanation that Gideon and I haven't been getting any for the past two days and that's why we're irritable asswipes.

That may have been the first time I fully understood why Gideon sometimes wants to maim Alistair. I even considered doing it myself. Just a little bit. He wouldn't die from it or anything.

Anyway, Gideon's so used to being the grumpy bastard himself that he has no patience when other people are in *slightly* unhappy moods, and so he called me all sorts of names and demanded I get out.

Don't worry, though—I got the last word when I announced I was going home to work with Noah and he realized he could have seized the advantage to walk out, blame me, and spend the afternoon with Sam. Seeing that look on his face did almost as much to improve my mood as getting home to find Noah taking a swim break.

Naked.

Of course, the downside of a naked swim break that somehow turns into a fuck on a sun lounger while I promise that none of the other buildings around us can see the terrace and pray to any deity that may exist that he never finds out otherwise is that you have to make up the time lost. Which is why Noah and I are still working at nearly seven thirty.

We would probably have been finished by now, except I can't concentrate. The minutes are ticking down to when David and Elinor will be springing their trap. They should be nearly in place around the compound now, although of course they've gone non-contact. So, you know, I have no way to know what's going on. If things have gone horribly wrong. If they're *dead* and Tish is on the loose, hunting down my lover who I've finally found after centuries of searching.

That last bit was a bit more dramatic than I intended. But the thought of losing Noah sends chills through me like I've never experienced before.

"Okay, that's it. We have to find a way to shut your brain up before I lobotomize you!"

Ah, the dulcet tones of my love.

"What?" I'm a little hurt. I haven't even spoken for the last thirty minutes.

"I can hear you thinking, Andrew. You can't sit still, and I swear, if you sigh one more time, I'm putting duct tape over your nose and mouth. You'd think you were fucking auditioning for the role of the big bad wolf."

It takes me a few seconds to get that reference—when you predate children's fairy tales, they don't always become enmeshed in your brain—but when I do, I throw up my hands. "Forgive me for having a soul!"

He rolls his eyes. "Come on, get dressed."

"Why?" I cross my arms over my chest, but I definitely do not pout.

"I left some notes I need at the office, and we both

need to eat, so we're going to the office, and then while I go up to get the paperwork, you're going to get us takeout from that Sri Lankan place you love."

As if on cue, my stomach rumbles, and he grins.

"It'll do us both good to get out, and fuck knows you need a distraction," he continues, but I don't need any more convincing.

Twenty minutes later, I find a parking spot just yards from the entrance to the building that houses the CSG. There's hardly any traffic in this area at this time in the evening, which meant a speedy journey and also allows me to better judge the danger level.

Noah leans over the center console and kisses my cheek, shocking me so much that my breath stutters. That kind of casually affectionate gesture is new for him. I really like it.

"Go get dinner. I'll meet you at the restaurant."

I hesitate, because since this whole mess started, he hasn't been alone in a public space, and while I know the CSG offices are secure, the street between here and the Sri Lankan place two blocks over is not.

He huffs, knowing what I'm thinking without me having to say a word. "Fine. I'll wait for you in the building lobby. But as soon as I see you coming, I'm coming out."

"I can live with that," I concede. The shared lobby isn't as secure as the CSG offices, but a security swipe card and code are needed to gain access after hours, so he'll at least be behind locked doors and have some warning if someone tries to get in.

We part ways, and I spend the walk to the restaurant trying not to think of all the things that could go wrong for David and Elinor. By the time I get there, I've given up on that and am actively counting off all the things that could go wrong for David and Elinor. I'm up to thirty-eight when I go up to order.

I sit in one of the chairs for people awaiting takeout, counting myself lucky there's one free, and am just about to resume counting—I wonder how many things I can come up with?—when my phone rings.

It's Percy, and my heartbeat picks up. I answer on my way to the door, waving with one hand to the cashier so she knows where I am, and tapping my Bluetooth earpiece with the other.

"Percy, hey, what's happened?" The glass door closes behind me, and I move a few paces down the sidewalk, out of the way of traffic and away from listening ears.

"Hold on, I'll conference you in." He sounds grim, which is a very bad sign. "Andrew, are you still there?"

"Yes. What happened?"

"Are you somewhere private? This is a conference call with everyone on the team except Elinor."

My throat closes. "Elinor…" I wheeze, just as I hear a shout from Alistair.

"She's okay." That's David, rushing to reassure us all. "Andrew, are you somewhere secure?"

"I'm on the street outside a takeout place," I say, looking around. "But nobody's close enough to overhear. What happened to Elinor?"

"Ambush," he says grimly. "The doctor's with her now, but he says she's going to be fine. Concussion, and fractures to three ribs and her left ankle. Some bruising. She's been in and out of consciousness, but I've been assured there's no major head trauma."

"Fuck. Fuck!" That's Gideon, eloquently vocalizing what we're all feeling.

"You're sure she's okay?" Alistair demands, his voice rough with worry for his cousin.

"Yes. Our field medic was in the second car and was able to get to us pretty much immediately. The emergency clinic doctor did a more in-depth assessment, and I had a CSG doctor called in to see her as soon as I woke up. She's going to need rest and healing, but she'll be fine."

I barely have time to feel relieved before the rest of his words sink in. As soon as he *woke up*?

"David!" The exclamation comes from several mouths.

"I'm fine," he promises. "A minor concussion, not even worth keeping me for observation, and my left wrist is sprained. The concussion from the blast knocked us all out."

"Start at the beginning," Percy says. "From the moment you went dark."

"It's not that interesting. Everything was going as planned. The only change was that the van we'd originally intended to take to the compound had a flat tire and nobody could find the spare. We need to have a serious talk to the crew here, because that's just shoddy."

"Noted," Percy says a little dryly, and I can tell he's wondering, as I am, if David's head injury might be troubling him more than he thinks. "So you took a different vehicle?"

"No. I mean yes. There was another van there, but Elinor thought it seemed a little too convenient that nobody could find the spare tire for the van I'd checked over personally, and Andrew's instincts were screaming at me"—he's definitely not thinking right. David would never normally say something like that—"so I commandeered SUVs instead. Because Ellie was with us, we needed two, which turned out to be a good thing. Our attackers didn't seem prepared for two vehicles."

"It does make a leak seem more likely, though," Sam comments grimly. "And worse, someone actively working against us from inside CSG."

"How did they get you?" Gideon asks.

"We were on a very lonely stretch of road," David continues. "We came around a bend and they had a truck across the road, blockading it. I don't know exactly what weave they hit us with. I only had a second's warning, but it looked… different somehow. It didn't actually hit us, anyway. Thanks to Andrew's warning, I had some very complicated defensive weaves around the cars. But the concussion wave from the impact knocked all of us in the car out, and then the car went off the road and hit a tree. We're lucky none of us were injured worse."

"You're lucky they didn't try to finish you off," Alistair points out.

"Oh, they did. I wasn't awake for that bit, but our second car got some warning when we lost contact with them, so they came around the bend ready for anything. Apparently the attackers were chipping away at my shield in an attempt to get to us when they were taken out. Three were killed in the scuffle, but two are still alive. I'm told one is even uninjured. I've put them on suicide watch with people I trust, but I'd appreciate if you could get a personally vetted team out here to take them into custody for questioning."

"Have we had any reports on Tish?" I ask. "This doesn't make sense. If he knew our plans, that you were coming, and has the resources to stage this ambush, why is he holed up with a bunch of human cultists?" My instincts are screaming at me, and the frustration of not knowing why is killing me.

"Nothing," Percy says, and there's that tiny trill of power in his voice that he gets when he's in full communication with the magic. "I'll reach out to the human government now, but I think we have to assume their agent has been compromised."

"I think so," David agrees. "It's been several hours since the initial attack. You should have had some kind of warning by now. I've got someone calling our contacts in the clan Sam's father is part of," David says. "If Tish heads that way, they'll be ready. But Andrew's right. We thought we'd cut him off from all his resources and contacts. If he can still muster this kind of force, I would have expected him to be safely hidden in another lab bunker."

"We've missed something," Sam bites out. "What the hell—"

"Ward breach at the office!" Percy's shout cuts through my head like a knife.

"Noah's there!" I cry, spinning and taking off at a dead run. I can hear their voices still, but I'm not listening. Fuck, I never should have left him alone. Who could this be? Surely not Tish—how would he have gotten across the country so fast? And why would he be trying to get into the CSG office?

But who else could it be?

I push myself to run faster. It's too fast—any human who sees me will know something's not right. But I'd rather deal with the fallout from potential exposure than subject Noah to being in Tish's hands.

"Andrew! Wait! Don't go in alone!" Gideon's yell cuts through the chaos of my thoughts as I round the corner where the building is. "I'll meet you in the lobby."

I'm not waiting for him.

Of course, as I approach the building and watch through the glass walls as he flashes into place, I remember that he can teleport.

Reaching the glass after-hours door, I prepare to blast right through it, but Gideon's already there, holding it open.

I don't break stride as I head toward the stairwell. One glance at the dark elevator panels tells me they're all locked down just as they should be. Gideon falls into step beside me.

"Percy can't get hold of building security," he mutters. "There's a team on the way. We protect Noah first and try to hold them here."

I nod curtly, saving my breath for the five flights of stairs ahead.

By the time we've managed three, I'm aware via the chatter in my ear—Percy never ended the call—that half a dozen demons from enforcement have arrived and are following us up the stairs. Building security still cannot be reached. And Noah's not answering his phone.

But nobody's tried to leave the building.

So what the fuck is going on up there? Maybe they don't know he's there. Maybe he's hiding so well, they're just doing what they came for—whatever that is—so they can get out before we arrive. They have to know a ward breach would have us here within minutes, so whatever they're doing, they should be trying to leave soon.

I push myself to run faster, but even with the power

of my years, my stamina can only take me so far. Gideon yanks me to a stop as we make the turn to the fifth flight of stairs, and while I want to shove him away and keep going, I make myself be reasonable. We're both breathing hard, and we need to be ready to tackle anything when we enter the offices.

Silently, I count to ten, forcing myself to regulate my breathing and using vampire mastery to settle my heart-beat. It's not the safest thing in the world to do, but I'm not an inexperienced baby.

In my ear, Percy says, "Noah's okay, Andrew. I'm getting a very strong message from the magic that he's unharmed. I-I think he's telling it to tell me. But… I'm not sure where he is. Be very careful going in; something odd is going on."

I look over to Gideon, who nods, pointing to his ear. Together, we creep up the last flight of stairs and pause by the door. It opens directly into the CSG reception area.

Gideon holds up three fingers.

My fangs descend and claws slide out.

Two.

I brace myself.

One.

He yanks open the door and I hurtle through, senses on high alert, aware of Gideon two paces behind me.

There's no one here, but I can sense the broken ward… and smell burnt hair?

Fuck me, Noah's using fire. That means they found him. But then why is it so quiet?

Gideon grabs my arm before I can take off out of reception.

"Wait," he mutters. "Was the ward breached from inside?"

I freeze, then focus my attention on it. The after-hours ward that protects CSG is a work of art. It was created by a team of sorcerers over months and is so delicately interwoven that it should have taken hours—or days—to break through. Percy should have had much more warning of what was happening, and the team of sorcerers attempting to break in—because that's what it would take—should still have been here in reception working on it when we arrived. An actual full breach within seconds like this shouldn't be possible.

But Gideon's right. I can't see weaves the way a sorcerer can, but even I can tell that the breach in the ward came from the inside. So... Noah breached it?

The world spins around me.

Why would he do that?

Actually... why *would* he do that?

I look at Gideon. "Why would Noah breach the wards from the inside?"

Percy replies. I'd almost forgotten he was still listening. "To warn us."

Gideon shakes his head. "That doesn't make sense. The *ward* should have warned us. It's supposed to notify you when someone tries to breach it—which it did. It wasn't created to guard from the inside, but if someone was trying to get in from the outside, you would have been advised." He shakes his head again. "We can talk about this later. We need to clear the offices."

"There's no one here," I say absently, still studying what I can feel of the ward while part of me itches to race out and find Noah.

"You can't know that. They could be hiding."

Gideon sounds impatient, and I give him a scathing look.

"My adrenaline is through the roof right now. I can hear the heartbeats of every person in this building and some from the street. Trust me, there's nobody on CSG's floors except us. Everyone else is in the stairwell coming up or the lobby." If I'd been calmer before, I could have saved myself that run up the stairs.

"So where'd Noah go?"

I push aside the surge of fear. "Abducted." The word hurts my throat. Fuck. That's his worst nightmare, and I failed to protect him from it.

"Okay, but how? You were here in under a minute. There's no way they could have gotten Noah down five flights of stairs and away from the building without you seeing them as you approached."

He's right. There would have been something—a vehicle speeding away.

"Did they teleport?" There could have been demons with them. But again, why were they even there? And why did Noah need to breach the ward from the inside for it to alert Percy? Were they not trying to get in, just standing in reception having a chat?

Gideon seems to focus for a second. "If they tele-ported, it wasn't from here. There's no residue at all. Plus, the wards that prevent direct teleportation in and out of these floors are still intact. They would have had to be in the elevator or stairwell to do it."

We were just in the stairwell, so he would have noticed that, but the elevator... I glance at it. The panel is still dark. Definitely locked down.

"This makes no sense."

The door to the stairwell opens as the demons from

the enforcement first responders team arrive. They stop when they see us just standing there.

Gideon takes over, directing them to spread out and search every office for anything that could tell us what happened here. I notice a couple of them doing a double-take at the ward.

I just can't follow this through. Percy seemed sure that Noah breached the ward from the inside to warn us. That kind of makes sense—after all, if Noah was already inside the ward, what other reason would he have to breach it? To let others in? But why? If they wanted access to information, Noah would be better served hunting it out himself. Until a few days ago, he spent all day, every day here. And what other reason could there be for accessing the offices after hours?

No, whatever happened, it wasn't Noah betraying us. So that must mean he was warning us... but again, why? What was happening that he needed to breach the ward to warn us? Even if for some weird reason it wasn't alerting Percy, he would have been safer to stay behind the ward and call us.

There's another minor commotion behind me as the stairwell door opens for another enforcement team, this time a mix of species since they didn't teleport. Gideon begins giving out more orders. In my ear, Percy advises that he's just a few minutes away.

"Dammit, who beat us here?" someone whines, and it's so out of place that everyone else falls silent. I turn around and identify the culprit as a youngish hellhound —at least, he's the only one going as red as a tomato. "Sorry," he mutters. "I was just sure we'd get here first."

"You thought you'd beat demons who can teleport?" I ask dryly, walking back toward them.

Three other shifters stop dead on their way out of reception.

"What?" Gideon asks immediately.

"Only demons have been here recently, sir?" the most senior asks, taking a long sniff.

Gideon and I exchange glances. "On our side? Demons, Andrew, and a human," he replies. "Any other scent should be at least"—he glances at his watch—"an hour and a half old, probably more. Who else do you smell?"

"Sorcerers," the man says instantly, sniffing again. "Four… no, five of them. Three hellhounds, all from the same pack environment. Burnt hair and some smoke—but I can't smell matchwood or accelerant. And…" He shakes his head as though trying to clear it. "The scent's a bit muddled. The human was definitely here too, but there was someone else." He looks around at his team. "Anybody?"

A few others sniff the air as well. "Maybe the human was wearing cologne?" one of them suggests. "And I can smell grass."

I squint at him. "By grass, you mean…?" Surely our intruders didn't stand around getting high?

He looks confused. "Grass. Green stuff? Grows… well, everywhere that's not a city block. Like a lawn?"

"Thank fuck for that," Gideon mutters, telling me I wasn't the only one stymied. "Okay," he raises his voice, "so we have five sorcerers, three hellhounds, and something unidentified. And at least one of them was at a park or somewhere that has grass recently. Correct?"

There are some doubtful looks and a few more sniffs, and I swear to fuck, for the first time ever, I wish Alistair would turn up. Hellhounds drive me insane.

"It doesn't exactly smell like cut grass." The team leader inhales so deeply, I worry he's going to start coughing.

Gideon opens his mouth, and I hastily leap in. I've seen that look on his face before. It never ends well. "Thank you. We'll let you know if we have more questions." It's better if we wait for Alistair and take advantage of his nose—and then he can deal with his brethren.

The hellhounds disperse to carry out their orders, and I look over at Gideon.

"This is fucked," he says bluntly.

Before I can answer, Percy's voice in my ear says, "We're unlocking the elevator and coming up."

Gideon and I both turn to look at the panel as it lights up. "We're right here waiting," I tell Percy. "Who's with you?"

"Alistair and Sam and half a dozen enforcement agents."

"Ask the agents to wait downstairs," Gideon says. "Let's not disperse this scent too much more before Alistair gets a chance to smell it. There's already been a lot of people through here."

"Consider it done," Percy says, and then the sound cuts out as he mutes his phone again.

"Sam should have stayed home," Gideon grumbles. I say nothing, because at this moment, I really wish I'd made Noah stay home.

The elevator doors open, and Percy and Sam hang back and let Alistair exit first. He walks right past us without even a glance of acknowledgment, his expression one of laser focus as he inhales.

"Three hellhounds," he says at once. "From a West

Coast pack. Give me time and I'll remember which one."

West Coast, huh? Maybe the reason Tish fled there was because he had allies. Could the cult have been a decoy?

A lot of work for a decoy, though.

"Noah was here," Alistair continues. "And a couple of those fireballs he's so fond of. He was…" He shoots me a glance. "He was afraid, but not a lot. I'm getting a lot of adrenaline from him, though."

Good. He was prepared to fight back. *Please let him be okay.*

"Five sorcerers." He hesitates.

"What?" Percy asks, stepping out of the elevator with Sam on his heels.

"One of them smells familiar. It's the same scent that was all over Sam and the lab in the bunker."

My heart stops.

"Tish?" The question bursts from multiple mouths.

Alistair shakes his head. "I can't say for sure. I've never met him. I just know that I smelled this sorcerer in the lab, and he'd touched Sam."

"Definitely male?" Sam asks sharply.

Alistair nods. "Yes. Male, fully mature but not elderly, and very worked up about something." He sniffs again. "But he wasn't using sorcery while he was here. In fact, none of them were." He scrunches up his nose and sniffs again. "Hold on, I want to shift and see if I can get a better handle on this."

He shifts, and while he's sniffing around in his waist-high hellhound form, Sam says, "I can't be exactly sure who came near me while I was unconscious"—Gideon growls—"but Noah said the lab assistant who ran the tests that night was a woman, remember? I think Tish was the only male sorcerer who came near me in the bunker."

"If it's not Tish, it's someone in his inner circle," Percy says. "Regardless, their presence here combined with the attack on David and Elinor is a clear sign that Tish has been playing us." His face is like stone.

Realizing the conference call has been disconnected, I ask, "How did you convince David to hang up?"

"He's coordinating on the West Coast," Sam replies. "Looking for Tish's allies. I think he also decided to interrogate the prisoners himself. Last we heard, he was demanding a doctor to heal his concussion."

"*David* did?" Complex healing is one of the rarest sorcery abilities and is only used for life-threatening injuries. Some of us who are more highly placed at CSG can overrule that if healing a more minor injury is important for government business, but we don't take advantage of it often... and to my knowledge, David's never done so.

Sam shrugs. "He's worried about Noah. And Tish is dangerous."

I can't argue with that.

Alistair shifts back to his biped form. "I don't know what the fuck is going on here, but it's seriously messed up," he declares. "There was someone else here, but I've never smelled anything like that before. As far as I can tell, they were the only one doing any kind of sorcery or magic."

"Sorcery *or* magic?" Percy asks sharply. "Were they a sorcerer? Or perhaps a human with magic? We've been assuming that Noah is the only one who's explored that gift, but Tish could have been ahead of us there too."

Alistair shakes his head. "I don't know. I don't think it was either. I've literally never smelled a being like this before. I'm saying sorcery or magic because it kind of smells like the residue of both, and it's definitely from this one person. Could they be some kind of genetic cross Tish developed?"

A sorcerer-human hybrid? It shouldn't be possible. I wrack my brain to remember what David said about Tish's research, wishing he was here.

Percy shakes his head slowly. "No, I'm sure there was nothing like that in the notes we seized."

"There also wasn't anything about these supporters on the West Coast," Gideon points out. "We thought we got all the compounds in that area."

"What else did you smell?" I demand. How can we possibly find Noah with no information?

"Grass," Alistair says succinctly. "Fresh, still growing, but it was a type I've never come across, so not a common lawn variety."

"Still growing?" Sam asks incredulously. "Like, they brought a planter box of exotic grass in here with them?"

He shrugs. "I can only tell you what I smell. There's a difference between the scents of cut grass and uncut."

I look at Percy. "Are you sure Noah's okay?"

"Yes." He sighs. "It's the strangest thing. I keep getting little nudges from the magic, giving me a feeling he's fine. Every few minutes. It's never done anything like that before."

"Maybe Noah's sending you the message?" Sam suggests. He shoots a quick glance around to make sure nobody else is within listening distance. "Using the magic to let you know he's okay."

Percy spreads his hands. "Your guess is as good as mine."

"Is it just a feeling that he's fine?" I persist. "Do you get anything else we could maybe use to find him?"

He grimaces. "I tried, Andrew. I'm trying to get an idea of location, but the magic just… slips away."

Hopelessness swamps me, but I shove it away. Noah's fine. He's maybe using the magic to send us messages. I have to do my part at this end so we can bring him home.

Alistair is now wandering the perimeter of the reception area. "Well, this is interesting and creepy. Gideon, are you absolutely sure they didn't teleport in and out?"

"Positive," he says immediately. "There's no residue at all in here, and those wards are still active."

"They are," Percy agrees, nodding. "There's no sign someone even tried. Why?"

Stalking back across to where the broken ward is, Alistair paces off a rough rectangle that covers the area from just a few feet in front of us, along the length of the ward for a few yards, then on the inside of the ward for maybe four feet. Then he turns and heads toward the hall that leads off to private offices. "Noah was here, leaning against the wall," he says, sniffing again. "He came down this hallway, but he definitely stopped here." He takes another step, and the wall is suddenly blocking most of him from view.

"Hiding," Gideon says grimly.

Alistair nods. "They saw him, though. Two of the hellhounds were over here as well." He takes a few more steps, moving out of sight, then comes back. "They stopped a few feet up the hall, so I'm guessing that's where they grabbed him."

I hiss.

"I'm sorry," Alistair says sincerely. "I'll try to be more sensitive."

Closing my eyes, I suck in a deep breath. "You're fine. So they went through the ward after he breached it —how did he breach it? It was coded to let him through for those nights he and David stayed late. Even if he shoved through from the inside, it shouldn't have had any impact. And he couldn't have done that from over there."

"The magic?" Sam asks, looking doubtful. "If he breached it on purpose to warn us, would he have used the magic to punch through it?"

We all look at Percy.

"I suppose it might be possible. We don't ward against the magic, because supposedly nobody can wield it. And the inside of the ward would be more vulnerable anyway."

"We still don't know why, though." Gideon's frustration is clear. "Why did Noah breach the ward to warn us of intruders who hadn't tried to breach the ward? Percy, aside from the obvious damage, is there anything wrong with it? Any reason it wouldn't have alerted you to an attempted breach?"

Percy opens his mouth, studying the ward, but Alistair butts in.

"Sorry, Percy, but right now, this is more important."

"What is?"

Alistair gestures to the area he paced off before. "Aside from the two hellhounds who came this way, none of the intruders left that space."

I look at the space. Then I turn and look at the door to the stairwell behind me. The elevator. And I remember that Gideon had to open the after-hours lobby door for me to enter the building.

"How did they get in?" I ask Percy. "We didn't stop to check. Loading bay?"

"The team downstairs hadn't ascertained that before we came up," he says. "I'll check with them now."

"You're not hearing me," Alistair snaps. "They. Didn't. Leave. This. Space." He paces off the rectangle again. "Their scent markers are all here. None of them are over toward you. And that's even with all the people who've tracked through here since then."

Sam squints at his best friend. "You're saying they didn't come up the stairs or the elevator?"

"That's what I'm saying."

I look at Gideon again, but he's already distant-eyed, his brow furrowed. "Are you—"

He shakes his head slowly. "There's nothing. Absolutely no sign of a teleport." He turns to Percy. "I'm going to test the wards."

"Is that necessary?" Percy sounds alarmed, and I get it. Attempting to teleport in an area that's warded against it is, by all accounts, painful.

"We have to eliminate the possibility."

Sam opens his mouth to protest, but Gideon doesn't wait. He flickers slightly—a sign of a failed teleport—then makes a sound of… well, pain. I grab him before he collapses and lower him to the ground.

"They're working," he groans as Sam rushes to kneel beside him.

Percy nods. "And I can clearly see your blocked attempt on the wards. Nobody tried to teleport in or out before Gideon, not since we had the wards checked and reset three months ago."

We all look toward the breached ward and the space Alistair is standing in.

What the fuck is going on?

And how can I rescue Noah if there's no way to track his abductors?

# CHAPTER TWELVE

## Noah

HOLY FUCKING SHITBALLS, this can't be real.

I reach out to the magic for the millionth time in the past few minutes, just to reassure myself it's still there. I do not want to be all alone in this... place. Wherever it is.

Holy fucking shitballs.

At least I can reassure myself Tish and his goons didn't get what they wanted from CSG. They got me instead, which isn't great, but I'm going to have a plan any second now. As soon as I think of something. In the meantime, I nudge the magic again, picturing Percy in my mind's eye and thinking about telling him I'm okay. I don't know if it's working, but I'm going to keep trying, because I'm pretty sure Andrew is having an aneurysm right about now. Either that, or he's gone on the warpath and is ripping apart anyone who stands in his way. Knowing that gives me a warm feeling inside.

Honestly, when I first heard voices coming from the executive reception, I thought Andrew had ditched the idea of dinner and come up to keep an overprotective eye on me. That irritated me, and I went marching down the hall to give him a piece of my mind. Fortunately for me, about halfway there I realized that voices meant more than one person, and some strange instinct made me slow down, then stop before I was in sight.

Lucky instinct, more like. Because about five seconds after that, I recognized Tish's voice. It'll be burned in my memory for eternity, and not gonna lie, I nearly lost it and freaked out. I'm so fucking proud of myself for holding it together, even if I was dumb enough not to go right back to my desk and grab my phone to call for help.

At that point, I wasn't too worried. The after-hours ward at CSG is serious business. The first time I had to pass through it, David and Percy had to do all kinds of work to make it happen. And unlike a lot of wards, you can really feel this one. Crossing it is like walking through a wall of Jell-O. Or what I imagine walking through a wall of Jell-O would feel like, seeing as how I've never tried it. Has anyone?

So I figured I was safe on the inside of the ward, and based on what I'd been told, I knew it would activate and alert Percy if they tried to get through it. Which was what convinced me to stay put and listen to what they were saying instead of going to get my phone and call Andrew. Tish was supposed to be on the other side of the country, about to be taken into custody by David and Elinor. That he was in the CSG offices told me something had gone seriously wrong, and I could only hope my friends were okay.

Tish and one other person seemed to be talking about what they needed to find. It didn't make a lot of sense to me—of course, I had to read between the words.

I guessed that "that trumped-up figurehead" was Percy, which meant they were planning to head for his office and would have to come down the hallway I was hiding in. There was something about contacts and maps and a seal—which I really hoped was a seal of office and not the marine life type of seal—but the part that seemed strangest to me was the complete lack of any urgency. Either they were just standing around talking, or they'd started working on breaking the ward but weren't worried about working fast. Based on what David and Percy had told me, that wasn't right. The ward was supposed to notify Percy immediately of any attempt to breach it. There was supposedly a team of enforcement demons on standby to respond to any call from Percy—not to mention the senior investigative team. Andrew was literally two blocks away. A call from Percy would have had him moving right away, especially since he knew I was in the building. So why weren't Tish and his friend worried?

That was what convinced me to peek very carefully around the corner to see if I could work out what was going on. And what I saw horrified me.

Tish was there, and a lot more people than I'd expected. They were all damn quiet. But the shocking part was what one of them was doing to the ward. It was… fuck. I can't see the individual weaves of a ward like sorcerers can, but right then, I could. Because it was glowing bright violet. And one of Tish's goons— although this one was a lot smaller and slimmer than the rest—was *parting the weaves*. I don't know how else to describe it. Nothing was being broken; nothing was being unpicked. The purplish glow was coming from the hands of the goon, and where it touched the ward, the strands of the weave were elongating, stretching, and the extra length meant they were able to separate from each other and form a gap while the overall ward remained completely intact.

Thinking about it now, I don't even know if that's logical. I have about a million questions to ask David about the logistics of the ward reacting that way, never mind *how* it was actually done and what the purple light was. Fuck, I really hope David's okay and that he just turned up to the cult's compound and realized Tish was gone.

But as the gap in the ward slowly got bigger, going from the size of an apple to a grapefruit, then picking up speed and becoming the size of a watermelon in half that time, I reacted, reaching for the magic and visualizing myself punching a hole through the ward.

I didn't actually think it would work. My reasoning —limited as it was in a split-second decision—was that any assault against the ward would set it off. I didn't intend to actually breach it. Maybe the inside isn't braced as much as the outside? Or maybe the ward isn't designed to stand up against human magic, since nobody really uses it—not combatively, anyway. Whatever the reason, I bashed a hole right through the ward where purple-glow guy was doing his thing.

They spotted me then—no surprise, the way purple-glow guy was carrying on—and two of them shifted into hellhounds and came through the hole in the ward after me. I still wasn't that worried. I figured they had to leave ASAP unless they wanted to be caught. So these hellhounds could come after me, I'd distract them for a bit, then they'd race out—hopefully right into the arms of the demons who would be teleporting into the building within seconds.

I'd retreated a few feet up the hallway and conjured a couple of fireballs to throw at the hellhounds—which gave me way too much satisfaction—causing one to yelp and hesitate but sadly missing them both, although I think I singed some fur. Add "practice aiming fireballs" to my to-do list.

Then shit got real. Tish yelled, "Grab him!" I had two seconds to wonder why they weren't already on their way out before the hellhounds shifted and took me down. I didn't stand a chance against them—they were bigger, faster, stronger—but I *still* wasn't that worried. By then, demons had to be mere seconds away, and I was sure Andrew would be right behind them. Tish and his goons would walk right into their arms. Maybe they'd try to use me as a hostage, but with a few moments to prepare, I'd set them all on fire and walk away whistling. I might even ask the demons from enforcement if they had any marshmallows, and tomorrow, the gossip in the office would be about how badass cool I am.

I was mentally rehearsing the marshmallow line and struggling lightly against the hellhounds' hold—to keep up appearances—when they shoved me through the hole I'd made in the ward. FYI, not as big as I'd thought it was. And yes, I made an inappropriate and poorly timed joke about holes as I was being pushed through, which might be why the goons on the other side were so rough when they grabbed me. Or they might just be assholes. I vote for them being assholes.

The two hellhounds shifted, jumped through the

hole, and shifted back, and then, I kid you not, purple-glow guy started glowing again and *a fucking portal opened*.

That's right. It was some real science fiction shit. And it's definitely not something sorcerers can do. Part of my research into human magic was extensively exploring what abilities sorcerers have and looking for historical events that show humans once had a matching ability. The only species that can circumvent having to travel in real time and space is demon, and there are limits on teleportation. Portals? No fucking way.

Tish went through the portal first. Two of his goons followed. Then they shoved me through, and this time, I wasn't struggling lightly for show. There was some real kicking and screaming going on. The screaming stopped when one of the goons punched me in the face—I hope the dumb motherfucker broke his hand on my jaw—but I kept on with the kicking and struggling right up until purple-glow guy stepped through the portal and it closed.

Which brings us to now. I'm huddled on a floor that feels like stone but is an iridescent green color. Should I be worried about radiation? I'll put it on the long-term list. Short-term, the conversation going on above me is of more interest. Also, if you match the fact that I didn't think stone came in that color with the portal, it could mean I'm somewhere very not where I should be.

Purple-glow guy is talking, and he doesn't sound happy.

"…assured us you could get the seal. That's why we have been assisting you. Now one of my brethren is dead, this creature"—he nudges me with his toe, and I fight down the urge to kick him back—"is here defiling our home, and we still do not have the seal. My lord is going to want blood for this."

Ah, it sounds like Tish has found people who think just like him. The whole bit about one of his brethren being dead worries me, though. Dead how? Fighting David's combat sorcerers, maybe? Portals would explain how Tish managed to cross the country without us knowing. But who are these portal people?

I sneak a quick glance around. The room is pretty plain. It's about twenty feet square and seems to be constructed entirely of the same green stone, with a solid wood door and no windows. There are some light-balls hovering up near the ceiling to provide illumination, and the only furniture is a wood bench against the wall beside the door. The lightballs are interesting, because they look almost exactly like the ones I create. Sorcerers can weave light, but the end result looks a little different. I can't explain how—you have to see it. Although, now that I think about it, Andrew said he couldn't tell the difference between my lightballs and what David wove. Maybe David and I could see the difference because we wield the power? The same way Andrew can identify blood type by the scent of it, whereas everyone non-vampire needs to use a micro-scope and know what the fuck they're doing.

Not important right now. What matters is that those lightballs look a lot like mine, which means someone here can manipulate existential magic.

Is purple-glow guy human? Could I glow too if I knew how?

I sneak another look at him while Tish argues about how they couldn't possibly have known I would be there and that what happened at the ambush wasn't his fault.

I keep listening—"ambush" worries me—but soak in as much detail of purple-glow guy as I can.

He's not human. Not unless he's one of those die-hard *Lord of the Rings* fans who have surgery to change the shape of their ears. Can you say pointy? There's also something *other* about the shape of his browbone and eye sockets. At first I thought it was the shape of his eyes and the way they were set, but it's the bone structure itself. In fact, he looks pretty much like every movie depiction of an elf ever, only shorter. The high-cheek-boned, hollow-cheeked, slender look never really did it for me, but I can't deny he has a certain magnetism. This close, he smells kind of… summery. Too bad I'm going to rip off his leg and shove it up his ass if he nudges me with his foot one more time.

Whatever species he is, I can't reject the possibility that he can manipulate existential magic just like I can. Does that mean he can sense when I do it? Whatever he was doing to the ward before wasn't something I felt, and those lightballs aren't pinging on my magic radar either. Which could mean that people who use the magic can't feel/see each other using it, or it could mean that he's not using the magic.

I have no answers, but I do have a slight headache from trying to reason this out.

Drawing the magic more tightly around me, I try again to send a message to Percy. *I'm fine.* I need to come up with a plan, because I am not staying a prisoner of Tish for a second longer than I have to. The biggest issue is that I don't know where I am. What if that portal took us to a different continent and landed us in the middle of a jungle? Or Antarctica? I can probably use the magic to fight my way out—as long as there aren't a hundred guards outside that door—but then I have to find a way to survive and get home, and me against Antarctica is not going to go well for me.

I do like penguins, though.

The other issue is that if I use my magic against Tish, he'll know I have it. I'm not sure yet if either of the hellhound goons has mentioned the fireballs, but I'm positive I was far enough up the hallway that he didn't see them himself. We do *not* want Tish to realize that humans can manipulate existential magic. Fuck only knows what he'd do with that knowledge, but it would be bad for humankind and the community.

So for now, I need to be patient and gather some information. And hope Tish doesn't know who I am.

As if on cue, a hand grabs my upper arm and hauls me to my feet. I pretend to stumble and stomp hard on the foot of the hellhound holding me. Just because.

"Noah Cage," Tish says, looming forward, eyes taking in every single inch of me. My skin crawls, and I look away, doing a quick assessment of the group. The sorcerers and purple-glow guy are gone, leaving only Tish and the hellhounds. "You're supposed to be dead. I had paperwork confirming you were euthanized and cremated. It was signed off by my senior lab techs."

I shrug but say nothing.

"How are you still alive, Noah?"

"Your lab techs always were sloppy," I say in a bored tone. I can't let him guess about the magic. It's my one advantage, and it's only good if I'm conscious. If they decide to knock me out, I'm done for.

I will not let Tish win. I'm stronger than him.

He tilts his head, still studying me in that creepy way. "That would take sloppiness to extremes," he muses. "I suppose the guards at the compound were equally sloppy, to let you escape?"

Relief hits me like a truck. He doesn't know I was stuck in that place for a year. I can make this work for me.

"That was just good luck for me. They happened to get distracted right when I was trying to work out how to get past them." I mean, the distraction was Gideon and about a million enforcement agents raiding the place, and it was after I'd been wandering through the compound for months, but still. "It helped that everyone thought all we humans were dead by then. Nobody expected anyone would be trying to get out." *Shut up, Noah.* Don't babble. Keep cool.

Purple-glow guy comes back in. "We need to free this room for others," he says. "Come."

Tish turns away and follows him out. I'm eager to see what's on the other side of the door and would happily have walked out after them, but my hellhound guards have decided that carrying me is their preferred option. They stand on either side of me and grab my arms and lift. These guys are definitely not CSG trained —they've left my legs free to kick at them and potentially trip them, and they've also not thought about how we'll get through the door three abreast like this. If I wasn't so keen to see what's outside this room, I could do quite a bit of damage to them. I've been training with Andrew and the team a lot lately, and they're teaching me and Sam hand-to-hand fighting. I'm not good enough to take down trained professionals, but these guys? And with the magic to back me up? I'm confident I'd at least have a shot. If I'd known this back at the office, I'd have put up more of a fight.

Sure enough, we get all tangled up at the door, and they have to put me down and let me walk through. Outside is a corridor, still made from the same green stone and completely bare. These people have clearly not got any kind of flair for interior decorating. Andrew would hate this place.

Fuck, I hope he never has to see it.

Down the hall we go, and into another room. This one is about three times the size of the other, fully furnished as a sitting room, and has a massive bank of windows on one wall. Windows that draw my attention immediately as I search for any clue to give away my location and help me come up with a plan.

I'm fucked.

Like… "there's no hope" kind of fucked.

Unless you know of somewhere on Earth where the sky is purple and grass is orange? Anywhere? No?

So, yeah… fucked.

Could I be on the spiritual plane? Is that even possible? I didn't think they had things like grass and buildings there, but… I pinch myself, but my body feels solid to me. Just to check, I pinch the hellhound gripping my arm.

"Ow! What the fuck is wrong with you?" he bellows, drawing everyone's attention to us. I widen my eyes as far as they'll go and bite my lower lip like I'm trying not to cry.

"You're hurting me," I whisper.

He raises a fist. "I'll show you hurt, you little human scum."

"That's enough," Tish orders. "Don't damage him; I'll need him."

Great. What a lovely and reassuring thought.

The hellhound shoves me into a chair that's surprisingly comfortable, but I sniffle and wince like I'm in pain.

"So, Noah," Tish begins somewhat pleasantly. "You were going to tell me what you've been doing since you left my compound."

I sniffle again. "Data management." I have to be really careful how I answer his questions. I know hellhounds can smell changes in physiology that can indicate a lie. Not all of them are trained to recognize it for what it is, and I've been through so much shit tonight that I probably stink of adrenaline and other body chemicals already, but I can't take any risks.

"Data management?" He sounds skeptical.

I nod. "After I got away, I met some people in the woods who wanted to know everything I could tell them about you and the labs. As a thank you, they helped me find an apartment and gave me a job doing data management."

The next few hours are tiring. Tish asks question after question about my health, from weight changes to dietary and sleep habits. He wants to know if I've been for any medical tests. If I've developed any extrasensory abilities. How's my sight? My hearing? My sense of smell? He even has one of his hellhounds cut himself to see if I react to the blood. Clearly he remembers enough about my file to know I have a vampire ancestor.

Then he turns his questions to Percy and the others, and I make myself give the most evasive, inane answers I can. I have to stall him while I come up with a plan, and if I refuse to answer and he tortures me, I'm screwed.

"Why were you in the CSG offices tonight?" he

finally asks, after getting nowhere trying to pump me for security information.

"Working," I say promptly.

His eyes narrow. "After the ward was activated? How were you going to get out? For that matter, how did you breach the ward?"

Crap, I'm going to have to tell an outright lie. *Keep cool.* I pull on the magic just a tiny bit, trying to make it understand that I want to seem like I'm telling the truth. "I threw my phone at it," I say blandly. "Did you happen to grab it? I really need to make some calls."

"I didn't see a phone," Tish says suspiciously.

"So you didn't bring it along, then?" Holy Jesus fuck, I need to stop sweating. It's going to give me away. I pull just a bit more of the magic, wishing I knew more about this kind of biology and how to stop the chemical cocktail brewing in my body. *I need to be calm* is all I can think, but thankfully, that's enough for the magic to do its work, and most of my tension eases.

He chortles. "Even if I had, it would be useless to you here." He seems like he's about to continue his interrogation, but the door opens right then, and purple-glow guy comes in.

"My lord will see you now."

Annoyance flashes over Tish's face. "I'm in the middle of debriefing the human."

Elf man's gaze turns glacial. "My lord will see you *now.*"

Tish hesitates an instant longer, then capitulates. "Fine, but I need somewhere secure to put the human."

Purple-glow elf man nods. "There's a linen closet with a lock on the way to my lord's chambers. Your animals can stand guard also."

The hellhounds scoop me out of my chair while I'm still processing that. A linen closet with a lock? What the fuck? Who locks a linen closet?

Sure enough, about a mile of hallway and six turns later, I'm standing in a small closet lined with shelves while the purple elf closes the door. A second later, the lock clicks.

Huh. I guess it's better than a dungeon?

There's no light in here, but it takes me only a second to conjure a lightball and start searching for anything that might help me. No luck—the shelves are stacked with sheets, towels, and blankets, but nothing else. Who keeps *only* linen in a linen closet?

I sit on the floor and think about my options. It's pretty clear that wherever I am, it's not on Earth. Theoretically, there's no reason why those portals couldn't lead to other planets. I could be galaxies away from my home right now, which is a really awful thought and one I push to the side. So... if I'm not on Earth, I definitely can't count on a teleporting demon to rescue me. They'd have no reference point to teleport to. Even if I escaped Tish, I'm at a severe disadvantage—and there's no way for me to know if I could find someone friendly who would—or could—open a portal home for me. Maybe the purple elf is the only one with that ability.

That leaves me with waiting until Tish decides to use me as a hostage or pawn and takes me back to Earth—*if* he doesn't decide to just kill me—or...

Or what?

There's really only one option if I want to take control of this situation. Of course, it might kill me, but I'll probably end up dead anyway if I stay with Tish.

I swallow hard. The last time I tried teleportation, it

was a small bowl over a distance of twenty feet, and it left me in pain and exhausted for days. I lost muscle mass. Teleporting my whole body over a distance I probably couldn't comprehend even if I did know it... well, I might not make it. I probably won't.

But I have to try.

I draw the magic around me, as much as I can, as close as I can. I send another message to Percy: *I'm coming. Be ready.* I open myself to the magic, letting it take me over in a way I never really thought possible. And I concentrate on going home.

# CHAPTER THIRTEEN

## Andrew

"...NOT TALKING," David's voice says through the phone on Sam and Gideon's coffee table. We retreated to their place to regroup, leaving CSG security and enforcement to secure the office while we try to work out what the fuck is going on and where Noah could be. "I think we need to get a warrant and bring a judge in to find the truth."

I pace restlessly across the carpet. "On what grounds? We've got nothing to connect them to Noah's disappearance or the attack on the office. And without that, no judge is going to grant a warrant to invade mental privacy." As a rule, our judges tend to be vampires, and the truth is gotten directly from the source.

Gideon shakes his head. "We still have to try. Those two hellhounds in custody are the only link we have to finding Noah right now." We all look at Percy. "Is he still okay?"

Percy shrugs helplessly from his seat on the couch.

"No change that I can tell. I'm trying to get the magic to tell me more, but…"

Yeah. If only existential magic was actually able to communicate with us and gave a crap about individuals.

I flex my fingers and make myself take a deep breath when I realize my claws are out.

"Let's apply for the warrant," Sam suggests. "The worst they can do is say no. In the meantime, we can go over it all again. Either they found a way around the teleportation wards—"

"Without any demons," Alistair interjects.

"—without any demons, or—"

Percy's wordless shout cuts him off and brings the enforcement guards waiting in the entrance hall bursting through the doorway. A second later, a body materializes at my feet.

It's so emaciated, it takes me a second to realize it's Noah.

"Medic!" Gideon roars as I drop to my knees and gather Noah carefully in my arms. "Secure the lucifer!"

An enforcement field medic rushes forward as two of her teammates take protective stances around Percy and the others check the rest of the house for surprises. I can hear Noah's heartbeat, but it's so weak.

The medic, a sorcerer with a mild healing ability, says, "He needs a hospital. He's not wounded; he's dehydrated and malnourished." She looks me in the eye. "He needs a hospital *now*."

---

TEN DAYS LATER, I'm still sitting by Noah's bed in the CSG enforcement clinic, listening to him breathe and waiting for him to wake up. At least he's not on the respirator anymore. During those first few days, while the doctors tried desperately to get enough fluids and nutrients into him to keep him alive, we had to rely on modern science to help.

I haven't left this room since he was brought here. Part—most—of it is because I need to know he's still alive, but officially, it's because Noah is the only witness to the attempted break-in at CSG, which makes him a target. I'm not risking him. I don't even use the bathroom unless one of my teammates is here to sit with him.

We've taken to having our status updates here. It's secure enough, and this way, Noah can be a part of it. Percy says the magic is being even more clingy and protective of Noah than usual, and that it seems very determined. I think that worries him—it definitely worries me.

"How's he doing?" David walks in and comes to stand beside me, looking Noah over clinically. He has no healing ability, but I know he can see the weaves the doctors are using to maximize Noah's nutrient intake and help rebuild his muscle mass. "He looks better than yesterday."

It's true, he does. And yesterday he looked better than the day before. He's still painfully thin, and he's going to have to do a lot of work to rebuild his strength and muscle, but the almost desiccated, skeletal look he had when we brought him in is long gone.

"His fingers were twitching before," I report. "Without the machines, I mean." The doctors have been using electrical impulses to stimulate the new muscle, but that was this morning, and I definitely saw his fingers move this afternoon.

"That's great." He goes around the bed to sink into the chair on the other side. "Did the latest brain scans show anything new?"

I shake my head, gently stroking Noah's hand. "No. Everything still looks the same. We just need him to wake up."

"Whenever you're ready, Noah," David teases. "Don't think I'm not going to yell at you for teleporting just because you've been unconscious for over a week."

That's our best guess, by the way. We still don't know how anyone got into CSG or how they got out with Noah, where they went, or what they wanted in the first place, but it seems pretty obvious to us that Noah teleported away to get back to us. He has the same after-effects as last time, except on a much more massive scale, which makes sense given he moved a bigger object over what we believe must have been a greater distance. Well, it pretty much had to be, unless his abductors had him stashed in Gideon's LEGO room. We don't know how he knew to come to Sam and Gideon's house, although David's theorized it might be a location thing —perhaps his kidnappers hadn't gotten too far from the office, after all. Sam and Gideon's place is the closest to CSG headquarters, and might therefore have been the closest safe place for him to go. We have no clue, and the only way we'll find out is when he wakes.

Which he will.

He has to.

"Aidan arrived last night," David tells me. "He and Percy were still discussing plans when I left the office."

Our warrant application was declined, which in any other situation I'd say was the right decision. Deep down, even as angry and unreasonable as I'm feeling right now, I know it was right. Those hellhounds have the right to be charged and tried according to our law, and we can't definitively link the attack on David and Elinor—who's fine but pissed as fuck—to what happened at the office. Sure, it would be an incredible coincidence if the same person or people—Tish—wasn't behind them both, but right now, we can't prove anything.

Unfortunately, that still left us with two hellhounds who might have vital information but weren't talking. So Percy called Aidan, who's the species leader of all shifters. He flew out to Portland to talk to the hellhounds himself—and if that had no effect, compel them to speak. Fortunately for them, they gave in and answered his questions. Unfortunately, they didn't know much. But it turns out they're from the same pack as the hellhounds Alistair smelled in the CSG office, so Aidan spent several days visiting that pack to see if he could find out more.

"Still no obvious links to Ti—" I break off when I feel movement against my hand and look sharply down at Noah.

His eyelids flutter.

"Fuck me," David says, scrambling out of his chair. "I'll get someone."

I lean forward, gaze intent on his beautiful face. This is the biggest reaction he's had. "Noah," I croon. "Can you hear me? Please wake up."

Another flutter, another twitch of his hand… and then his eyes slit open and he squints.

I reach over and slap the light switch beside the bed. Half of the lights in the room go out. "Hey," I manage, trying not to cry. "You're back with us."

"An… rew?" he croaks.

"Yes, it's me. I'm here."

His mouth stretches in a lopsided, weak attempt at a smile. "I—fucking—win." He closes his eyes again and his breathing deepens, but it's different this time. He's just sleeping.

He wins.

---

It's another eighteen hours before Noah is alert and aware enough to hold a proper conversation, although he drifted in and out of sleep quite a bit during that time. He's still incredibly weak and has very little muscle strength, but after a battery of tests, the doctors are satisfied that he has full brain function—well, for a human, anyway. All he needs is high-nutrient food, rest, and extensive physiotherapy, and he'll be able to resume his life.

"Are you sure you're up to this?" I ask, not for the first time, but I don't want him to overdo. He's already tried several times since he became coherent to tell me what happened, but I insisted he needed medical clearance first.

"Shut up and sit down," he orders, talking a little slower than usual, his words sounding clumsy, but then reaches out—slowly and shakily—to hold my hand. He takes a deep breath, then looks over at Percy.

"I had to breach the ward because Tish was there with an elf and he was stretching it open."

I blink.

"What?" Elinor says dumbfoundedly. "I think my concussion might not be healed yet." She only arrived a few days ago, having had to wait for medical clearance to fly. The doctors healed her broken bones to a certain point that made them stable, but she still has a cast on her leg and some tenderness in her ribs.

Noah moves his head slightly as if to shake it, then grimaces. Slowly, he walks us through what he saw, and I begin to wonder if maybe the brain scans missed something important. Then he gets to the portal, and I look at Percy. He needs to stop Noah so we can call the doctors in.

To my shock, Percy's gone pale. Not in a "damn, you have a traumatic brain injury" way, but an "oh no, the elves are coming through the portals" way. And I'm not the only one who's noticed.

"Percy?" David asks sharply.

Percy shakes his head. "Let him finish."

Noah's eyes widen at this tacit acknowledgment that Percy knows more than he expected, but obligingly continues.

"…and then they locked me in the linen closet and I decided to try to teleport home," he concludes. "I'm sorry I didn't stick around and try to get more information, but I wasn't sure when I'd have an opportunity like that again."

"You did the right thing," Sam insists, squeezing Noah's foot through the blanket. "We wouldn't even know this much if you hadn't come back."

There's a general murmur of agreement, and Noah manages a small, uneven smile.

"So." He looks at Percy. "Where was I? On a distant planet? Was I so far, light from that sun hasn't reached our planet yet?" He seems a little too excited by this idea.

Percy clears his throat. "Actually, you weren't on another planet at all."

Noah's face falls. "But… the grass was orange."

"Sorry, I meant you weren't on another planet in this universe." Before I can fully take that in, Percy continues. "You were in another dimension."

"Say what?" Alistair's jaw has dropped, but awareness is dawning in David's eyes.

"I thought those were myths," he says sharply. "All the archives mark them as folklore."

Spreading his hands, Percy says, "And they may be. This is something I didn't know about until Noah was speaking and the magic… gave me the information. The portal was opened between our dimension and theirs by a member of a species that lives there. And those portals used to be quite common, but that stopped around the time of the species wars. That's it. That's all I know. We're going to have to dig through that folklore and see if we can verify any of it as being factual."

"The magic won't tell you anything else?" Gideon asks, sounding more off-balance than I've ever heard him before.

Percy shakes his head.

"So what we know," Sam says slowly, "is that at least one elf or group of elves from another dimension have teamed up with Tish for reasons that aren't clear and can use portals to move around at will?"

"That sums it up." David rubs the bridge of his nose, no doubt thinking of all the research ahead while we wait for Tish to make his next move.

"I don't think they can use the portals just anywhere," Alistair says. "If they could, why not go right to Percy's office? Or at least to the inside of the ward. Whatever power these elves have, the wards do have an effect on it."

"That's something, at least," Elinor grumbles.

David stands. "I think we should let Noah rest while we put together a plan to tackle this research and shore up our defenses. Noah, as soon as the doctors say you're up to it, you'll be in charge of the folklore challenge."

Noah manages a small, slow nod. "I'm in."

The team disperses, saying their goodbyes and heading back to the office. When Noah and I are alone, I smile at him.

"I'm so glad you're awake. Let me recline the bed for you so you can sleep."

"Don't you fucking dare," he drawls, tripping over the words. "I'm not sleepy yet."

"You need rest," I chide, but I leave the bed alone and reach for my water bottle instead. The thought of elves from another dimension popping in and out of portals has made my throat a little dry.

"I love you," Noah declares, and I spit water across the bed. He laughs, a slow *heh heh heh*. "If I'd known you'd react like that, I'd have told you while the others were here."

"Very funny." I want to hit the call button and get him a dry blanket ASAP, but I also really want to hear him say it again. "Are you… Do you…"

"Are you at a loss for words? This day will go down in history." The movement of his mouth is not quite a grin, but the sparkle in his eyes says it all. "I love you, Andrew. I know our relationship is still new, but for a while I didn't think I'd get the chance to say it, so I'm seizing the opportunity now."

All the feelings I have for him rush up in me, wanting to burst out. My fangs descend as though I'm an out-of-control adolescent.

"You're sure?" I choke out, and then at the look on his face, "I'm not doubting you. I just… I'm so much older than you. You've been through a lot, but most of your life is still ahead of you, and I'm coming to the end of mine."

"You'll still likely outlive me," he points out. "Are you really trying to talk me out of loving you?"

"I love you," I burst out. "I love you. I've waited over eight hundred years to feel like this. I've loved before, but nobody's ever been you. I think I started to love you when you broke my nose."

He laughs again. "I can do it again anytime you want. Now kiss me, damn you, because I can't move that far yet."

So I do. And when my fang nicks his lip, he mutters something about sneaky vampires and deepens the kiss.

---

Want an Andrew and Noah bonus scene? There are two ways to grab it:
Subscribe to my monthly newsletter
(bit.ly/LouisaMBonus)
OR
Join my Facebook group, RoMMance with Becca & Louisa (look for the pinned post).

# HI FROM LOUISA!

Hey folks! I hope you enjoyed *One Bite With A Vampire*. You can download an Andrew and Noah bonus scene by subscribing to my monthly newsletter (bit.ly/ LouisaMBonus) or joining my Facebook group, RoMMance with Becca & Louisa (look for the pinned post).

Book three in the Hidden Species series, *Hijinks With A Hellhound*, is Alistair and Aidan's story and you can find it here.

If you'd like to try more of my work, check out my website: www.louisamasters.com All my books can be read as standalone, but you'll meet recurring characters and can follow their journeys through the series.

And I'd love to see you in my Facebook group, RoMMance with Becca & Louisa!

Hugs!

Louisa xx

# ALSO BY LOUISA MASTERS

*Here Be Dragons*
Dragon Ever After
The Professor's Dragon

*Hidden Species*
Demons Do It Better
One Bite With A Vampire
Hijinks With A Hellhound
Sorcerers Always Satisfy

*Met His Match*
Charming Him
Offside Rules
Between the Covers (M/F)

*Joy Universe*
I've Got This
Follow My Lead
In Your Hands
Take Us There

*Novellas*
Fake It 'Til You Make It (permafree)
Out of the Office

After the Blaze

# ABOUT THE AUTHOR

Louisa Masters started reading romance much earlier than her mother thought she should. While other teenagers were sneaking out of the house, Louisa was sneaking romance novels in and working out how to read them without being discovered. As an adult, she feeds her addiction in every spare second. She spent years trying to build a "sensible" career, working in bookstores, recruitment, resource management, administration, and as a travel agent, before finally conceding defeat and devoting herself to the world of romance novels.

Louisa has a long list of places first discovered in books that she wants to visit, and every so often she overcomes her loathing of jet lag and takes a trip that charges her imagination. She lives in Melbourne, Australia, where she whines about the weather for most of the year while secretly admitting she'll probably never move.

http://www.louisamasters.com

Made in the USA
Monee, IL
22 February 2024

53942876R00173